T0106152

STEVE MARCO

ARDENT RISING

iUniverse, Inc.
New York   Bloomington

Ardent Rising

This is a work of fiction. All of the characters, names, incidents, organizations, and dialogue in this novel are either the products of the author's imagination or are used fictitiously.

iUniverse books may be ordered through booksellers or by contacting:

iUniverse
1663 Liberty Drive
Bloomington, IN 47403
www.iuniverse.com
1-800-Authors (1-800-288-4677)

ISBN: 978-1-4502-5761-9 (sc)
ISBN: 978-1-4502-5819-7 (ebook)

Printed in the United States of America

iUniverse rev. date: 10/28/2010

FOR CARA

ACKNOWLEDGEMENTS

With many thanks:
To my darling wife, who was always
patient and supportive.
To my parents, who always believed.
To my sister, who always made me feel like a hero.
To the Bellarmine Escapism and Strategy Team, lifelong
friends who gave me a place for my ideas to play.
To you, for taking a step into my world.

ONE

It was so much work to get one damn piece of paper.

"Behold your destiny," Sophia proclaimed, mocking Dante in a grandiose voice. She beckoned to him, standing with her back facing the vibrantly dressed mechanical fortune teller. The tiny slip of his fortune rested tightly between her first and second fingers. She smirked at him, extending her hand outward, offering him the fortune. Dante reached out for the paper, only for Sophia to yank it back with an abrupt swipe of her hand. Her light features shifted from mock innocence into complete mischief. She hopped around, spinning past, daring him to pursue.

Dante lunged forward towards Sophia's delicate, outstretched hand, only to come up short again as she bolted away quickly. She bent over slightly, just enough, and called out. "Sorry *Seraph*, you'll have to be quicker than that. Come on!" She vaulted away into the crowd. Dante frowned to himself and moved to intercept her, slipping close between the droves of people separating them.

"Will you ever stop calling me that?" Dante replied as he passed close to her laughing form, only to see her slip away yet again. The crowd was overwhelming his vision and masking his target.

Sophia laughed and shook her head. "I like calling you Seraph. It sounds a little dangerous, maybe sexy, even. Don't you agree?" She danced around, weaving backwards through the crowd. She moved like she was playing the role of Moses, parting the Red Sea of carnival patrons. They opened up the space as if she had commanded them with some strange magic. "Catch me if you can!" she shouted out to him.

Dante's spiky hair fanned out as the chilly wind ran through it. It was autumn in Louisville. With the wind blowing, he had to squint his eyes to focus on Sophia, who had evaded him as she backed her way into the sea of the crowd. The annual carnival in Waterfront Park was in full swing. The blue sky, blast-white clouds and modest skyline cast a vibrant scene for the carnival goers.

Maybe feeling sorry for him, Sophia returned to Dante's presence. Stepping out in front of him, Sophia closed the distance but continued to evade Dante's attempts at pursuit with a bilateral weaving through and through the crowd. "Is there any particular reason why you stole my fortune?" Despite her attempts to widen the gap between them, he was gaining ground on her. At this point there were only about fifteen feet and a couple of dozen bodies separating them.

"It's called fun, Seraph. Maybe you should try it. I can see the headlines." Sophia made a banner with her arms. "Salvatore College's own Dante Rubicon finds fun in his last year. Instead of sitting on his ass in the library, the resident bookworm *actually* steps foot off campus and does something *not* involving books. Live at seven."

Dante sighed. "That's quite an imagination you have there, Sophia." It wasn't in his best interest to let her know that he secretly agreed. The school year had been particularly stressful already. This little outing to the park was the first time he had been off campus in nearly a month.

"I know. It's part of my charm." She was still mocking him, but the battle wasn't over yet. He sprinted forward in another attempt to reach her again.

Another reach, another grab, and yet another miss. Dante nearly growled at Sophia's taunting laughter. She couldn't get away with this. He'd never hear the end of it.

Using one of the more oblivious carnival goers, one with her hands completely filled with a giant teddy bear, Dante hid himself for a moment from Sophia's sight. In the instant of his invisibility, Dante caught up to her, snatching the fortune out of her hand with a proclamation of triumph. Sophia half-heartedly clapped, a bored smirk on her face. "Well, I wasn't going to keep it anyway. Your destiny is your own. Right, Seraph?"

Dante just nodded, not really sure what she was talking about, but then she threaded her fingers through his. Dante looked up at her, a little confused, and her eyes softened. He blushed slightly and let her lead him through the crowd. The downtown skyline passed in front of them as the pair rounded the corner of Waterfront Park.

"I'm glad we did this," Sophia said, leading the two of them up the path towards the carnival rides.

"Me too," Dante replied. "I haven't seen you in the student center in a couple of weeks."

"I know. I've been busy with some… work stuff," Sophia stated, a little weakly.

"You never told me you had a job," Dante questioned.

"There are a lot of things I have never told you," she said with a chuckle. "Some of them would make you blush."

"Sounds like a challenge to me," Dante said. It sounded like she was flirting with him. That was a good thing.

"Play your cards right and you might just get an education," Sophia teased. Dante cheered internally, though on the exterior, he merely smiled.

Sophia's steps ceased abruptly, nearly knocking the two of them together. In front of them was an old style carousel. The golden apparatus looked like it had seen its glory days at least thirty years ago, but it was a heartfelt touch bringing her back to entertain children, like a grandparent rocking an infant.

Sophia's eyes were alight with humor, and her mouth crooked into a small, yet wicked smile. She looked every bit the cat who ate the canary, and Dante sensed, from the look she shot his way, that he might be a singing meal with feathers.

"Oh no, you can't be serious," Dante said, his eyes going wide.

"Come on, Dante. It's my favorite thing. You're going to come ride with me, aren't you?"

"I think I am far too manly to ride a carousel."

She whisked her shoulder length red curls away and reached out to him. "Please?" she whined again. Sophia dipped into her pockets, pulling out two tickets. "My treat, Dante. Come on."

"I'll just wait for you over here," Dante concluded. He started to walk away. Sophia took three long strides and pressed herself up to him in a manner which allowed for no resistance.

Dante just stopped. Overloaded from his senses, his mind was futilely attempting to process the input. Her hair rested on and around his chest, and her skin smelled like strawberries plucked in the morning dew at the height of their potency. Not one reasoned thought could be generated in his head.

"So," she said, chewing on her lip, which was drawing Dante's eyes, "You and me?"

"You and me?" Dante repeated.

"On the carousel?" She tapped his nose and stepped back, a Cheshire cat impression replacing the seduction. "I'll owe you one."

Dante managed to shake his head. "Don't think I won't collect," he replied, his voice taking a slightly off-key wavering tenor.

Sophia made a gesture of a bow, lowering herself slowly. The movement showed off the strappy pink tank top she was wearing. It was a little low cut in the front, but only just enough to stand out a little. A solitaire diamond leaped towards the earth before being snatched back by a length of silver chain.

"I'm counting on it," she said in a voice of velvet. "Please?"

Before he knew it, he was sitting down on one of the damn riding horses on the carousel. He took a spot in the interior row, trying to keep himself as invisible as possible.

It wasn't easy, but Dante could see Sophia at the edge of his vision. She was far ahead of him, her legs wrapped around a model Arabian stallion, her head back in happy laughter as the ride continued. Around the third turn, something caught her eye. Her entire demeanor immediately transformed from joyous to pensive, with a slight frustration and maybe a little fear.

Her eyes traveled backward. Dante saw her meet his gaze, and instantly her face cracked a smile. It was fake, not a little fake, but *completely* fake. Something had scared her, and it was something she didn't want him to know about.

As the horse he was riding slowed, Dante already hopped down and started to search for Sophia. He had lost sight of her as the ride stopped, her horse landing out of his field of vision. He felt a gentle tap, then a quick swat to his leg. Like any real man, he jumped in shock.

Sophia's eyes looked back from his. Mirth lit up her features. "Aw, I can buy you another ticket if you like," she laughed, stepping closer to him as he hopped down from carousel's edge. There was no dignity in a response, so he replied with a shake of the head. She retaliated with a quick raspberry, bringing a slight scowl but more of a smile to his face. Taking his hand again, Sophia walked the path to the exit.

Sophia was still leading the couple, moving them down the long path from the loud rides to the clear and cool waterfront. The pair walked down, taking care to not get separated in the huge crowds that were taking their sweet time negotiating the somewhat significant grade towards the water.

Immediately past the exit to the rides, Sophia dragged him towards one of the smaller side paths. Her eyes darted back and forth, as if she were checking against some kind of attack. Tension hummed in her shoulders as they bumped together in transit. Her hand, still cemented to his, felt clammy.

"What is it, Sophia?" Dante asked as they walked.

"I'm looking for some privacy," she said. This was a little strange. "I owe you one, remember?"

"I thought we had more carnival to visit." This didn't add up. She was acting strangely. He'd known her for over a year; this wasn't right.

"The carnival can wait," she said, pulling him towards another section. There were several tents set up with various toys and gifts for sale. Sophia dragged them into one of the unattended ones.

"Sophia, what's going on?" Not that Dante would complain about getting with the girl of his dreams for a little alone time, but this wasn't right. He knew it, deep within his bones.

"For once, Dante, just shut up and go with it," she replied. She pressed her lips to Dante's, taking him completely by surprise. Almost a full second passed before Dante even managed to close his eyes. A spark of static danced on his lips, causing him to flinch. Sophia skipped back after a moment with wide, beseeching eyes.

"What the hell?" Dante snapped.

"Static electricity," Sophia replied evenly. "It happens from time to time." She leaned in again.

"Hate to interrupt." A woman stepped through the edge of the tent. It was a sultry sort of woman facing them. Her posture betrayed a soldier's stance. She looked like a blade wrapped in silk.

"Oh, hi, Rachel," Sophia said with a smile. "What are you doing here?"

"Looking for you. Who's your friend?" Rachel replied.

"Rachel, this is Dante. Dante, this is Rachel. She's my lab partner in physics class." Sophia gestured to them both, and Dante shook Rachel's hand.

"It's nice to meet you," Dante smiled.

"Likewise," Rachel replied. "I'm sorry, but would you mind if I borrowed Sophia for a second? I need to talk to her about a... class I missed."

Dante looked between them. Sophia looked like she was about to be executed. It must be some horrible class. "Sure," Dante said, "I'll just be outside."

Sophia smiled. "It won't take long. I'll come get you in a few."

Dante stepped out of the tent. The entire thing didn't make sense. Things had been going so well. He could hear that they were speaking, though since they were whispering, he couldn't understand them. There was a small vent in the top of the tent. The tent was near a small rock outcropping that would serve as a stand if he wanted to eavesdrop. Dante took special care, and maneuvered himself to observe discretely.

The view of them was decidedly confrontational, with Rachel chastising Sophia in an authoritative stance. It looked like a school teacher was trying to explain to a first grader why it was important to turn in her homework on time. Sophia, on the other hand, played the part of an angry child trying to avoid being dragged back indoors before the sun went down in the summer.

Rachel handed Sophia some sort of parchment. It looked like a scroll, belonging in the renaissance far more than in the light of the modern day. She tore it open, probably breaking a wax seal or something. She started to read it before the scroll was completely unfurled. Rachel put her hand on Sophia's shoulder, and Sophia's expression shifted from intensity to rage to misery.

When the end of the scroll was reached, Sophia looked like she was on the verge of tears. The two of them whispered some more, this time far more hurriedly. Rachel pulled Sophia into a hug, and the pair hung together for a while.

As the two of them embraced, Dante stopped thinking he was investigating and started to feel like a voyeur. He hopped down from the rock and leaned back against the tent wall. He crossed his arms, and set himself up as if he had been there the entire time.

Sophia and Rachel only kept him waiting a few more minutes before they walked outside. The previous adversarial attitude had evaporated, having been replaced with a very powerful sisterly energy. Rachel projected a small, tight smile at Dante as she passed by, not breaking stride. Sophia put a fake smile in place and took Dante's arm as the two of them walked away towards the center of the carnival grounds.

"Hey… are you sure you're all right?" he said soothingly. The tone of his voice only seemed to put her back on edge. Her entire body snapped taut and she was a little shaky. She nodded again and kept walking. A few minutes later the pair had found themselves in front of the funhouse.

"Rachel's dad is really sick," Sophia whispered. Her eyes low. "They're not sure if he's going to get better, that's why she missed our lab class."

Dante's expression softened. "I'm sorry, Sophia. Do you know him?" She nodded, though the gesture appeared to be somewhat mechanical.

"Yeah, he would bring stuff for me and Rachel in the dorms. We live on the same floor." She smiled self-deprecatingly. "So that's why I'm a little upset."

"Makes sense," Dante replied. They passed the side of the funhouse and made their way to the food court of the carnival. Dozens of different scents and smells wafted up from the edge, blanketing Dante's senses in funnel cake and cotton candy.

"Do you want to go back?" Dante wanted to know.

"No, I'm enjoying being here. Give me a few minutes and I'll be back to normal." She snuggled up to him, clinging to him like he was a life raft in a flood.

Ignoring the sensory overload, Dante pushed forward. He was stubborn when things didn't add up. Even though there was a lot of emotion in her story, it didn't make sense. He really needed to get to the heart of the matter.

"Sophia, what's with the scroll?" Dante whispered. Sophia's eyes got big and darted around.

"Come on. There's a lot more carnival to go through before it gets dark," she said. She stopped a moment later, an inspiration in her mind. Her face got serious and intense.. "Or would you prefer we continued what we started in the tent?" she said. The statement came out of the blue, though she forced a smile afterward.

"What *is* going on here, Sophia? This isn't you. I've known you for nearly a year, and you've never acted like this." As exciting as it would be for Sophia to continue what she started, Dante couldn't shake the nagging feeling that something was seriously wrong with her.

"Maybe I've been hiding more from you than you realize." She put on a perfect, sultry smile.

"Or maybe something is wrong and you're not telling me." Dante refused the bait.

"I'm okay, Dante, really..." she replied. Her tone was not very convincing. "I don't want to think about it right now. Let's get moving." Sophia dragged Dante back over. "I'm hungry, we need snacks," she said, and pulled him over towards the food area. By the time Sophia was done, she had coaxed him into buying her two sugar covered funnel cakes, a roll of cotton candy, and a giant bucket of soda.

The frivolity of the display was nice, as Dante attempted to balance all of the stuff Sophia had handed him as they ran the gauntlet of the carnival food court. His expression was somewhat of a ruse, as his mind was elsewhere. The key to everything was that Sophia didn't answer his question about her disposition. He was sure that there was *far* more to this story.

He wasn't one to let a mystery stand. Dante was about to confront her when he stumbled, narrowly avoiding dumping the cotton candy all over the place, along with the popcorn, chocolate and fifteen other things he was saddled with.

"Why am I carrying all this?" he growled.

"Cause you look cute carting all that stuff around," she winked. Sophia slipped away again, waiting for Dante to catch up, only to take flight in a series of moves designed as stall tactics. It was pretty obvious how hard she was trying to make him drop the subject, but whatever it was on that scroll, it really upset her, to the point of crying in Rachel's arms. After devouring the bulk of the snacks, they continued on their way.

The walk down the hill towards the unexplored part of the carnival was travelled in silence. Sophia held onto Dante's now freed arm like there was nothing holding her up except what strength he shared with her. Every so often, there was a slight sniffle coming from Sophia's direction, and she blinked a lot in a vain effort to keep the tears hiding there from obscuring her vision.

As the last cake was chomped down upon, the sky was turning amber. The sun began to retreat from the park. This was the cue for many of the crowd to scramble intently back to their cars, causing a big traffic nightmare between the main highway and the access road to the park. As Dante stood up from the picnic table where they had made their home, Sophia took note of the dying daylight.

"Do we need to go back now? I'm not ready," Sophia asked meekly.

Dante replied somewhat quietly, "We can leave later. I've got nowhere to be, you just let me know when, okay?" Sophia seemed pleased, though still sad. She yet again gave the impression of a child wanting to stay outside five minutes more in the summer, as if she was hesitant to return to the real world.

"Where would you like to go? I think they're starting to close the carnival," he said. The sounds of pickup trucks backing into the side entrance of the park were a complete giveaway. She led him towards the river.

"I want to walk down to the pier."

Dante agreed, and he followed her over to the water. Surprisingly, the Ohio River was quite clear, especially by this point as the sun had dipped below the western edge of the horizon. The entire river came alive as the city skyline opened up its lights to the fading sky.

They walked on the shore towards the west, heading towards Main Street and the business district. "I love the night on the river," Sophia began, looking around, waving her free hand as though she was searching for the right words. "Everything seems so much more alive when the sun goes down. Do you know what I mean?"

"I like the night," Dante began, "though I have to say I like the day more," he concluded. She seemed puzzled by his response. "Especially this day," he said, earning himself a smile. "There aren't a lot of people around." Sophia raised an eyebrow. That sounded like the beginning of a very cheesy come on. He slapped himself mentally and recovered. "What I mean is that during the day, the world is crowded with people. Everyone is going around, living their lives. It's nice to see that. We're all a part of it, in a sense. In this world, none of us are really alone."

Sophia blinked, seemingly processing that information. She pulled Dante a little closer before she spoke. "But we are all alone," she said to herself, quietly enough that he could barely hear her. Dante searched her eyes, silently pleading for her to tell him what she meant by that comment. He was nearly desperate to understand about the scroll, about the pain in her eyes at the thought of going home.

"I'm sorry?" he queried.

"You're getting pretty philosophical on me, Dante," Sophia responded with a forced bright response. "I'm just glad to see all the slobs having a good time," she trailed off, a little unconvincingly.

"Sophia, something is going on. If I can help, I'd like to." Dante squeezed her hand gently. She seemed to puzzle this out for a moment and then turned to face him. "Is this about the scroll?"

"You're just not going to let that drop, are you?" Sophia snapped.

Dante looked a little confused at the strength of her response, but he continued. "Not planning on it, no. You really seem like you need to talk about it. You can tell me to shut up about it and I'll do that, but I can't help you if you don't tell me."

"Dante, have you ever made a mistake, but it started so perfect that you didn't realize it *was* a mistake, and by the time you did, it was far too late?" She turned her head, looking out to the nearly clear waters of the river.

"Sure, I think everybody has," he replied. "Dealing with regrets is a part of life, I guess."

"Oh no, it's not that," she quickly replied. "I mean, I don't know."

"What do you regret?" he asked, raising her chin to meet his eyes. She shook her head. "Sophia, if you're in some sort of trouble..."

She cut him off. "Look, I can't talk about it," she said in frustration. "Can we just stay like this, enjoy the moment for a little while longer?" Sophia put her head on Dante's shoulder, leaning into him and holding him close. He nodded and drew her closer, bringing up his arms to envelope her. They stayed that way for awhile, until the full moon rose over the city.

A sound awoke Dante from their warm connection, snapping to and holding his attention. As he turned towards it, a familiar shadow approached. As his eyes began to adjust to the darkness in that direction, he felt his head go light. A soft *I'm sorry* was the last thing Dante heard before the darkness enveloped him.

⁖

As Dante regained consciousness, a fleeting dreamlike memory remained in his mind for a moment. It was of a large stone room, with many people gathered around him. The image vanished as soon as he became aware of the outside world, but it felt like it was important for some reason. There was a man there, standing out in the center of the room, underneath a vibrant skylight.

"Welcome to the Amphitheater, Truthsayer," the man said. Dante saw a flash of light from a sword the man was carrying, and then the dream ceased.

Dante felt a small breeze on his face when he regained consciousness. The air was sweet smelling but too sweet. It was as if a bottle of perfume exploded on the carpet all at once, bathing the air in a sensation of vanilla and rosemary. He felt silk on his face. Only shadows crept into his vision through the material.

Two men, at least it seemed like they were men, were quickly carrying him, one by each shoulder, down a long, nearly silent corridor. The thick thuds of their footsteps echoed in the hall. Too groggy to even speak, Dante just remained still and let the parade go on.

A large door squealed open, and Dante was slammed backward into a damp concrete wall. Two large manacles locked into place around each wrist. A couple of experimental tugs on the restraints indicated that there was entirely no way he could get free. He couldn't even move the shackles; they felt like they each weighed over a hundred pounds.

"Oi! Who's there?" a smooth English voice came from somewhere in the room. The voice was like a train, soft at the beginning and loud and alarming at the end. Despite the icy, overwhelming fear, Dante could estimate that the other man was about ten feet away. His voice carried a hint of confusion, suggesting that he was unaware of his surroundings, most likely blindfolded as Dante was.

"Dante Rubicon," he replied, not really expecting that to mean anything.

"Yeah? Dante, from Dr. Kann's Web Design last year?" the voice responded.

"That's right," Dante returned, his voice finding purchase. "Do I know you?"

"Max Doggery," the Englishman returned. "Did you just get picked up?"

"Yes, from the carnival," Dante returned.

"Bugger me, the Waterfront Carnival? Blimey. I've been here for days," Max spat back with a quickly hushed voice. "Quiet. You stay cool, kid."

Dante thought that he must have been near a window or a doorway to a hall, since the click-clack of footsteps passed every few seconds. He could hear people talking, but the language was unfamiliar. It sounded a little like the Latin he took in school, but with a more lyrical and rounded sound. As he concentrated, the language inexplicably cleared, and he could understand the words within the heavy accent. "He defied the harvest. That is beyond the ability of even the most powerful Ardent."

A second, younger voice responded. "You've heard the legends as well as I have, Eric… Could he be one of the Ancients?"

The first man replied with a bellow, "It doesn't matter what he is. Lord Lucien has demanded an audience with this prisoner. Tell the Minister as soon as the bastard wakes up."

"There is no need, he just did. Send for the Minister now."

Dante felt his adrenaline begin to spike. The panic coursed through his veins like warm blood, and he shook a little as the boot steps around him continued. "Max," he began.

"Shush," Max replied, cutting Dante off. "We've got company."

A minute later, Dante heard a female voice that sounded sweet and innocent, yet determined and professional. The voice came from the edge of the hall. Dante assumed she was about thirty feet away and moving towards him. Panic rose in his gut, and bile started to crawl up his throat.

The unknown woman entered the room a few moments later. "Wait outside," she commanded. The heavy thud of boots confirmed to Dante that the guards had left.

"Max?" she whispered. Her voice seemed very familiar. "You need to stay still. You're only going to hurt yourself if you keep fighting us." More thrashing sounds were the response. Max apparently didn't like the suggestion.

"Rachel, you can just go to hell. You betrayed us! You gave up our location!" he roared. The words were murderous, each one like a knife poised at her throat.

The response was unfazed. "You know better than that. Damn it, Max, it was either this or an execution squad. Now stop this shit and listen. I'm going to get you out of here, but you need to cut the crap and be patient. This isn't the time for one of your lame-ass plans. Just stay quiet and do what I say."

A couple more steps resonated in the room and Dante felt his blindfold slip away. His eyes, quickly adjusting to the darkness, were met with a soft expression covering veiled ferocity. Dante couldn't help smirking. "So, Rachel, I didn't think it was time for lab class already."

"Oh wonderful, we have another smartass. Don't start with me. Sophia's bringing Max a little something to get the two of you out of here, so just don't move, and for the love of heaven, keep your mouth shut, okay?"

Biting back a really good retort, Dante just sat there like a statue. After a couple of moments he nodded his head robotically. "That's a boy…," said Rachel. "Just be cool."

He scanned the area and found himself in a small apartment room. There was something off in the surroundings, a lack of feeling perhaps. The carpeted floors and tan walls looked like they were slapped right over the cold tiles of a dungeon. The inherent warmth implied by the modern furnishing was lost as if it was never there. It was all a deception, nothing more.

With a quick splintering sound, the door opened. Two men who could only be described as brutish stepped into the room first. They were wearing large gold bracers on their left arms and black, wide-lapel suits complete with a scowl. Rachel stepped over to the wall, lowering her head in supplication.

Rachel spoke softly as a third man entered. "Lord Lucien."

Max reflectively struggled against his bonds. It was an emotional response, as if he were recoiling in front of an open flame.

Lucien was dressed formally, if simply. The suit was coal black, the color matching his eyes. The cut of the cloth was as sharp as his expression. A peak of gold lined his arm, a gauntlet similar to his servants' resting there.

"Hello, child," Lucien said as he walked around Max's chair. There was no response, only the slight grunt as Max seethed in his captivity. "It's so wonderful to see you again. I've missed you."

Without warning, a distortion rang through Dante's ears. A thousand nails on a thousand chalkboards screeched in his mind. Reeling from the pain, his head was thrown back as he clenched his teeth, trying to bite back a scream.

Lucien turned slightly in the most minor acknowledgement of the pain behind him. Shifting his weight slightly, he continued his speech. "I'm eager to have you back. There has been much strife between us, but we need no longer harbor the ill wills of the past. All I need are the pass codes to the rebel safe house and all will be forgiven."

The distortion crashed again, a little weaker then the first time, but still enough to cause Dante to retch. He choked back the bile rising in his throat from the pain. He cursed out loud when he stopped coughing.

"Stop it, you bloody bastard!" Max shouted.

Lucien smiled like a shark. "You don't believe me, Max? I know you don't. You'll understand soon enough," he replied. There was no pain this time. Dante involuntarily winced, expecting more pain, but there wasn't the tell tale sign. Confusion rang in his ears instead. The searing cacophony subsided.

Dante continued struggling against the bindings but they were too strong, and he was too weak to free himself. He kept his eyes low, trying to be inconspicuous. Max shook his head. "Give you the pass codes? Not in this lifetime, asshole."

Lucien's voice had all the smoothness of a chiseled rock, and all the delicate softness of concrete. His anger came through for the first time. "I'm hurt, Max, but nevertheless, it's the truth. Just say the word and I'll let you go."

The chalkboard's scratching symphony returned. This time Dante actually screamed. It was too much for him to take. It was the purest pain he had ever experienced. He teetered on the edge of consciousness, but barely managed to stay awake.

"Damn it, Lucien, what the hell are you doing to him?" Max shouted.

"I've not done anything to him," Lucien replied with a hint of bewilderment in his voice. Dante was roaring out loud, but the monster in front of him didn't even seem fazed. He wondered how many people this man had tortured down in this place. "He will be fine. I will see to it personally."

Another screeching klaxon racked Dante's mind, and he roared again in fury.

"Quit lying, you bastard!" Max commanded. The bonds holding Max were even more secure than the ones with which had contained Dante. The Brit couldn't even move.

The pain subsided again. Max's words still rung in Dante's ears.

The pain came every time Lucien lied. He could perceive it. Dante had a superpower.

He had a truth sense.

Oh, shit. This was completely insane. No time to think too much about it, though. On the very slim chance that it was real, embracing the madness might be the only way to get out of there alive.

"You're going to harvest him, aren't you?" Max spat.

Lucien answered, "That is not my intention."

Pain shrieked again in Dante's mind, but he managed to clamp it down by focusing on the words Lucien spoke. "Are you into snuff films or anything?" Dante asked. "Is my Senior Seminar class going to see this on the internet? Would you mind fixing my hair first?"

"Don't be melodramatic, boy. I'm not going to kill you." More pain. *Another lie.*

"You don't lie so well," he said, a smile sneaking through his lips. Lucien's face lit up in shock at his audacity. "So... what's your story, Lucy? You the head of some bizarre cult who sacrifices hapless carnival-goers for a big demon slug in the ground or something?"

"You have a very impressive imagination," Lucien said, leaving Max's side and moving towards Dante. "Watch your tongue, boy. You are in the presence of greatness."

"Don't talk too much about me," Max chimed in. "Do you still make the knights recite that God-awful oath every morning? Personally, I thought it was a little pretentious, especially when we had to drop to our knees in the middle..."

"Still your tongue, traitor, before I remove it," Lucien snapped. "Your defiance has gone on long enough, Doggery. I will enjoy eating the marrow from your bones."

"Now that, I believe," Dante said wryly.

"Yeah, he's really forthcoming, isn't he?" Max chuckled and looked back at Lucien. "I'm sure you would enjoy eating me. I'm a part of a balanced breakfast, after all." Lucien stalked over to him, and the room clamored with the sound of a backhanded slap. Max's face opened into a near beaming smile. "You hit like a three year old. Sissy."

"We'll see how brave you are when I eat your soul. I shall savor the taste immensely, though I have more pressing matters to attend to at the moment. I'll leave you to count down the remaining minutes of your life." Lucien spun on his heel and walked out of the room. Rachel and the other two men followed swiftly behind. As the heavy door shut, they could hear the dust falling from the ceiling.

"That doesn't sound good," Dante summarized. Max chuckled for a moment, then his voice got very, very serious. It was not final exam serious, but military, life or death, storm the beaches, serious.

"We have maybe four minutes before Lucien walks back through that door. Once that happens, we're completely buggered." Max started checking over his bonds. "We need to get out of here now. Are you an Ardent?"

"Am I a what?" Dante replied.

"Ardent... you know, empowered, Royal magic, big shiny gauntlet?"

"I don't have a freaking clue what you're talking about."

"A latent, huh? Well, keep trying with the cuffs. I'll see if I can get my access device to power up." There were several whirring and spinning sounds coming from Max's direction. After a couple of minutes, Dante saw Max slump in his chair. "Shit. My interface coupling has been removed from my gauntlet harness."

The footsteps up the stairs became audible again. Dante heard the sounds of movement and people arriving around the spiral staircase leading to their location. Fear gripped him, and he began to struggle violently against the chains holding him. "We gotta get the hell out of here!"

"Oi! What the hell?" Max bellowed again, almost in an aggressive manner. Dante responded by roaring out in horror.

The door burst open a second or two later. Two guards raced to Dante, pinning his arms, securing him, and one guard commanded Dante to be still. A chill caused the guard's voice to shake. It was more likely, Dante thought, that Lucien's reward for failure involved more of a horrible death than simply a written warning.

Dante ignored the guard's fear. His own panic drove through his system, adrenaline amplifying his strength. Fight or flight had switched over to the latter, and every watt of power within him was pushing towards escape. His arms flexed and the heavy metal bonds snapped into nothing. Dante raised his hands in shock.

Sophia burst into the room, followed by Rachel. When he saw her, Dante roared, "How could you do this to me?"

The statement stopped Sophia in her tracks, until she caught sight of Max. Sophia dove at him with a snarl on her face. She yanked his chair back, flinging it towards the wall, and Max collapsed to the floor. As he raised his voice in protest, Dante saw Sophia stealthily place a small device in the palm of Max's hand.

Scared and more than a little pissed off, Dante grabbed the guard pinning him, finding the meaty arm trying to hold him back against the wall. He moved his hand to the guard's wrist and pulled on it with all his strength. The guard fell to his knees with a sickening crunch. His face lit up if he was electrocuted, a seizure quickly followed by a scream.

Dante stood up, his legs shaking slightly. His movements were detached and robotic as his mind began to process the horror surrounding him.

"Oi, lad!" Max shouted, struggling against the bonds. "Mind getting me out of this?"

Dante reached over and grabbed the bonds. With a slight effort, they popped open. Not a half second passed before Max was on his feet, eyes scanning the room. With first guard passed out, the other one raised a blade, only to be struck from behind by Rachel, who knocked him out with a single strike to the head.

Max began to pull various electrical components from his pockets and the lining of his coat. A couple of the devices looked like small video game cartridges, along with a motorcycle riding glove inlaid with circuitry. The pieces clicked together with a practiced motion. The result was an electronic armlet, cascading with electrical wiring and extending over half of Max's forearm.

The strange apparatus flashed with a bluish hue and spark. The lightning traveled up his arm and stopped at the large crystal at the end. The device had a small keypad mounted on the inside. Tapping on the keys, Max looked up for a moment before continuing. "Seal the door, Dante."

Rachel shook her head. "Nice try, Max, but there are jammers here. You won't be able to teleport out." She cracked the door open and gestured for Sophia to follow. "Stay here. It's safer right now, but we'll go and get them deactivated. Keep trying." Max opened his mouth to say something, only to be cut off by Rachel, who appeared to have experience in doing so. "Don't start, Max. You'll never get out alive if you charge forward, and you know it." She smirked at the slumping of his shoulders. "Have faith, big guy. I'll see you on the other side."

Sophia reported, "The coast is clear, Rach. We should go now." The two women ran out, but before Sophia left, she turned to Dante. "*Now* seal the door," she said grimly. Dante nodded, quickly pushing the oak door closed. After the door slammed shut, he locked the latch and broke the handle off, effectively destroying any chance of forcing the door open without busting it down.

A loud pounding started on the door and shouting seeped out from behind it. Dante jumped at the sound. Max typed on the keys of his armlet. "There are two goons smashing on the door. We don't have much time."

Dante moved forward. "How is it coming over there?" He pressed to the door. "Figure a way out of here?"

Max replied with a negative, "Nope, only one way out and it's still blocked. Jammers are still going. We're stuck until the girls get the interference taken down." Two large crunches rattled the door, projecting into the room. The heavy oak door showed the impact points bleeding through on the interior side.

"Shit!" Dante spat as the door lurched on yet another impact. "This isn't working, man! We can't wait!" Fear flickered in his eyes. Max threw up his hands, half in exasperation and half in apprehension.

"What do you want me to do?" Max shouted. "I can't very well smash through this bloody concrete!" Max's eyes flashed big for a moment. He rattled on the keyboard, typing frantically.

Dante paced the room and looked out at the speckled concrete wall which was his resting place earlier. The wall was pitted, but appeared solid. The mortar was still intact, save from a spider web crack from where the guard slammed into the wall. "Max? What about this crack?"

Max looked up. "Nah… nah… it's too small, I can't blast it open." Dante looked at him with confusion. "Wait… if you widen the crack, I might be able to get through it."

Dante's hand traced the spider pattern. Max looked over to him, running some calculations on his apparatus. He nodded, stepping back. Max was seemingly calm amidst the sound of the prison door caving in behind him. "Are you suggesting I hit this concrete wall?" said Dante.

"Don't think too much. Just do it. It's the only way out of here," Max snapped, continuing to type on his arm computer.

Dante stepped backward, keeping the crack in the center of his vision. There was a momentary flash of the absurdity of flinging oneself at a concrete wall. The next crash from the door behind him shook those thoughts away. Whatever awaited him on the other side of that oak door was far more terrifying than a self inflicted concussion. His steps towards the crack were first unsure, but the fear tensed his muscles and drove him forward.

The concrete made a sickening crunch on Dante's impact. The sound shook the room, the echo nearly deafening. A cloud of gray billowed in the air, surrounding Dante like a long cape. The cloak lifted, and a jagged six inch crack in the wall greeted Dante.

Max didn't waste a moment. "Stand aside," he said in a short, clipped tone. As Dante moved, a light blue flash leapt from Max's outstretched arm, slamming into the weakened wall. The wall literally exploded, moonlight seeped through, but before Dante could admire it, Max grabbed him by the shoulder and dragged him through.

"Do you know the way home?" Dante questioned. Behind them, the door smashed and the footsteps were moving forward with express speed.

The former prisoner looked up at Dante. "I just need a couple of moments to calibrate this locator. We're clear of the jammer now." Max pulled a card less than two inches long out of his pocket and attached it to his armlet device.

"What is that, a memory card?" Dante asked. The sounds of ricocheting bullets responded to Dante's question, and the two began to run in a full sprint. They were outside in the country. Trees shielded them from the shooters' sight as they ran forward towards freedom.

Max said nothing, but after a moment, he completed his calculations and flipped a switch. Blue light enveloped them both, and in an instant, Dante was standing in the quad of his school. He fell over on the ground, oblivious to the scant number of preoccupied passers-by.

Max extended his hand to Dante. "Come on champ, the party's not over yet."

Two

Dante took Max's arm. He nearly pulled Max to the ground as Dante leaned on him to get up.

"Can you walk?" Dante asked, seeing Max's weakened state.

"I bloody well have to," Max replied. "We stay out here, they're going to find us. We have to get indoors fast."

Dante stood quickly, "Here, lean on me." Dante hoisted him up.

Max leaned on him to keep standing. "The dorms, let's head to the dorms."

"Ok," Dante said. "Who's looking for us? Is it that Lucien guy?" he continued.

Max nodded, "Yep. He's got a hard-on for killing me, and I can't imagine he likes you too much either."

"Terrific," Dante spat as they moved towards the access roadway to the dormitory. "Mind telling me what the hell is going on?"

"You've got a power, right?" Max said. "Don't bullshit me either Dante, I saw you smash that concrete wall."

"Didn't realize it until tonight, but I guess so," Dante replied.

"You're an Ardent," Max said. "I'm one as well."

"I take it this Lucien person is an Ardent too?" Dante questioned, looking around the path ahead of them.

"Yeah, he's a Royal Lord, kind of a king of Ardent." Max said while rolling his eyes.

"What's his beef with you?"

"I used to work for him. He was a dick of a boss," Max grumbled.

"Obviously," Dante deadpanned. "Not to go all selfish on you, but what does this have to do with me?"

"I'm not sure yet," Max replied. An alarm began to wail on his arm computer. "Shit! They've found us." The pair of them had nearly reached the outer doors to the dormitory.

"What do we do?" Dante said, nearly dragging Max along as the door came into view.

"Get us inside. We'll head into the basement study lounge and blend in." Max pointed at the doors which were nearly within reach.

Dante slammed the doors open and pulled Max down the stairs to the basement. The corridor was well lit, but there were no other students around. "Shit," Max spat, "No one's down here. We need to hide."

Ducking around the corner, the two of them quickly dove into one of the study rooms.

Max looked down at his gauntlet, "They've entered the building. Two of them went up the stairs. Two of them are advancing downstairs."

"What is that?" Dante looked at the glove. He didn't get a good look at it during their escape, but there were readouts and a screen built into the device. It looked like a piece of science fiction attached to a long motorcycle glove.

"It's my conduit. It's how I work my mojo," Max replied.

"A conduit?" Dante asked.

"A source of focus for your power. Everybody has one," Max answered. "Except for the Ancients, that is. Be cool. They're right outside."

As they waited, Dante saw two shadows pass near the doorway. The lights were kept off in the study room, and the door was locked. After a moment, the goons passed by the window on their way to investigate the rest of the floor.

"I think we're safe for the moment," Max said. "We should get to a common room. If we stay in the populated areas they won't be able to get us."

"Why?" Dante asked.

"It's one of their laws. They can't mess with normal people. If we hide in a place where norms can see us, they won't be able to snatch us up. It's forbidden for them to use their powers in front of regular joes."

"Damn. Okay, let's move." Dante let Max lean on him as they struggled up to the stairwell. Slow and mindful of Max's injuries, they successfully made it to the common room.

Dante deposited Max on one of the side couches in the center area. The room was located in a connecting walkway between two separate dormitories, with a big screen TV and pool table in the middle. On the side of the room was a small kitchenette, and a set of vending machines which had seen entirely far too much use in the last decade.

The room had some people in it. Most of them were watching TV, and one was cooking a frozen burrito. They seemed to ignore Dante and Max, which was definitely a good thing.

Dante jumped right in. "Okay, who were those guys?"

"Ardent knights, they serve Royal Lords like Lucien," Max said.

"Is that like a job?" Dante wanted to know.

"More like enlisting in the military. Lords find people who haven't awakened to their power yet. We call them latents, and the Lords feed them a bullshit line to get them to serve." Max answered, scanning the room, smiling at the occasional student passing by his field of vision. Surprisingly, no one seemed all that interested in the weird conversation the two of them were having.

"What kind of line?"

"That they're gods, they can make all your wishes come true, blah, blah, blah, shit like that," Max waved his hands around.

"Was that the line they gave you?"

"Pretty much," Max shrugged.

"What did they offer you?"

"Immortality."

"Did it pan out?" Dante asked skeptically.

"Yep, got the brand and everything," Max replied, pulling up his sleeve and showing an old scar in the shape of a sigil.

"You're shitting me," Dante replied.

"Nope, I'm a hundred years old next month. I joined up during the Great War, in the twenties."

"Kind of a big birthday, I'll get you a card."

"Very nice. Anyway, Lucien and I had a falling out during the Blitz, in the Second World War. I saw him for the monster he really was, and he saw me as the free-spirited rebel I really was. It was a real fun time for revelations, let me tell you."

"You're really serious," Dante stated.

Max nodded. "I really am." *No pain.* He was telling the truth.

"Damn. Okay, I take it you had to run?" Dante asked.

"Oh yeah, but before I did, I set up a few other groups to raise hell with Lucien, his flunkies, and the rest of the Royal Lords. We put together a little underground railroad of sorts, right after the war. It made me one of Lucien's least favorite people. Which, after all, was part of the fun." Max replied, occasionally looking down at his arm device to assess the movements of the knights as they searched the dorms.

"So there are others, like you, who are fighting Lucien," Dante said. He looked around, still anxious that they would be in deep shit if the knights rushed in.

"There are a few groups. Louisville has one, led by a guy named McCray. Most of them are former knights like yours truly, though some of them came into power naturally and have been hiding ever since," Max replied. "We steal information and route it through the different groups, making sure our folks stay clear of the Lords' manipulations."

The room had filled up a little, as some sporting event was starting on the TV. Dante walked over to the vending machines and picked up a soda. "You want anything?" He said back to Max.

"I'm good," Max said after swallowing a couple of pills. "I'm surprised that Rachel isn't involved in the search; she's their student contact."

"How do you know her?" Dante said, popping the soda open.

"She's one of ours, one of McCray's rebels," Max said, looking down for a moment. "She volunteered to spy on Lucien eight years ago. Because of her, a lot of people are alive today that Lucien would have harvested or enslaved."

"Sounds pretty heroic," Dante said.

"It is. You have no idea how much danger she's in every day," Max replied.

Dante sat down. "What about Sophia?"

"I have no idea. I didn't know she was Ardent until I saw her in the dungeon a few hours ago," Max responded, looking humbled.

"You know her, though," Dante stated.

"Yeah, from one of the classes that I'm a teaching assistant for," Max answered. "She's the one that lured me into being nabbed."

"How do you mean?"

"She invited me to see this movie at the indie theater up the street. She gave me this line about how it would only make sense to watch an English movie with an Englishman. When we entered the theater, she must have drugged me or something. I passed out. When I woke up, I was in that dungeon."

"Yeah, she got me too," Dante volunteered. "It was the same set up, except for me it was at the carnival."

"If it makes you feel better, she was most likely given a commandment to do it," Max said, "Lucien does shit like that all the time. Sometimes he just does it to test the loyalty of his flunkies. Don't take it personally."

"I'm pretty sure that Rachel handed her the order to get me. Do you think they're working together?" Dante asked.

"Possibly, if Sophia were commanded to get us, there isn't a lot she could have done without getting herself killed. Allowing the arrest to happen and then helping to break us out might have been the only way," Max said. "Or she could be playing Rachel to gain favor with Lucien. We just don't know."

"Rachel seemed to trust her," Dante suggested. "That's something, right?"

"She did," Max replied. "It's a good sign. I take it you and her are an item?"

"Not really. We've been friends for a while now," Dante answered uncomfortably. "I don't want to imagine her as some sort of evil cultist or something."

"We'll need to get the truth out of her," Max said, shifting the topic around. "Looks to me like you'll be able to help with that."

Dante looked confused. "What do you mean?"

"You seemed pretty sensitive to the bullshit lies Lucien was spewing," Max said with a slightly triumphant grin, "You're a Truthsayer, aren't you?"

"I don't know," Dante replied. "Is that rare?"

"As rare as hen's teeth. The only Truthsayers ever recorded were Ancients, and they're supposed to be extinct."

"Are they immune to the harvest, because I overheard one of the guards talking about that?"

"They were reputed to be, yes."

"What's the harvest, anyway?"

"Think cannibalism, without the mess," Max replied. "The Lord literally sucks out your life force until there's nothing left."

"Shit. Okay," Dante said, shaking off a cold chill. "That's nasty."

"Yeah," Max said. "I've seen a few harvests in my day and to be honest, I still have nightmares about them."

"So, if I'm an Ancient," Dante said, changing the topic away from horrible life-force-stealing-death. "What does that mean?"

"I have absolutely no idea," Max said with a wry expression. "You have to understand, there is virtually no factual evidence about the Ancients. There are only stories and half spoken accounts. The Royal Lords burned every bit of information they could get find on the subject."

"Any idea why?" Dante asked.

"Something about their origins," Max answered, "That's the prevailing theory going around the water cooler."

A series of beeps started on Max's armlet. He looked down, at first in confusion, then with a determined anger. "We've got company, Dante," Max said.

"Shit. What do we do?" Dante wanted to know.

"Be ready. They can't take us in view of the norms, but they may try something else."

As the door to the stairwell opened, Dante expected to see one of the goons from the dungeon earlier. He was surprised as Sophia stepped through the door.

Her expression was grim, and perhaps a little scared. Her voice was neither. "Dante, we need to talk," she said.

Dante frowned. "Words every man wants to hear."

THREE

"Are you alone?" Max wanted to know. Sophia walked into the common room with a slow, steady pace. A couple of the students watching the TV eyed her, but said nothing. Sophia glared at them in response to their ogling.

"Yes, the other knights have left the campus." Sophia said, leaning on the armrest of the couch where Max was sitting. Dante wandered over and leaned on the other side.

"Are they going to come back?" Dante asked. He folded his arms in a defensive gesture.

"Eventually, but you're safe for the moment," Sophia replied. "I'm sorry I got you into this, Dante."

"I'm not even sure I know what *this* is." Dante replied.

"Where's Rachel?" Max interrupted.

Sophia looked up to Max. Her green eyes flashed and her lips drew tight. "She wanted me to give you this." Sophia tossed a memory stick to Max. "She said it was very important."

"What happened?" Max questioned, putting the memory stick in a small exposed slot on his armlet. A computerized voice stated that the data was decrypting.

"During your somewhat less than dashing escape, I was working on getting the jammers down. Rachel used the chaos to break into one of Lucien's personal databases. She didn't say what she found, but it was important enough that she ordered me to get it to you immediately."

Dante stayed back, listening. Sophia's entire posture was rigid, like she was barely holding it together on nothing but willpower.

"Lucien brought us both in front of him. He held me responsible for your breakout. Rachel came to my defense, stating that she was the ranking knight in your capture, and therefore should be the culpable party." Sophia lowered her eyes. "Lucien harvested her right there. Two of his lackeys held me back so I could do nothing but watch her die. He then sent all of us after you two without an explanation."

"Son of a bitch," Max spat. "I can't believe it."

"So that shit on the memory stick better be important, since she died protecting me in order to get it to you," Sophia said angrily. "And I'm done with your damn crusade, Max," She glared at him. "I just want out."

"I didn't know you were *in* the fight," Max said.

"For a little over a year now, Rachel is-was--my mentor."

"You're one of the rebels," Dante said.

"Correction: I'm a *former* rebel," Sophia spat. "So leave me the hell alone Max. I've done enough."

Max shook his head. "So you're just going back to Lucien now, be his lap dog, after he killed Rachel?" There was anger in his voice, and it was building quickly.

"No, shithead. I want out, and I'm going to get out, and I'm not going to let your jihad screw me out of my freedom."

Dante looked between them. "Wait a sec. Rachel died for this info. Before we get all pissy, let's see what she thought was worth dying for."

"Fine," Sophia replied.

After a couple of minutes, the armlet completed the decryption and the data started coming in. Max began to scan it. "These look to be analyses of energy prominences in the area. Basically, it's an elaborate radar map of all the Ardent in Louisville. There are some of these signatures that are different from the others. I can't decipher them. The date on this scan is yesterday afternoon. One of the odd signatures is at Waterfront Park standing next to a normal Royal Ardent signature."

"That must be you and me, Dante," Sophia said. "From everything we saw, you're quite a bit different from the ordinary."

"One of the goons called me an Ancient," Dante answered.

"That would help explain the strange signature," Max said. "This came from some system that performed the scan in real-time, meaning every single active Ardent within a fifty mile radius can be isolated with this technology, anytime."

"What does that mean?" Dante wanted to know.

"It means that every rebel and hiding Ardent is easy pickings for Lucien."

"If he has this technology," Sophia chimed in, "why did he have us search for you?"

"He's probably trying to keep it a secret, even from his own people," Dante proposed.

Max nodded. "Also, there are references in this data illustrating that Lucien is contemplating going to war with the other Lords. With this scanner, he would have a significant advantage over them."

"He could kill them all in one fell swoop. The rebels would be sitting ducks," Sophia said grimly. "What about jammers? Could they be used to hide the rebels?"

Max scratched his head and then proceeded to enter in some new numbers. "Standard teleport jammers are completely useless, but with a little modification, maybe we can make something that can mask an Ardent energy signature. Conceptually, each one would only work on a single person, and only for a very limited time, say, fifteen minutes at most."

"That's not enough time for *anything*," Sophia summarized. "They're screwed."

"We need to do something, right?" Dante questioned, as he looked between them.

"Yeah, though it's going be very rough," Max replied.

"What do you have in mind?" Sophia wanted to know.

"We destroy this real-time scanner. We get the rebels together to help us break into Lucien's lair and secure the device. I could run a program to really mess it up, even if we can't break the device physically."

"Goddamn it," Sophia said. "You'll need someone on the inside to lower the security in order to get in, won't you?"

"It would make our chances of success far better, yes," Max replied.

"Fine. I do this, Max, your rebels get rid of Lucien's new toy, and I get out of this business," Sophia demanded. "I just walk away, understand?"

"That's the plan, Sophia. You have my word on it." Max said with a determined voice.

"All right, but we do this my way," Sophia commanded. "Max, you go to the rebels and get us some reinforcements." She turned to Dante. "Dante, I'm going to train you on your new powers." She smirked. "We need to see what you have."

"How dangerous are we talking here?" Dante asked.

"On a scale of one to ten: fourteen, champ," Max said. "But Lucien already wants you dead, so you're not going to make things worse by helping us."

Dante nodded. "Well, that sucks." He raised his eyes. "Oh, what the hell. Yeah, I'm in."

"Good," Sophia smiled. "Rest up tonight, big boy, because tomorrow you belong to me."

"I thought you'd never ask," Dante replied.

．．

True to her word, Sophia was knocking on Dante's door at eight am the next morning. She was dressed to work out, with yoga pants, sneakers and a tank top. Her reddish hair was pulled back into a ponytail, and her expression was an odd mixture of seriousness and amusement.

"Morning, Seraph," she said. "Are you ready for me?"

Dante raised an eyebrow. "It depends. What are we doing today?"

"I thought we'd get breakfast and then go to the gym. It's not open for a few more hours, so we'll have the perfect privacy to work you out on your more than normal abilities."

"Okay," Dante said as he grabbed his coat.

The walk over to the cafeteria was made in relative silence, though before they made it to the doors, Dante spoke up. "Hey, I just wanted to say that I'm sorry about Rachel," he said softly. "She sounds like she was something."

"She was," Sophia replied. "Lucien's going to pay for what he's done. That's not the first time I've seen him do something like that. He's a monster."

Dante nodded, and opened the door for her. She smiled weakly, probably fighting back tears, or perhaps rage - knowing Sophia, probably rage.

The two of them picked up their meals and sat at a table at the far corner of the cafeteria. There was a wall completely made of glass, which shined so much light into the cafeteria that overhead lamps weren't necessary.

As they sat down, Dante spoke again. "So how did you get involved in all of this?"

Sophia stopped for a moment and took a big gulp of her coffee. "It's kind of a long story."

"I've got time," Dante replied. "That is, if you're okay with telling me."

"Sure. It started a few years ago," Sophia said, tugging a little bit on the end of her long ponytail. "We bumped into each other, literally. On my birthday, me and a couple of my girlfriends snuck into this dive of a nightclub on Bardstown Road. You might have heard of it, Bloodlines?"

Dante shook his head, "Nope, but I don't really get out much. You know that."

"We're going there tonight. It's a well-known Ardent hangout," she said with a smirk. "I'll finally get to see if you can dance, Mr. Seraph."

"Lovely. Anyway, you were saying?"

"The place looked like it belonged in a macabre painting. There were all manner of wild things going on."

"I didn't think you were a goth. You certainly don't dress like one," Dante said with a grin.

"I was back then. You should see the PVC, leather, and corset collection I have from those days."

"I thought we were working out today," Dante chuckled. "Though I'll take a rain check if it's all right with you."

"Asshole," she said with no venom. "So we snuck past security. In retrospect, they probably let me in because I was a latent, and then we proceeded to go crazy on the dance floor."

"The owners were Ardent?"

"Yep, and several of the bouncers," Sophia answered. "I ended up dancing with some guy, and he started to get frisky. Lucien walked up to us and told the guy to get lost."

"It doesn't sound like a place a Royal Lord would have been caught hanging out in," Dante summarized. "They seem to be more the tea and crumpets kind of folk."

"Not usually, but since there was a latent in the house, namely me, he came down to recruit. People with the talent are very rare."

"I see," Dante replied. "Go on."

"He said that he ran a courier business, and could use someone to help move packages around town. It sounded a little weird to me, since there is such a thing as the post office, but I was so totally enraptured with him that I just accepted. He met with my parents the following week and for some strange reason, they were okay with me doing this work."

"Lords have mind control?"

"They do, or maybe he was just persuasive. Either way, I got a really cool summer job, and had a totally hot boss."

"Do you know why he did it that way?"

"Yeah, I do. He was waiting for my power to awaken," Sophia said. "There's no way to tell when a latent will get their powers. It didn't take long for me though. I got them about two months after I started working for Lucien."

"What can you do?" Dante asked.

"Oh no, that comes later. I show you mine after you show me yours." She winked.

"Well, if you're going to be like that," Dante huffed. "So, what happened *after* you got your powers?"

"When I became a full-fledged Ardent, Lucien gave me more responsibility in his organization. He assigned Rachel as my mentor, and she taught me how to use the new abilities," Sophia said, twirling the straw in her orange juice.

"I take it you didn't like what you had to do," Dante said. "You mentioned that on the night of the carnival."

"Yeah, it sucked," Sophia replied. "When I think back, it had less to do with what I had to do, rather it was what he wanted me to be."

"What do you mean?"

"First off, I was a goth chick. I liked it. It was what I was comfortable with. One day I was just told that it wasn't appropriate for my mission and I had to change *everything.*"

"Your mission?"

"Apparently Lucien thought something big was going to go down at this college. He appointed me as the official recruiter/spy. I was supposed to identify any latents on the campus and report their identities to Rachel, who would arrange for an introduction with Lucien."

"Doesn't sound too bad," Dante said as he raised an eyebrow.

"I thought the same thing at first. About a year ago I found out what happened to the people who refused. Rachel showed me. They were either brainwashed or harvested. Have you ever wondered why there are so many accidents outside the campus on the main road?"

Dante thought for a moment, "There's at least a few of them each year. They've been working on getting that traffic light added to help with that."

"That's all bull," Sophia said. "While not all of them, the majority are latents being taken out. When I learned about that I went in search of the rebels. Thankfully for me, Rachel was one. We kept each other's secret."

"Was I supposed to be brought in for the same reason? Is that what was on the scroll?"

"No, you didn't get the pitch. He just wanted to kill you. I didn't much care for that," Sophia said with a look of disgust. "In case you've been wondering, I didn't ask you to the carnival to nab you."

"Oh yeah?" Dante asked. "Why did you then?"

"Maybe I'll tell you someday, but we've got to get to the gym before the place opens. Let's move it, *Seraph*."

∴

Sophia walked up to the gym door first with her bag on her back. Dante scrutinized the doors as he came up behind her. They were not quite as solid as the doors holding them prisoner in that dungeon, but it would make a real ruckus if he had to break them open.

She slung her bag with one hand, holding out her other one. "Take my hand," She said with a grin. "That is, if you want to live."

"That isn't even the least bit funny," Dante made a face. He complied, however, and in an instantaneous flash of blue light, they were inside the gym. Dante shook his head from the slight disorientation. "You can teleport like Max can," he said in wonder.

"Yep," Sophia smirked. "It's one of my many talents."

"I'll refrain from commenting."

"Nice one. Very clever," Sophia said. She flipped the light switches on and the entire gym awakened. The world was bathed in white light. Sophia led him towards a set of mats at the far end of the gymnasium. They were a little different than the others. The mats and the walls surrounding them looked far sturdier than their normal counterparts.

"You are in for a treat, Seraph," Sophia said, her hand presenting the room to him. "We can go pretty hard in here. This area has been reinforced with Ardent power. The walls, mats and beams don't break very easily. It's a great environment for a big, strong, tough guy like you."

"Okay, so what do we do first?" Dante wanted to know.

"To start, I'll put up a force field. You hit it as hard as you can. We'll see how strong you are," Sophia chuckled. She rolled up her sleeve and ran her hand along the exposed flesh. A gold armband appeared out of nowhere, coming into existence with a bluish shimmer.

"What is that?" Dante asked.

"It's my conduit," Sophia replied. "All the Lucien's bitch knights have one just like it. If you destroy the armband, the schmucks won't be able to work any of their Ardent mojo. Remember that."

With a practiced gesture, Sophia rolled her shoulder and pushed her arms out. Blue light seeped from the armband like water from a pouring pitcher and froze into an energy shield affixed in front of her.

"Okay. Hit it, stud."

Dante tapped the field experimentally. The bluish light shimmered and felt completely solid. "All right, if you insist." He reared back and slammed his fist into the shield. It collapsed immediately. "Hard enough for you?" he said in satisfaction.

Sophia's face went slack in shock. "Damn," she said, "Yeah, I guess that will do. We'll need to see how fast you are next."

"How do you want to test that?" Dante wondered. "Do you need a stopwatch or something?"

Sophia made a face. "Not exactly. You ever do any martial arts training?"

"Yeah, in high school," Dante said. Reaching into his pocket, he put on a pair of sunglasses. "I can honestly say, 'I know kung fu.'"

Sophia rolled her eyes. "Cute. Come on, big man, I want you to take me."

"Excuse me?" Dante pulled the sunglasses off his face. His jaw hung slightly open. "You don't mean?"

"Come at me, try to take me down," Sophia clarified. The gauntlet on her arm glowed again and a long spear-like appendage grew out of the end. At its extension, it was a completely formed *pata* weapon. The device was three feet long with a glove and blade forged together.

"You're serious?"

Sophia laughed, "Aw, you're not scared of me, are you?"

Dante raised his arms in a fighting stance. "You asked for it." He rushed forward towards Sophia quickly, reaching out to grab her arm. Sophia smirked and slammed the flat of her blade into Dante's legs, knocking him face first onto the ground.

"Not so quick, are you, stud?" Sophia teased. "Care to try again?"

"You bet your ass," Dante replied. He pushed himself up and rushed at her a second time. This time, he attempted a vault sideways in the middle, bringing his legs up in a horizontal cartwheel.

"I love the whole twirling thing," Sophia said. She stepped to the side and slapped his legs again. The force of the impact spun him around and slammed him down on his back.

She walked by and stood over him. "Try again," she said. "This time, try to concentrate a little more, okay?"

Dante stumbled back up. "Okay, maybe I can't move any faster." He dusted off his pants. "Can we move on to something else?"

"There's no way you're getting off that easy." Sophia shook her head. She closed the distance with Dante and put her hand on his chest. "Don't be such a wimp." She narrowed her eyes and put her hand on her hip. "If you are an Ancient, you're supposed to have powers of speed and well as strength. We need to know exactly what you can do if we're going to be able to bust up that scanner."

"You know, for a race which was forbidden to be discussed, the Ancients seem to have a lot of fans."

"Yeah, well, I read banned books in high school too."

Dante threw his hands up. "How can you be sure you're right about these powers?"

"It's the Truthsayer-ness. That one is definitely an Ancient-only thing. So quit your belly-aching and get back to it."

Dante grumbled to himself, but complied. Sophia strode away and got into position.

"Don't think, just focus," she said.

As he sprinted towards her, time seemed to slow down. Sophia was moving at a progressively slower speed. Eventually it appeared to Dante that she was nearly standing still, like a video moving at one frame per second.

Dante stepped over the lance, one leg after the other, as it was frozen in a swing at the level of his shins. He grabbed Sophia by the shoulders. Dante then stepped forward, wrapping his leg around hers. It was a simple takedown, the opposing force pushing Sophia to the ground.

The one part he didn't consider is that when it came to martial takedowns, he was very out of practice. During the maneuver, Dante lost his balance and landed on top of her.

As his focus wavered, time returned to normal. Dante grinned down at Sophia. "Gotcha," he said triumphantly.

"Not bad," she said, her face flushed. "I barely saw you move."

"I guess you were right."

"What was that?" she said innocently. "Speak up. I didn't hear that last part."

"I said, I guess you were right," he replied with an exasperated sigh.

"Now that you have me, what are you going to do with me?" Sophia whispered.

"I hope I'm not interrupting the... training," Max said, wandering up to the two. Dante vaulted off of Sophia like a bottle rocket. He landed on his behind a few feet away. Sophia leisurely sat up and burst out into laughter.

"Your timing is impeccable," Dante growled. He stood up and walked back over.

"I need to go visit an old friend of mine. I thought it would be good for you to meet her," Max said. "Her name's Janet, and she's a rebel, one of McCray's gang."

"She? Hmm…" Dante said, looking over a Sophia with a conspiratorial wink.

Max was quick to respond. "It's not what you think. We're just mates." Pain wracked Dante's head from the lie. *It sucked.* He had to figure out how to control the reaction. Dante certainly didn't want to go through life falling down every time someone told a fib.

"Max, you do realize who you're talking to, right?" Dante raised an eyebrow.

"Hell, that's going to get really annoying," Max replied, making an exaggerated frown. Sophia laughed quietly, letting her smile annoy Max further.

"Think about how it is for me. I may never be able to date again," Dante replied, half seriously.

Sophia smirked. "Oh, I think you'll do all right." She turned to Max. "Are you going over to see your girl now?"

"Yeah, she's up at the school," Max replied. "You guys done with your, ahem, *training* for today?"

"Smartass," Sophia took Dante's arm. "Let's go then." She picked up her bag and headed out. The group passed through the newly opened doors, since the gym was now open, and followed the walkway to Max's car. Sophia opened the rear door and all but pushed Dante inside. Max came around and took the driver's seat. He started the car and took it away from the campus.

During the drive, Sophia struck up a conversation. "You're quite the lady-killer, aren't you, Max?"

Max chuckled, "It's the accent, you know. Gets 'em every time."

"Ever have an issue with the whole immortality thing?" Dante said, more thoughtfully. "Can't imagine that being too easy to deal with."

Max thought for a moment and responded quietly, "Well, having lived for nearly a century, I can honestly tell you that *any* relationship with a woman is hard. I take it you've never had a serious lady-friend?"

Sophia chuckled, "This conversation has just turned interesting. Answer the man's question, *Seraph*."

Dante shook his head. "That's just mean. No, I haven't."

Max laughed, "Hey, man, I knew it from the beginning. It's written all over you."

"Ass," Dante stated.

"Touché, though you are right. It's hard to explain to someone that you're going to remain young while they head towards Social Security. It's even harder if you don't tell them. Then you have to pretend to age, or fake your own death every now and then. All of it just to make sure your appearance makes sense with your identity."

"Sounds lonely," Dante replied.

Max nodded in agreement, "Yeah, yeah, it can certainly be that way. I think that's why I made this identity to go back to school with. You know, to be around people again. Hey, we're here."

Dante stepped out of the car in front of a martial arts school. A stylized crane was perched over the top of the place with the words **Free Crane Martial Arts** set in red letters right beneath the bird.

Max knocked on the door, while tapping a couple of keys on his armlet. "I need to send the pass codes in." He explained. A shrill beep followed. "Access granted."

"My turn." Sophia tapped her forearm, after which her gold gauntlet shimmered into existence. A positive bell sound followed. "I'm good, too."

Max looked at Dante, who obviously didn't know what this was all about. "Each rebel has an authorization code. It prevents knights from sneaking into rebel safe houses. The houses are set up with defenses should any knights try to break in or sneak past security. We've been verified, and I let them know you're my guest," he said. The door opened. A teenager and a woman in her thirties were standing there.

"Mark, Janet," Max said, "Good to see you."

Mark smiled. "Likewise, Max. How have you been?"

"I've been good, Mark, thanks."

Janet cut into the conversation. Her tone was not pleased. "Why are you here, Max?"

Max was a little surprised at the reaction, but answered quickly, "This is not something we should discuss on the street. May we come in?"

"Sure," Janet said, leading the group inside. There was a main area with clean white mats and a touch of padding underneath. A row of colored belts caught the light above a set of training mirrors. The group ended their journey at a small office in which Janet stepped behind an oak desk.

"Okay, so we're inside now." Janet was clearly not happy. "So… talk."

"Hey, lady," Dante said. "No reason to be like that."

"I'm sorry, but who the hell are you?" Janet snapped in response.

"This is Dante," Max said. "He helped me escape from Lucien's dungeon."

"Not bad, kid, but keep your trap shut regarding things that don't concern you."

Dante glared. "This is ridiculous."

"Janet, Rachel's dead," Max said abruptly. "Lucien killed her last night."

The older woman deflated. She closed her eyes for a moment and lowered her head. "What happened?"

"She discovered something in Lucien's databases and sent me out to get it to you," Sophia answered. "In order to do that, Rachel protected me from Lucien's misplaced wrath, and got killed in the process."

"Damn it," Janet spat. "What was the information?"

Sophia looked at Max, who answered, "Lucien has developed some kind of Ardent scanner. It gives him the ability to detect every Ardent in the city. Jammers don't seem to stop it, either."

"What's the range?" Janet wanted to know. She pulled out a pad of paper from her desk, and started making notes.

"A radius of fifty miles," Max answered, "at least."

"Shit," Janet growled. "So I take it you've come here to tell us we need to get the hell out of town?"

"Far from it," Max answered. "We're going to destroy it, and we want your help."

"Where is it?" Janet asked.

Max tapped a few keys on his armlet. "According to the data retrieved from Lucien, it's in a warehouse on Seventh Street and Wilkerson."

"That's a four story building. That's also a fortified installation for Lucien's servants. What kind of hair-brained plan could you dream up that would allow us to destroy that device and get out of there alive?" Janet demanded.

"We're going to leverage Sophia's access to get us inside, but we'll need rebel backup to make sure that we can make it to the device before getting overwhelmed by Lucien's knights."

"So you want to use us as cannon fodder?" Janet snapped. "There is no way I'm asking any of my rebels to do that."

"I'm still a knight in good standing," Sophia chimed in. "This plan can work, we just need some support."

"I can't believe you are suggesting this," Janet growled at Max. "You should know better, Max. It's suicide, plain and simple."

"On the contrary, it's a good plan, and if we don't do something, we'll need to abandon Louisville for good," Max summarized. "Lucien's been anxious to give us dirt naps for years. He'll make good on it now."

"Then we abandon the city," Janet responded. "We'll set up somewhere else."

"That's completely insane," Max answered. "What happens when he finds us again? And again? Lucien is power hungry. He's not going to stop until he takes the whole bloody country."

"Not my problem, Max." Janet shook her head. "We just need to keep moving."

"Would you at least take the request to McCray? He may want to weigh in on the attack."

"It's not worth his time," Janet said. "Now if we're done here, I've got evacuations to arrange."

"We're not done here, not by a long shot," Max growled.

Janet cut him off. "Oh, yes, we are. Time for a reality check. This is my place, Max, and these are my people. They're not yours and, to be frank, you haven't been involved in the Ardent Rebellion for three damn years. So don't waltz in here like some kind of king, expecting us to just bow to your whims. You're not a hero anymore, Max. You're not even a sidekick. You're on the *sidelines*. You run around with your own plots, but time and time again, you fail the people who rely on you the most."

Max snapped, "Go then, run away with your tail between your bloody legs. See if I lift a finger for your stupid ass again." He stalked out of the office and sped out the door to his car.

Dante and Sophia looked at each other. Sophia walked out first, Dante following quickly behind. Janet remained behind her desk, barely acknowledging the departures.

"Well, that could have gone better," Dante said.

"She's scared. All the rebels are," Sophia replied. "As they should be, but you can't just run from Lucien forever. He finds you, no matter how far you go. He's a persistent bastard."

"Shit," Dante spat. "That sucks."

"It truly does," Sophia answered. "There's not much we can do about it, though."

Thankfully, Max hadn't driven off without them. Dante and Sophia took their seats in silence, and Max sped away from the school without a word.

Finally mustering up the courage to speak by the time they reached the interstate, Dante spoke, "You all right?"

"An assault on the installation is out of the question," Max answered, brows creased in concentration. "Without rebel support, we would be overwhelmed the moment we teleported in. Not to mention we'd alert all sorts of police and authorities who might rip open our little secret world if we got into a real fire fight."

"We can still succeed if we move by stealth," Sophia responded. "We have a few other constraints, but if we timed things right, I could sneak you guys in and get you out before anyone's the wiser."

"How do you suppose you can do that?" Dante asked. "We'd be doing this completely alone. I don't know about you, but I'm reluctant to go up against an entire unit of those punks again."

"Leave it to me." Sophia nearly smirked. "I need to do some homework first, but, I'm telling you, we can do this."

"Meet up with you tomorrow then?" Dante said eagerly. "Is that enough time?"

"Oh no, mister, you're not getting off the hook that easily," Sophia said. "We have a trip to the most-enjoyable Bloodlines tonight."

"You're taking him there?" Max said. "That is hilarious."

"What's that supposed to mean?" Dante said, his ego slightly bruised.

"Oh no, it's okay, I'm sure you'll be fine," Max said with a chuckle. He looked at Sophia. "I expect pictures."

She nodded with a sly smile. "Oh yeah, it will be one for the record books."

"Perfect, just perfect," Dante groaned. "What time?"

"Just after nightfall, wear something black." She winked. "This is a *goth* club, Dante. Keep that in perspective when you pick your outfit."

"As long as you do too," Dante replied.

"Oh, I don't think you'll be disappointed."

Slicking back his dark hair one more time, Dante stood in front of Sophia's dorm room door. The long black coat, complete with black leather pants and a dark grey shirt, was totally not his style, but Sophia was pretty specific as to the wardrobe requirement of their destination.

He knocked on the door only once. The door opened slowly, revealing Sophia in a whole different way.

Her heels were tall enough that she was looking him in the eye. Her legs were covered with tight, shiny black pants, which traced every contour of her well defined legs. Her torso was covered in a frilly blood red construction. It was tight enough to leave little to the imagination. A large choker was latched around her neck. Her lipstick was red, her eyeliner black. Her hair was done up in a twist, completing the ensemble.

Sophia cocked her hip to the side, presenting herself. "So, are you disappointed?"

"Not even a little bit. You look…" Dante said in awe.

She smiled, very pleased. "Amazing? Auspicious? Delectable?"

"Yes, yes, and… well, I did eat before I came by."

"You look pretty auspicious yourself. The leather pants do good things for you."

"Well, I didn't want to stand out at this place," Dante said.

"You will, but not for the reason you're worried about," Sophia replied. The pair of them walked outside, heading towards the parking lot. The rising moon reflected off of Sophia's skin. She looked like she was glowing. Dante shook his head to avoid staring.

"Come on, I'll drive."

It was Dante's turn to smirk. "Oh no, there's no way."

"What do you mean?"

"Hi, have you met me? I'm an Ancient, remember?"

"Why thank you for that wondrous revelation. So…"

"So, my way of transportation is cheaper, more fuel efficient and a hell of a lot more fun."

"You can't teleport, so what on earth are you talking about?" Sophia asked.

Dante looked around. Thankfully it was pretty quiet. There was no one else in sight. He scooped her up in his arms. "Think you can navigate from the air?" He said triumphantly.

"Wait, are you saying you can *fly*?"

"I just found out this afternoon," Dante replied. "Pretty sweet, huh?"

"That is freaking unbelievable. Are you sure you're up to this?"

"I think I'll be able to manage. I should be able to avoid any birds on our way."

"If I get bird shit on this outfit, you are in trouble," Sophia warned.

Dante leapt up into the sky and kept going. Sophia clung to him tightly and yelped. Dante chuckled as they split through the first layer of clouds. "It's okay, Sophia, I'm not going to drop you."

"I'm not scared, smartass. You just surprised me," Sophia snapped.

"*Sure* I did. It's okay, baby. I'll protect you."

"You're so manly," she drawled. "I am all a-quiver by having your strong arms around me."

"Don't you know it," Dante said with a grin.

"Do you know how fast we're going?"

"I don't have a speedometer, Sophia," Dante said. "Though I think we're moving faster than the cars down there."

"Wait, there it is. Take us down. Land in that alley, behind the club." Sophia pointed to the location and Dante complied. The pair touched down quietly and undetected.

She led him forward, taking his hand immediately upon landing. They could hear the bass from the sound system outside the building. The music was dark, heady and exotic. It certainly fit the profile of a gothic style, heavy metal club.

"Hey Joe, haven't seen you in a while," Sophia said to the bouncer at the front door.

"Hey it's the big S," Joe said with a smile. "Long time, no see. Who's your friend?"

"This is Seraph," Sophia said, ignoring the look that Dante gave her. "Seraph, this is Joe."

"Nice to meet you, Joe."

"You too," Joe replied. "You guys looking for the coven?"

"At some point, but mostly we're just hanging out," Sophia said. "I'm showing my new boy here the ropes."

"Cool. You two have fun now, you hear?"

"Will do. Thanks Joe. See you later." Sophia smiled, leading Dante into the club.

"Seraph?" Dante questioned.

"Do you really want them to have your real name?"

"No, I guess not."

"Besides, with the outfit, the name is very hot."

"I aim to please."

"You do." She pressed up against him as they maneuvered up to the bar. The pair ordered drinks and took a scan of the room.

"So, what's the coven?" Dante said, nursing his drink slowly.

"It's a long story, but the leader is a man named Dmitri," Sophia said. "He's a bit of an information broker, though he's occasionally worked with the Lords in a more direct capacity."

"Does he file their taxes or something?"

"More like enforcing their commands. I need to find him before we leave," Sophia explained.

"Shit, what are you looking for?"

"With the scanner active, we need to know if Lucien has been moving to engage the other Lords. Dmitri would know. I can't risk asking someone in Lucien's employ, as it could blow my cover."

Dante looked around. "Do you see Dmitri?"

"He's over there." Sophia pointed at a pair in the corner. There was a man latched on to a girl's neck, giving her a hickey.

"What's he doing?" Dante looked in disgust. Even over the loud music, Dante could swear that he heard slurping noises.

"He's feeding from her," Sophia stated. Her tone was flat, as if it was a completely normal occurrence.

"Excuse me?" Dante nearly choked on his drink.

"Yeah, that's kind of a long story, too. Dmitri is a vampire, Dante."

"A vampire," Dante said, saying the words out loud to assist in his processing of them. It didn't work. "A vampire?" Dante looked stunned. "You're serious? There are *vampires*?"

"Oh yeah," Sophia replied.

"You mean, turn into bats, vampire?"

"No, they can't do that," Sophia answered.

Dante kept going. "Burn in the sunlight?"

"Nope, they just lose all their powers."

"Stake through the heart, long in the tooth, vampire?"

"Yep," Sophia said, "though a stake through the heart pretty much kills anything."

"That's disgusting."

"Yeah, it's not pleasant to try to break through the rib cage."

"I don't mean that. I mean watching Dmitri make a meal of that girl."

Sophia raised an eyebrow, "Out in public? They're getting bold."

"That sucks," Dante said. "Literally. We should do something."

"Let's go say hi," Sophia said, running her hand down her arm, summoning her gauntlet into existence. Dante nodded. Sophia led them both through the crowd towards the corner.

Sophia grabbed Dmitri's shoulder, shaking him enough to get his attention. Dmitri retracted his fangs and turned around. The blond prey wobbled on her high heels for a moment and fell. Dante caught her and urged her into a chair.

"I think she's had enough," Sophia smiled. "You're too rough on these mortals, Dmitri. They just can't handle you."

"I've not met a woman who could," Dmitri said, wiping his mouth with a quickly reddening handkerchief. "It is most agreeable to see our favorite knight of Lucien. How have you been doing, my dear?"

"I'm very well, good sir," Sophia said smoothly, allowing Dmitri to kiss her hand. Despite himself, Dante bristled. He glared at the vampire.

"Now, what have we here?" Dmitri said. His mouth was still tinted red from his interrupted meal. "You're impetuous, aren't you? What's your name, boy?"

"Seraph," Dante said.

"Well, how biblical," Dmitri said sarcastically.

Dante was direct. "You always try to eat your guests?"

"Not always, but when I do, I assure you they don't mind," Dmitri replied. A lie rang in Dante's head. He gritted his teeth and nodded slowly.

"We're here for information, Dmitri. I was hoping you'd be able to help us out," Sophia said, taking the focus off of the confrontation that was brewing in front of her.

"I am always willing to help our friends in the Royal Compact." Dmitri urged them to sit. "What may I help you with?"

"Word on the street is that war is coming," Sophia said. "Have you heard of movement from the other Lords?"

"Ah yes, I have heard of such tales, but far more in the province of your Lord, rather than the others. There is talk that he has a special detection method which allows him to know the location of any Ardent in the region."

"Interesting," Sophia said with a sultry tone.

"Yes," Dmitri replied, taking Sophia's hand again. "As always, my coven will remain neutral in the affairs, unless secured by one of the Lords."

"I was under the impression that Lucien had you on permanent retainer," Sophia stated.

"We are...eager to renegotiate the contract." Dmitri smiled a shark's smile.

"I'll pass that along."

"Please do. We would very much like to serve Lord Lucien again," Dmitri said. "Now, if there is nothing else, I would like to return to my evening."

"Thank you, Dmitri," Sophia said.

"As well to you, my lady." Dmitri kissed Sophia's hand again and then departed. He vanished quickly into the crowds of people on the dance floor.

Dante looked up at Sophia, scowling. "You're going to need to disinfect that hand, you know."

"Are you jealous, *Seraph*?"

"Possessive," he replied. "Big difference."

"Kinky. I've never been possessed before, I might like it."

"Ha, ha. You're so funny." Dante frowned.

"Of course I am." Sophia looked around. "Are you ready to leave?"

"I guess so," Dante answered.

"I'm not. You still owe me a dance." Sophia took his hand and led Dante onto the dance floor. "Come on, Seraph. Show me what you got."

And he did.

Four

"The plan is pretty simple," Sophia said on the next night, with the authority of a professor as she stood in front of a whiteboard.

The three of them had set up in one of the library's study rooms. Since it was after ten o'clock, the entire library was pretty dead, with only one librarian on staff. It was a good place to discuss clandestine plans, and they had vending machines.

"All right, on the third Saturday of next month, I'm going to enter the building at eleven o'clock. I'll start off in the main office and wait there for thirty-five minutes, acting like I'm reading some reports in my workspace. I'll add the detection device to a port on one of the workstations. The gadget will broadcast the sync timer with the main security system," Sophia said, pointing to the basic blueprint of the building on the whiteboard.

Dante groaned. This was worse than organic chemistry. "How come the detection device won't trip the security?" he asked.

Max raised his arm computer and showed off the circuitry. "This apparatus is keyed to the detection module, but the device isn't actually *doing* anything. It's not sending off any GPS coordinates, or interfacing with the security subsystems in any way. Its only job is to provide a relay for the apparatus in my tech here. That way, I can scan the systems remotely, and bypass the system as if I were standing in the room. It's how I am going to be able to time our entrance to the exact moment when the security system goes down."

Dante nodded. "Okay, moral of the story is that timing is critical. Got it."

"Good. Okay, that brings us to entry," Sophia continued. "I will go to the restroom on the basement level, and plant the second detection device there. It will serve as your entry point. I will return upstairs. The main system, jammers and security will deactivate for a fifteen minute maintenance window."

"That's why the specific day, there's a downtime in the system," Dante stated.

"Correct, that's when you both will teleport in. You will wait in the back of the restroom for a moment to avoid the patrol. You will then proceed to the server room. You will have the fifteen minutes to locate and destroy the scanner. That gives you just enough time to teleport out before the security system and teleport jammers go back online."

Max nodded, and smirked with a touch of a smug expression. "We'll activate the scan masking right before we jump in. If we're being monitored, they'll think we're still on campus. Fifteen minutes will be plenty of time."

Sophia didn't look convinced. "At the end of the maintenance window, I will signal an alarm upstairs, it should draw the knights away from your location. I'll provide information that it was a false alarm to the head knight in Lucien's court, cover our tracks electronically and leave when the whole thing is settled. Are there any questions?"

Dante mockingly raised his hand. Sophia smirked and called on him. He asked his question quickly, "So my entire role in this operation is to be the beat-stick in case something goes wrong and we need to fight our way out?"

"That's right. With Lucien away on business, and since he never goes there anyway, none of the other guards is as strong as you. If necessary, fight your way upstairs. Oh, and make sure if you run into me you attack me too. We need to reinforce that I'm still on their side," Sophia said, with a hint of a smile. "Don't worry, Dante. I'll go easy on you."

Max smiled. "Piece of cake, right?"

Dante shrugged. "So, what do we do until the third Saturday?"

"Well, I would think you'd want to study for your exams, but that's just me," Sophia chuckled. "I think we should train some more, you and I. The more skilled you are with your powers, the better our chances for success if something goes wrong."

"You're a glutton for punishment, huh?" Dante smirked.

"If by punishment, you mean inflicting it on you, then yes, I suppose I am," Sophia replied. Dante made a face.

"I think she won this round, champ." Max clapped.

"It's not over yet," Dante answered, his eyes never leaving hers.

∴

FIVE WEEKS LATER

"Wait, did you say *fly*?" Max said as he and Dante walked towards the library.

"Sure did. It was neat trick to pull on Sophia," Dante replied with a grin. "It didn't help me, though."

"I saw the crack in the gym wall. Did you do that?"

"Not on purpose. Technically Sophia did it using me as the projectile." Dante shrugged.

"Damn, she punted you right through the wall?"

"Yep, she's vicious," Dante said.

"Not that you mind, I'm sure," Max answered.

"I'm not entirely sure what you mean."

"You are seriously affecting my ability to live vicariously through you," Max said with a grin.

"It wasn't so long ago you thought she was a spy," Dante stated. "Now you're waiting for us to hook up?"

"Hey, I'll admit when I'm wrong. There's a lot of proof. She had the access codes to the rebel safe house. She's given me extensive knowledge of Lucien's holdings and resources. If Sophia is a spy, then I'm a goose."

"Where are we supposed to meet her?" Dante looked around at the dark hill behind the library.

"In that outcropping down there," Max said. "Look, there she is." Sophia saw them on the top and waved.

Dante looked to see if anyone else was around. Satisfied that they were alone, he jumped off the edge of the hill. He floated down, landing on the platform with barely a sound.

"Showoff," Max said as he slipped and slid down the hill.

"You boys ready?" Sophia asked.

Max nodded. "We're locked and loaded, awaiting your signal."

"Dante?"

"I'm set," he said. "Don't worry, I'll be fine."

"I know you will. Remember, if I see you, I'm going to attack you, so don't hesitate."

"I understand," Dante replied.

"See you on the other side, *Seraph*." Sophia summoned her armlet and a bluish shimmer enveloped her. She blew Dante a kiss as she vanished from sight.

"Not one word, Max," Dante commanded. Max just shrugged with a smirk on his face.

"I wasn't going to say anything, champ." Max grinned. Dante rolled his eyes.

Approximately a half hour later, Max's armlet began to beep.

"She did it. The first device has been planted." Max said evenly. "I am now getting data on the system clock. The jammers are going down. We're all set for the teleport."

Dante nodded. "Standing by."

"The second detection device has been planted. I'm getting the layout now." Max gestured. "This is it. Here we go," Max said and proceeded to count down the last two minutes, and when the end came, a faint blue light circled the two of them. The next second saw a bright flash project in front of Dante's eyes. When he next opened them, the world was a different place.

Dante's eyes adjusted. They were in a small alcove in what looked like a two person restroom. Max was next to him. The room was very quiet, with only the sounds of footsteps above disturbing the complete silence. Max stalked over to the door and peeked through.

"Masking devices are online and stable. I see the sentries. They're passing by now," Max said. Counting to five, Max opened the door softly and gestured for Dante to follow him. Using his arm computer as a guide, Max shuttled them to a security door at the end of a long hallway.

"It's locked. Access codes are needed," Max said. He clacked on his keypads for a moment and the door opened. "Twelve minutes left, we need to find the scanner."

Dante and Max had been given very clear instructions from the recovered data as to what the scanner looked like. The device was about as big as a dishwasher and shaped like a rough trapezoid with blue running lights across one side. In the center was a very large black crystal.

In the ten minutes which comprised their search, they found nothing that fit that description.

"I don't see it, Max. Could it be somewhere else in the complex?"

"No way, this is the only room with sufficient power consumption to have a device like that. I think this is just a server farm."

"Two minutes," Dante said. "We need to get out of here."

"Okay, stand by for teleport," Max said, punching keys on his armlet.

Nothing happened. "Max?"

"I'm getting a new reading. The jammers are back up." Max shook his head.

"We still had two minutes," Dante said incredulously.

"I think we've been discovered," Max said. "We're going to have to fight our way out. Dante, get ready."

Dante opened the door, only to see four armed men walking towards them. "Shit!"

Max shut the door.

"What the hell are you doing?" Dante snapped. "This is a dead end."

"I'm not getting riddled with holes, that's what I'm doing. Seal the bloody door."

Dante complied, locking the security door shut. "Terrific, now what do we do?"

"I try to find the jammer within the network and shut it down. You stand by that door and kick the shit out of anyone who gets through."

"We are so screwed," Dante summarized.

The door latch unlocked and the four figures behind it started to pile in. The first guard didn't even make it into the room before Dante struck him in the chin with a roundhouse kick. The impact spun the guard, tumbling him out into the hallway.

The second guard didn't make the same mistake. He opened fire with a bolt of lightning from his gauntlet. The bolt struck Dante in the chest and sent him hurtling into one of the server racks. Machinery and sparks flew as Dante struggled back to his feet.

The guard, impressed by his previous success, moved into the confines of the room, his arm raised to launch another electrical surge at Dante if he took any offense action.

Dante took a *very* offensive action. He accelerated to superhuman velocity and everyone around him began to move in slow motion. Dante jumped into a long dash which was made impossibly long by the power of his flight. He grabbed the guard from above, one hand on each shoulder. Dante spun around in a circle, taking the guard with him, releasing him at the apex of the spin. The guard was flung into the hallway, striking the approaching guards with enough force to knock them down.

Dante slammed the door shut. He smashed the control panel with his fist, hoping it would keep it from being reopened so easily.

"We're out of time, Max," Dante snapped. "Where the hell is that teleport?"

"I'm moving as fast as I can," Max rebutted. "It doesn't seem to be on the main system."

Something slammed into the door a few times, and the sounds of electricity arching off the door could be heard from inside.

"This door isn't going to hold long," Dante said.

"Champ, with all due respect," Max said evenly, "shut the hell up. I'm trying to work here."

A bluish shimmer appeared in front of the door. Dante stepped back. "What the hell is that?"

Max spun around and drew his armlet up in defense. "That's a Portalis effect. A teleportation portal."

A man stepped through. He was adorned simply but elegantly in a coal black suit. His neck had a red tie around it, and he wore a gold and silver gauntlet on one arm.

"Oh, bloody hell," Max stammered. "Lucien."

"Hello, Max," Lucien said as he walked into the room. Max responded by opening fire with a bolt of blue electricity from his armlet. The bolt cascaded through the air and slammed into Lucien, who ignored it without a care. "You should know better by now, son."

"I'm not your son, you bloody bastard," Max spat.

"Take him," Lucien said to the two remaining guards.

Dante stepped in front of Max to shield him. The guards grabbed Dante's arms from either side. Dante threw his arms out and propelled the guards into the opposite walls of the room.

"Ah, the Ancient," Lucien said.

"Back off," Dante commanded. He brought his hands up in a fighting stance. There was no point in subtlety now.

Lucien was not concerned. "Interesting. I had wondered if your power was equal to the myths. I am eager to find out."

Lucien rushed forward and struck Dante on the chin with a right cross. The force of the impact shattered the air and rattled the server racks. Dante spun and skidded onto the ground, landing on his face.

Growling, Dante leaped back up and approached Lucien with a punch of his own. Lucien grabbed his fist in mid-throw. The Lord then pushed down, pressing Dante to his knees. He resisted, and the floor beneath both of them cracked under the pressure.

Dante broke the grip and slammed his other fist into Lucien's throat. Gagging, Lucien slumped over, only to be struck again with Dante's knee as it came up in a strike. Lucien was thrown back, but remained on his feet.

"Impressive," Lucien said, rubbing his throat. "But not impressive enough." Lucian pointed at Dante. Lightning leapt from his hand and struck Dante in the chest. He came off the ground and slammed into the back wall. Sparks flew as the servers crashed down from the shelves, breaking on impact.

Dante spat a glob of blood out of his mouth. He staggered back to his feet. Max was grabbed by the two guards in the room and pinned in place.

"You are persistent," Lucien said.

"I'm just getting warmed up, asshole."

Dante rushed forward, lunging at the Lord. Lucien sidestepped the attack and slammed his hand into the back of Dante's neck. The Ancient slammed into the ground, chipping the tile on the floor.

"It appears that the power of the Ancients was overstated," Lucien said.

Dante tried to stand. A sharp searing pain indicated that his left leg was broken. He forced his way up, bones rubbing together, and leapt at Lucien with failing strength, striking Lucien's face with desperate ferocity. The impact knocked Lucien down, sending him skidding into a wall.

"Maybe not," Dante said, wavering on his feet.

Lucien soared out from the wall and struck Dante's ribs with his fist. He felt some of the them crack immediately. Dante attempted to raise his hand to strike Lucien again, only to have it snatched out of the air. Lucien bent his arm and snapped it at the elbow. Dante collapsed on the ground, barely conscious.

"Maybe so," Lucien smiled. He walked over to the sealed door and pried it open. "Sophia, you may come in now."

Sophia walked into the room. Her face was passive as she avoided looking at the bloody mess that was Dante. "My Lord?"

"You have delivered the traitor and the Ancient," Lucien said formally. "As agreed, I release you from my service. You may now leave with my blessing, my dear."

"Thank you, Lord Lucien," Sophia replied. "That is... most generous of you."

Dante tried to say something, but nothing came out. Max didn't have that problem.

"You bloody whore!" he spat. "How could you do this to him?"

Sophia looked at Max, her face a cool mask. "I'd worry about myself if I were you Max. I'd give you about five minutes to live."

Without another word, Sophia walked back out through the door.

"Now, Max, you and I have some unfinished business," Lucien said. He gestured to his servants. "Bring him here."

The two guards yanked Max forward, tossing him down in front of Lucien. The Royal Lord wasted no time and grabbed Max around the throat. He pulled Max to his feet and stepped towards a wall, slamming Max into it.

"Now, Max, there is some information I need from you," Lucien said.

"Go to hell," Max said.

"What do you know about the new Ardent race?" Lucien asked.

"I don't have the slightest idea what you're talking about," Max replied.

"Come now, Max. You expect me to believe that you don't know about something as monumental as the creation of a new Ardent race, when you are allies with an Ancient, no less?"

"I don't have a freaking clue, and even if I did, I'd rather die than help you enslave anyone else," Max spat.

A twinge of fire danced between the pair. Max screamed in agony as a thread of his life force was stolen. "The harvest. I know you remember it well," Lucien said amusedly. "You have one last chance to live, Max, or you will die here with your power used to destroy the rest of your rebel brethren."

"The Ardent will rise, Lucien," Max said, his teeth gritting against the pain. "I may be dead, but they're coming for you. Think about it, the Ancients are returning. There's one right there, and more are coming. You'll die and they will all be free."

"Take that thought to your grave, Max."

"Lucien, you will stop." A booming voice captured the attention of the room.

The two guards turned and pointed their gauntlets at the voice, projecting from a small shadow behind some of the rubble on the far side of the room.

Lucien tossed Max a few feet away. "Identify yourself, and bow before your god." He lowered his arm and a Roman-styled *gladius* sword materialized in his hand.

"You are not my god, Lucien, you are my lieutenant. Do you not remember?" The owner of the voice said, coming into view. The person was tall and powerfully built. The clear gray eyes were met by a head of long brown hair and a square jaw which would make him the envy of many a superhero. He was dressed in casual clothing, faded blue jeans, and a long tan duster. His expression was serene, though his face was stern. He gave the impression of a panther ready to strike with his every shift and movement. In the flap of air coursing through the room, a glint of metal could be seen on the edge of his hip.

"August," Lucien said, snickering. "You fool. Your lieutenant? I think not. You are nothing. You are my broken enemy from a thousand years ago."

"It was not always as it is now," August said.

"I believed your line to be extinct," Lucien summarized, walking towards August.

"You know now that it is not the case."

"What do you want here?" Lucien demanded.

"Release the boy and his friend," August answered.

"He is one of you, is he not?"

"Yes, but you knew that as well."

"Then I should kill him to make an example of the rest of your fragmented race."

August drew his sword. The blade was about three and a half feet long, adorned with ancient writing and a curved pommel. It rested comfortably in August's right hand. "It has been centuries since the *Ardent Vow* has tasted the blood of a Royal," August said. "Harm that boy any further and the burning of Rome will be a pale comparison to my wrath."

Lucien looked at his two guards. "Kill him."

The guards moved in, opening fire with their gauntlets, lightning striking August in fierce impacts. August remained unfazed. He vanished for a moment, no doubt moving faster than the eye could see. The guards' arm bands shattered, along with the bones underneath. August reappeared as the two guards slumped onto the ground.

"Time has made your soldiers weak, Lucien," August said, as the *Ardent Vow* gleamed in the light. "Do you dare to face me yourself?"

Lucien pointed his sword at August. "My blade has missed the blood of the Empyrial." He rushed, thrusting his blade forward. August parried the strike, spinning around and retaliating with a swing at Lucien's throat. Lucien blocked the strike and stepped back.

August pressed the attack, swinging in wide arcs, driving Lucien back. Their attention appeared to be diverted from Dante and Max, both of whom were trying to get their bearings.

Dante screamed as snaps and cracks shook his body. Max crawled over to him and pulled him away from the fight.

"Got you, champ," Max said, his voice strained from pain.

"Damn it, Max! It feels like I'm being torn apart."

Max tapped a few keys into his armlet and scanned Dante. "More like you're being put back together again."

"What are you saying?" Dante replied, gritting his teeth.

"You're regenerating," Max said. "It's a good thing too. Those broken ribs nicked a lung. You'd be choking to death on your own blood right now if you weren't an Ancient."

"That's just wonderful," Dante said.

A beep sounded from Max's arm computer. "Hell's bells," he said. "Hang on, Dante."

"What?" Dante said. Max tapped a few more keys into his computer and the world flashed blue again. When Dante opened his eyes this time, he was standing in the pit behind the school library.

"Sophia must have deactivated the jammers," Max said. "The detection device was keyed to her signature. It wouldn't have gone off unless she sent a message."

"So she didn't double-cross us," Dante said.

"No, but she could have played us to get herself released. We just don't have enough information to be sure."

"That's a conversation for later," Dante stated. "Right now, I'm just going to head back to my room."

A sound carried over their heads like the fluttering of wings on the wind. Dante looked around, but saw nothing. The two of them started walking back to their residence halls.

"I still can't believe I survived that beating I took."

"You were pretty bad off," Max replied.

"It is in your nature, Truthsayer." August's voice preceded his image as he moved into the light of a street lamp. His clothes had several rips, which combined with some dried blood, looked suspiciously like slash marks.

"I see you survived your duel with Lucien," Dante replied. "Thanks for the save, by the way."

"It was of no consequence," August said. "Our race is joined within life and death."

"Yeah, thanks also for the cryptic there," Dante said sourly. "Mind telling me what's going on?"

"You are the Truthsayer," August answered.

"And what does that mean exactly?" Dante wanted to know.

"You are Empyrial, one of the first race of Ardent. None have been born into this world in over a thousand years, save you."

"Then who are you?" Dante asked.

"I am August, Champion of the Council and Defender of the City of Rome."

"That's quite a title," Max chimed in. "Care to tell us what that means?"

"Once, long before the time of your grandfather's grandfather, I was the leader of the Empyrial Council's army."

"The Ancients," Dante summarized. "Were you at war with Lucien?"

"Not at first. We began our conflicts with true creatures of darkness."

Dante sighed. Just what they needed. More enemies. "What were they?"

"They were the Morte-Veras, our dark analogues. They waged war against all who lived in the light. In our earliest days on this earth, in battles which were not recorded in human history, we fought and died to keep the balance between order and chaos secure on the new soil of the world."

"How did you know first know Lucien?" Max asked. "You called him your lieutenant."

"Lucien was one of the children of the Empyrial," August stated. "The Royal Lords are the second race of Ardent, created by the Ancients in their war against the Morte-Veras."

"But just now, Lucien denied it, didn't he?" Dante said. He had heard some of it, but he was pretty beaten up by that point and didn't really trust his recollections.

"Yes, something happened to his memory," August said. "It happened with all the children. They rose up against us, called us enemies."

"What happened?" Dante wanted to know.

"Our children betrayed us, and laid waste to our citadel in Rome. The entire council was slain in the attack. Our people were scattered to the four winds. Then the Lords hunted us down, exterminating our entire race. Only I survived the purge of the Empyrial people."

"Sounds typical," Max said. "They don't share power well in *this* century. I can't imagine they'd do better in the old days."

"Indeed," August said. "Change is coming on swift wings. The Lord's reckoning is at hand."

"What does that mean?" Dante asked.

"The third race of Ardent is being born," August answered. "Look to them as allies in your war."

"Could you be any more cryptic?" Dante said sourly. "This doesn't help us at all."

"You will see, Seraph, very soon."

"Wait, how could you possibly know that nickname?"

"That will be revealed as well." With that last word and a nod, August vanished into the night. His form seemed to just flicker out, like a lamp from a switch.

Dante shook his head. "The man couldn't have left an email address or cell phone number?"

Max made a face. "He's no longer showing up on my sensors."

"What's the radius?"

"Three miles. He must have booked it somewhere."

"Okay," Dante said. "Now what?"

"I'm going back to my room to see what I've got stashed in my fridge. You interested?"

"Nah, I'll see you tomorrow. I think rest is in order. Spontaneous tissue regeneration apparently makes me sleepy."

"All right then, off you go," Max said. "I'll check in with you tomorrow." The pair parted ways on the road back to their respective rooms.

As his door clicked shut, Dante walked over to his bed and saw that it was occupied. Sophia was sitting on it, legs crossed, arms folded, and eyes determined, like she'd been waiting there for awhile.

"As if the night couldn't get any more interesting," Dante summarized.

"You don't know the half of it," Sophia replied.

FIVE

"So…" Dante said, pulling off his jacket. "I suppose you teleported in?"

"The residence hall assistant is a friend of mine. I told him I was going to surprise my boyfriend. She let me in with her spare key."

"Well, I can say I'm certainly surprised," Dante said. He sat down cautiously in his study chair. "What's up?"

"I came here to fill you in about Lucien's next move." A banshee's wail ripped through Dante's head. He gritted his teeth, only a few painful blinks telegraphing the pain.

His reply was short. "Try again, Sophia."

"What do you mean?" Sophia replied defensively. "Truthsayer, remember? That's not why you're here. So can we just get on with it? I'm tired."

"You know what? Never mind. It was stupid anyway." She got up and started heading for the door.

"Sure, go ahead and saunter away, like you did earlier tonight. See if I care."

"What the hell does that mean?"

"It means you left us to die in there." Dante rose to his feet, knocking the chair down.

"I did not," Sophia shot back, her voice starting to rise.

Dante made a face. "How do you figure that?"

"I deactivated the jammers and sent the signal to Max."

"Yeah, you're a real team player, aren't you?" Dante shook his head.

"Screw you. I saved your life," Sophia snapped.

"Lucien nearly beat me to death, Sophia." Dante's words were sharp, and fear leaked out. "Max said if I wasn't an Ancient, I would have bled to death on the floor of that warehouse," he said with his eyes lowered. "So forgive me if I'm not feeling generous right now."

"I know. I'm sorry," Sophia said. She turned around and walked back into the room, leaning on the edge of his desk. "For what it's worth, I really didn't mean for it to go down that way. I didn't know what else to do, but my freedom was right there, so I took it."

"At our expense," Dante snapped. He took a breath. "That wasn't fair. I'm sorry."

"It's okay, I'd be pretty pissed too if I were in your shoes. The thing is, Lucien had already found out about the break-in. Before you ask, no, I don't know how. He assumed I lured you both in there. I didn't lie. I just let him believe that."

"I thought he wasn't supposed to be there."

"He wasn't. He never goes there."

"So what made this time different?" Dante wanted to know.

"As I said, I don't know. Maybe he had surveillance on you and Max," Sophia replied, her fingers tapping nervously on the side of the desk. "With that real-time scanner in place, he could track your position anywhere."

"Shit," Dante spat. "That doesn't make sense. I thought the masking device would have prevented that."

"Maybe Lucien had a way around it," Sophia shrugged. "It doesn't matter. Turns out the scanner wasn't even there."

"Do you have any idea where it is?"

"Not a clue," Sophia replied.

"Terrific. The rebels are totally screwed, unless they can get out of town real freaking quick," Dante stated.

"Maybe not," Sophia said. Her face turned into a cautiously proud grin. "I wasn't able to get the scanner, but I did manage to copy the blueprints for the device."

"You think Max can make the masks work longer?"

"I would think so, yes," Sophia replied. "The data is encrypted, but Max should be able to crack it with a little time."

"That's real good. We'll get it to him first thing in the morning."

"Yeah, being harvested, even for a second, really drains a person. He'll need the rest."

"Understood. Thanks Sophia." Dante said, though her expression definitely indicated that they were not done. "So, do you want to tell me the real reason why you came up here?"

"It's really stupid," Sophia said.

"I doubt that. Why don't you just tell me?"

"We're square, you and me, right?" Sophia picked at the edge of her sweater, taking off an invisible piece of lint.

Dante put his hand on her arm. "Look, I'm just glad you're all right, Sophia. I'm glad we made it out of there." That statement earned him a smile.

"I don't like it when we're fighting," she said.

"Me neither. Except when we're training, of course," Dante commented.

"Good, I feel epically ridiculous for asking something like that," Sophia said, smiling softly. "Thanks for going easy on me."

"Don't think you're entirely off the hook. I have a question for you."

"Oh great. What's that?"

"Why did you ask me to go to the carnival, anyway?" Dante asked, as his expression softened and became reflective. "You never said."

Sophia smirked. "Why do you think?"

"I don't know. If you had to get me to Lucien, you didn't have to go through the motions of a date. I mean, you didn't with Max, right?"

She chuckled, and immediately Dante realized that he sounded completely jealous. He didn't bother trying to correct her notion, considering it was more right then he wanted to admit.

"No, I didn't take Max out. That was work." She looked into his eyes, in an expression more appropriate for a first date then a confession. She took a steadying breath, as the next words she spoke could either make things better or completely obliterate them. "Simply put, I've wanted to go out with you since we met, but you just couldn't take the hint."

His eyes got big. Despite the gravity of the conversation, or perhaps because of it, Sophia's face lit up with amusement at his expression. "You look surprised. You shouldn't. You had to know that I had a crush on you." Dante's mouth was agape, and he wordlessly shook his head. "You're pretty dense, you know that?" she added.

"I have been told that sometimes, yes."

"I wasn't on the job when I took you to the carnival. I really wanted to go out with you. When I saw Rachel while I was on the carousel, she gestured for me to see if you were a latent. That was the deal with the shocking kiss I gave you in the tent. I was checking you for the talent. I didn't get the order to bring you in for the harvest until Rachel slipped me the scroll. That's why I was so upset. The scroll told me to bring you to Lucien right away."

"I remember what happened after that," Dante sighed, a little wiser to the situation, but still confused. He took a step closer, so her face took up his entire field of vision. "I'm not sure exactly what's next."

"I want two things," she began, holding up her fingers. "First, I want *you* to save *me*. I can't do it without you. I want to be free of this damn Ardent life." She reached out and gently touched Dante's cheek. He leaned into her touch slightly, but his eyes stayed locked on hers.

"I thought you got released," Dante said. "You're already in the clear, right?"

"Not really, I guess you could say I have some karmic debt. I need to do something for Rachel, and for everyone else I've hurt by going along with Lucien for years. I want to balance the scales."

"And I can help with that? You saw what happened tonight when I fought him," Dante replied.

"You knocked him down, Dante. People think of him as a god, and you knocked him down. Do you know what that means?"

"He beat me within an inch of my life. I don't understand."

Sophia glided her hand down to his shoulder. "You still stood against him and lived to tell about it. A legend, an *Ancient* appeared to save you. Even though Lucien beat you up, you survived. You've done something that we all thought was impossible. Word is going to spread like wildfire."

"People talk, don't they?" Dante interjected.

"There's a lot of Ardent out there, Dante. Some of them don't understand their power. Some of them hide from Lords like Lucien. Some of them don't even realize that they even *need* to hide. Some try to help, like Max does, but they really can't do it on their own. They need more. You can bring them together, be their voice."

Dante placed his hand on her hand. "What are you saying?" Sophia turned around and moved closer, wrapping her arms around him. "Do you want me to be some kind of leader?"

"I told you once that your destiny is your own. It's time for you to take it. Be the leader we've been waiting for and the hero we've been dreaming of." She leaned in closer.

"And, throughout all of this, I just wanted to be with you, in the normal way when two people like each other do. The second thing I want is to kiss you, so in case you're about to ask me what I am doing, this is me, kissing you." She closed the remaining distance, pressing her lips into his with a tenderness which surprised him. He returned the kiss softly at first, deepening the kiss quickly after.

They parted after a few minutes. Dante had lost count, and Sophia looked a little dazed. He smiled. "This isn't exactly how I pictured this conversation going."

"Did you think we were going to fight?" Sophia said, still holding on tight.

"Most definitely," Dante replied.

"I'd have kicked your ass," Sophia said tenderly.

"You wish," Dante reached around and tapped the end of her nose.

"There's a cracked wall in the gym that says otherwise."

"Touché," Dante said, as he stifled a yawn.

"Am I boring you now?" Sophia chuckled.

"Hell, no. I'm just exhausted. It's been a long day."

"It has been one hell of a day. It's… wow, two in the morning. I'd better get back to my room."

"You're past curfew, how do you plan on sneaking out?"

"Oh, a girl has her ways," she said, bringing her gauntlet into view. "I've never been caught in the men's dorm after curfew."

"I'll bet you haven't."

"You want to join me for breakfast tomorrow?" she asked.

Dante nodded. "Of course, meet you at ten?"

"Sure."

"Later, *Seraph*," Sophia vanished in a ring of bluish light, leaving Dante with a head full of questions, which promptly left him as he collapsed on his bed, sound asleep in seconds.

∴

"That was nice," Dante said as he and Sophia left the cafeteria after breakfast, the next morning.

"It was, wasn't it?" Sophia said with a smirk. "Maybe we could have been enjoying this months ago if you had taken the initiative, mister."

"Oh, yeah, and you were throwing yourself at me the entire time during economics class," Dante said.

"Apparently that truth sense of yours doesn't get tipped off by your own sarcasm." Sophia smirked, lacing her hand in his.

"Not especially, it would seem. Otherwise I think my head would have exploded by now," Dante answered sourly.

"Yeah, that would put a serious damper on the day," Sophia said. "Speaking of which, when is Max meeting us?"

"In an hour or so. He wanted us to meet him in front of the library," Dante replied.

"Did he say why?"

"No, he didn't. Maybe he's sweet on the librarian or something."

"She is hot," Sophia said. "But he doesn't seem the type to go for the naughty librarian."

"You never know. I didn't realize I was into goth until recently," Dante replied.

Sophia smirked triumphantly. "Opened your eyes, did I?"

"You could say that, yes," Dante said. "I noticed you hung up the black leather in favor of your preppy outfit."

"Don't even get me started," Sophia replied, making a face. "I hate this look, but I'll attract attention if I go back to the dark side. We can't have that right now."

"I thought Lucien said you were released," Dante questioned.

"He did."

"Think he's watching you?"

"It's a definite possibility."

"Doesn't that put you in danger if he's tracking me already?" Dante asked, concerned.

"I'm not sure," she shrugged. "Want me to leave?"

"No way," Dante replied quickly.

"Then shut up and don't worry about it." She kissed him on the cheek. "I'm a big girl." It wasn't sufficient for Dante, but it would do for now.

Max scurried through the library doors a few minutes later. He was carrying a ton of papers and a few books. They were nearly to his chin and Dante wondered whether he was using some sort of Ardent power to keep everything from tumbling down.

"Aren't you a techie?" Sophia asked. "There's a lot of paper there."

"Har, har, you're a bloody riot. I'm surprised I didn't catch you two snogging."

"Do you have some purpose summoning us here?" Dante said, a little embarrassed.

"Yeah," Max said, dropping his books down on the table. "I think I've found something."

"Care to elaborate?" Dante picked up one of the books.

"Last night I managed to hack my way into the scanner feeds."

"I thought that wasn't possible," Dante said. The entire point of the raid was because it was completely protected. "Were you able to get this from the blueprints we sent you this morning?"

"No, unfortunately it's going to be awhile before I can decrypt that data. This is not from the control system at all, just the outputs. Since the energy is beamed all over the city, it was easy enough to piggyback a reporting subroutine."

"If you say so," Dante commented. "Do you know the scanner's location?"

"No, but I noticed that there was a dead spot in the signal. There is a small location in the city which is shielded from detection."

"Is there some kind of interference?" Sophia asked. "Or perhaps it's a permanent masking?"

"Could be either one, maybe. I'm not sure," Max replied.

Dante closed the book. "Where is it?"

"This is where it gets interesting," Max answered. "It's a single city block, and guess what's smack dab in the middle of it?"

"A strip club," Dante answered sourly.

"You wish," Sophia said. "I didn't realize you were into that particular form of entertainment, Dante."

He answered with a very significant blush.

"Anyway," Max interrupted before Dante made a bigger fool of himself. "Bloodlines is in the center."

"So Dmitri found himself a little oasis in the war, didn't he?" Dante said. It was another reason to hate that arrogant vampire bastard.

"I'm not sure. He could have discovered the scanner and rigged a defense against it on his own," Max pondered.

"Vampires aren't usually the techno types," Sophia said. "And Dmitri certainly wouldn't do anything that could get his hands dirty, but he might have access to other means."

"That's what I was thinking," Max said.

"So do we confront him?" Dante asked.

"Yeah, but it's a little trickier than that," Max replied, tapping a few keys on his armlet. "He's pretty powerful, and has several vampires at his disposal."

"Do you think it will come to that?" Sophia said. "He's been helpful in the past. Maybe I should go in first and see if I can get him to give up the info."

"I don't like it," Dante replied. "It's too dangerous."

"Easy, stud. It'll be fine," Sophia answered. "If I not, you and Max can swoop in with the cavalry."

"We should try the rebels again," Dante said, "unless all of them have left town by now."

Max smirked. "Actually none of them left town, including Janet. McCray, who is the actual leader, told her to sod off."

"Do you know where they're holing up?" Dante wanted to know.

"There's an old movie theater on Bardstown Road. It's the primary safe house. If they're anywhere, that's where they'd be."

"Some of them probably have day jobs, so we'll hit it tonight," Max concluded.

∴

Dante and Sophia sat on the hill behind the dorms, watching the sunset. The two of them were locked together when Max's car sped around the back driveway. The headlights woke them out of their embrace.

"Now, now kids… don't let me interrupt." Max beamed as he opened the window. His grin was so big that the light from the rising moon gave Dante a good view of his pearly teeth.

Max shut the car off and stepped out. He was wearing his normal trench coat, but it appeared as though he was wearing body armor underneath. The faint bluish glow of wires ran up and down the length of the jacket, and his gloves were humming softly in the quiet twilight.

"Shit, Max. I thought we were meeting in a couple of hours. You know, nightfall?" Dante said. Sophia laughed out loud and leaned over to his ear.

"Don't worry, Seraph. There'll be another sunset tomorrow. I might even let you take me out to see it," she whispered.

"I wish I was coming over just to play third wheel, but this is a business call," Max said, walking up. "Since we were going in to meet with the rebels, I took the precaution of reviewing the scanner feed around the old theater. I found several other Ardent moving around the place en masse. The rebels are under siege."

Dante and Sophia stood up as one.

"What are we looking at?" asked Dante.

"They appear to be powerful Ardent, eight of them in total. They've sealed the exits to the building and set up jammers to prevent escape."

"Lucien?" Sophia asked.

"Maybe. No way to be sure until we get there," Max answered.

"There's something you're not telling us," Dante said.

"I think they're vampires. Whoever it was, they sent bloodsuckers after my friends." His voice was grim. "McCray knows his little group is no match for eight powerful vampires. They've sealed themselves in one the theater rooms behind a powerful shield."

"I take it the shield will collapse eventually," Dante said. Max nodded. "Then we need to go in. How quickly can we get there?"

"It will only take a couple of minutes. We can teleport nearby and walk out on foot. Unfortunately, all the direct ways in are sealed so we'll have to *make* a way in. If they are vampires, they'll hear any attempt at entry. We'll have no way to get the drop on them."

"That's fine. We'll need to fight them anyway," Dante said. He looked at Sophia. "You in?"

She didn't waver. "I'm surprised you even had to ask. If it's Dmitri, I'm going to kick his sleazy ass."

"Champ, I hope you got your badass tricks handy. This is going to get messy," Max said. As Dante turned around, the dusk light shined down upon him, scoring a long shadow over the dark ground.

"I'm good," Dante said. "Let's go get them out." He opened the car door and got in the back. Sophia joined him there, nearly sitting on his lap, trying to stay close. Max chuckled, got in the driver's seat, and turned the car around towards the street.

Dante turned to Sophia so she could lay her head on his shoulder. Her eyes were far off, like she was gazing at some unseen horizon.

"What is it?" Dante asked, in a whisper. Sophia's eyes turned to him, and a delicate smile graced her features.

"Do you remember when I gave you your nickname?" she replied, her voice light but intense.

"Sure, in that seminar class, why?"

"It really suits you, especially now. I'm very proud of you."

"I don't what to say," Dante answered honestly.

"You're welcome," Sophia whispered, letting her fingers dance on the side of his face. Dante took her hand, securing it around his.

"All right, Max, let's do this."

Six

Dante didn't think it was possible to teleport the whole damn car.

The shadow of the city lamps coated Max's sedan as it progressed through the blue portal. Dante turned his eyes away from the bright flash. The rubber tires made a soft thud as the car jostled down onto the uneven pavement. When his eyes came back into focus, he noticed that the car was in an alley, and the familiar sounds of nightlife roared around him.

As Dante stepped out of the car, he realized that they were in the Highlands section of Bardstown Road. He could see the outline of St. Bernadette Church over the edge of the building on the right side of the alleyway.

"Come on. We don't have much time," Max said, hurrying.

Max went first into the street. He was itching for a fight, that much was very clear. His walk had changed from its usual jovial bounce to a regulatory military gait. His eyes darted back in forth in paranoid radar detection. His hands were open and outstretched, menacing in their apparent predatory state, and every so often, a wisp of blue light jumped from one finger to another.

Dante walked behind Max, adding a second pair of eyes to scan for hostiles. As they left the confines of the alley, the sounds and lights of the street hit them in full force.

It was not a quiet night. The honks of cars radiated as they tried to park at street meters. The laughter from roving packs of teenagers wandering around from shop to shop resonated against one hundred year old buildings.

Sophia followed behind, her hand gently placed on Dante's shoulder in an apparent attempt to stay with him through the weaving crowd. Her hand was a little clammy.

Max stopped the group in front of their destination. It was an abandoned movie theater from the 1930's. The old ticket booth stood in the middle between the two sets of doors.

Only pausing for a moment, Max continued on. Inspecting the door, he ran his glove over the side. A faint hum from the glove was followed by a shrill beep. He looked down at a technical readout on the edge of his glove. "The security alarms have been tripped. The barrier shields have gone up."

Dante pushed on the door. It was solid.

"Is it a pull door?" Sophia smirked.

"Charming," Dante said sarcastically.

"These doors are seriously reinforced. With the shield, they can withstand over twenty thousand pounds per square inch," Max said, at Dante's confused look.

"I guess I need to knock, right?" Dante said, rearing back his fist.

"Do your thing, champ."

Dante slammed into the door. A blue shimmer flashed around the outline, but the door itself cracked open slightly. He pushed hard on it, using all his strength. Eventually the entire door creaked open.

"Ate your spinach today, I see," Max said. The three of them entered.

The inside was in surprisingly good repair, considering the age of the place. The long red carpet was clean, and the twin spiral banisters were still white, defying time.

"This place had been used as a safe house for quite some time, hasn't it?" Dante asked.

"Yeah, it's one of the first ones in the city," Max replied.

A large crash came from the second floor, disturbing the dust and misting the air with a grey fog. On the edge of his vision, Dante saw Max heading up the stairs, moving fast. Dante jumped the stairs to reach Max, landing right next to him at the top. Sophia met them a moment later.

The simple internal doors were cherry red, like most of the other décor. A larger, white ornate door was surrounded by four people.

The four people were definitely vampires, or at the very least, they weren't human. In the midst of their conversations, roars and screeches were flung back and forth at the same regularity as the spoken word.

The vampires themselves were an odd mix of people. One looked like a varsity football player. Another looked like a goth kid. One of them looked like a glam girl wannabe. The last dressed like a soldier in camouflage pants and an olive drab t-shirt.

The glam girl saw the trio as they crept forward. Her blue eyes went big, and she bared her teeth, fangs and all. She roared, snapping around at attention. Goth Vamp had already gone through the door, leaving even odds to engage.

Max opened fire first. A shrill blue lightning arc struck Military Vamp in the chest, picking him up off the ground and slamming him into an adjacent wall. Pulling himself free, Military Vamp dusted the flecks of plaster off his shoulders. He bared his teeth and lunged at Max.

A few seconds before the creature reached Max, Dante slammed into the beast from the side, causing him to veer away. As the vampire skidded down to the far side of the hallway, a well placed grab dragged Dante along for the ride.

The football player rushed at Max. The vampire moved quickly, his movements blurred in Dante's vision. Like a rolling tidal wave, the bruiser plowed into Max, bringing him off the ground and slamming him into the adjacent red door nearly fifteen feet away. Max barely had enough time to put his hands up to shield his face.

The door held on the impact, splintering from behind Max's coat. Max slumped over on the floor like a marionette whose strings were cut. He was gasping for air, trying to stand back up as the vampire stalked over to him.

The beast had a smirk on his lips and rolled his sleeves back in an exaggerated attempt to intimidate. His cold blue eyes had changed into jet black orbs, and long sharp talons appeared on the edge of his fingertips. The creature bared his teeth, which were now elongated nearly four inches. He lifted Max off the ground with a large hand affixed to his coat. Max's head was pulled over as the vampire leaned down to bite. Max appeared to be unconscious, and his head lolled to the side from the angle he was being held by the creature.

Two arcs of blue lightning crashed into Max's opponent, striking the vampire directly on the left shoulder blade. The force of the blast knocked the creature forward, causing him to slump to his knees and fall unconscious. Max slipped free.

The vampire glam girl crawled up the edge of the wall to balance herself. Her eyes lost any hint of color and darkened to a completely raven black. She roared in a voice which was not quite human and vaulted over the edge of the balcony, performing what appeared to be an Olympic dive as she went over. She landed like a cat on all fours effortlessly. She didn't even look up as she ran towards the door. A red shimmer glowed and a portal appeared in the doorway. She lunged through it and vanished.

As Dante and Military Vamp both stood up after their shared impact, the vampire didn't waste any time. He reacted with a quick hook, his claws extended outward in a slashing maneuver.

Dante easily evaded the vampire's hand and took the inside block, making a swooping motion with his hand. He grabbed on and used the balance to hold the vampire. Dante retaliated with a side kick, propelling the vampire over the balcony onto the floor. There was a crunch as the vampire struck the ground.

As Dante watched from above, the vampire dove through another reddish portal in front of the door.

"The area is secure," Max said, pulling himself up to his feet. "Is everybody all right?"

"I'm good," Dante said.

Sophia walked up and patted Dante on the back. "I'm ready for more."

Max, seemingly a little perplexed, looked over at Sophia. "Thanks kid. You saved me."

"Don't think this means I like you," she said with a smile.

"We need to keep moving. One of them already made it through the door," Dante said, scanning the room.

"Hold on, champ," Max said. "There are two ways in. After this door there's a T-junction. One path leads around to the west side of the theater. The other leads around to the back side. By taking the back side entrance, we can come up behind them, with plenty of room to fight." Max punched a few keys on his armlet.

"The straggler went towards the west side, didn't he?" Dante questioned.

"Yes he did. We should split up," Sophia said. "One of us needs to follow the straggler, the other two to take the other way in."

Max nodded. "Sophia, you and I will take the back way. Dante, see if you can catch up to the vampire with some of that handy-dandy flying."

As the three parted company, Max and Sophia heard a scream from down the dark hall. The voice was young and female, probably no more than a teenager. Max shouted at the sound, heading towards it at breakneck speed. Sophia raced along after him, only a couple of steps behind.

The walkway narrowed into a tight corridor with only enough room for Max and Sophia to be shoulder to shoulder. The tight hallway forced the pair to slow down to avoid a collision.

Sophia and Max made it into the main theater. Crafted in the old style, the screen was designed to show Hollywood classics. The red carpet and drapes were worn, faded from a bright red to a dull wine color. The ornate wood had lightened from the exposure of too much stage light, bleached to a dull brown. There was a long staircase leading down an elaborate ramp to the front row. The area granted plenty of room to maneuver. The walkway was long and wide, allowing four people to pass side by side through the left and right sections of the theater. The room appeared deserted.

Sophia looked around, confusion written on her face. "Shit! Where's Dante?" she said. Her eyes darted around, making a circle with the rest of her. "He should have beaten us here."

"I'm detecting seven life signs in this room. They are minor rank threes and located in the service room on the side of the stage. I'm also detecting a couple of others, but it's strange. I can't get a good reading on them."

Sophia's eyes got huge. "I don't like this." She turned around and started up the stairs at full speed, taking the steps two at a time with a long stride. She slammed into the door. The door didn't budge. Sophia bounced off and fell forward, hitting the ground with a loud thud. She pulled herself up and pounded her fists on the door. "Max! The door won't open." Sophia ran across the back of the theater to the other set of doors, pulling on the handles. The doors remained still.

"We're screwed, it's a trap!" he started up the stairs to reach Sophia. The faint sounds of Ardent powers murmured around him. As he reached Sophia, four other shapes appeared in the periphery of the room. Max looked over at them. "I got four new contacts," he said, scrambling his fingers over his tech.

After the last keystroke, his eyes opened up as big as saucers. "Oh, bloody hell. All four of them have rank ten energy outputs."

Sophia sprinted over to him. "How big?" Her gauntlet shimmered and her sword pike spat out of the end of the armlet. She gave it a practice swing and turned back to Max.

"They're huge, like Lords almost," he said. Sophia gritted her teeth and readied her power.

"Shit," she said. "I hope Dante is all right."

"My, my, what do we have here?" Dmitri said as he emerged from the shadows. "Little bird, how did you find yourself here? Lucien won't be too pleased."

"I'm here on his business," Sophia said. "I was commanded to extend his offer of mercy to the rebels."

"Tut, tut, it's not polite to lie, Sophia. We both know that you've allied yourself with the Ardent Rebellion. Don't embarrass yourself further with such a pale deception."

"Screw you," Sophia spat.

"That's more like it." Dmitri grinned.

A striking blond woman emerged from the shadows. She was a vision, with full red lips and steely blue eyes. Her long legs were reflected in the subtle lamps, and she was dressed in an outfit more appropriate for the opera than for a brawl. "Well, hello, Max… it's been a long time."

"Carmen, so charming to see you again," Max said dejectedly.

Sophia shook her head. "Ex-girlfriend?"

"Long story," Max said as he looked back over at Dmitri. "Dmitri, so good of you to drop by, though I must say I'm surprised. I didn't expect that you'd be into this kind of work."

"And what, pray tell, do you think 'this kind' of work is?" The vampire replied.

Max grinned despite the situation. "Being Lucien's lapdog. Chewing on scraps from his table."

"Now, now, there's no reason to be rude," Dmitri said.

A dark haired teenager walked out from a shadow. She looked deceptively dainty, with a hint of Middle Eastern heritage.

"Adelai," Dmitri said, "welcome to the grand finale."

With a smile far older than her years, she winked at Max. "Thanks for coming to my rescue," Adelai said sweetly. "I wasn't sure you'd be able to hear me from the anteroom."

Max scowled. "I get the chump award for today."

"No joke," Sophia replied. "If we live through this, you and me are going to have a serious talk about your taste in women."

She turned her attention to Dmitri. "So what's the story?" Sophia questioned. "Are you really just following some mandate from Lucien?"

"Do you recall how, when we last spoke, I told you of our desire to renegotiate our contract with your Lord?"

"Yeah? And?" Sophia answered.

"And this was one of the stipulations," Dmitri replied. "By delivering the rebels to Lucien, our covenant will be assured and we will be kept out of the impending war."

"This is about Bloodlines," Max said. "You bought the ability to remain invisible from the Ardent scanner."

"Very clever, Max. Yes, that was the bargain. As part of the agreement, Lucien delivered to us a device that masks the scanner, as well as a method to utilize the scanner itself if the need arises. It allows us to stay one step ahead of the fighting, and remain blissfully uninvolved."

"Once he's done with the rebels, Lucien will come after you. Please tell me you're not daft enough to believe he'll keep his word," Max stated. He scanned the room, looking for any other exits. There were none, aside from the back entrance.

"Of that I'm sure, but we have a plan for that situation," Dmitri answered, smiling so his fangs showed in the light. "We will protect ourselves with numbers."

"During the war, you're going to turn people, make them into vampires."

"Yes, en masse," Dmitri replied, "with enough like-minded vampires, we will destroy the surviving Lords, ensuring our continued existence."

"Behind the cloak at Bloodlines, you can increase your numbers without Lucien being wiser to it."

"Yes, we will begin with the strongest of the rebels," Dmitri answered, "and for you there will be an honored place with us."

"Not really my style," Max said, shaking his head.

"Although I love the goth thing, I prefer to *dress like* the dead, rather than actually *be* dead," said Sophia.

"We will take you and your friend in the hallway, provided he lives. Donovan is quite strong."

"He's more than he looks, Dmitri," Sophia said, suddenly bold. "He's an Ancient, and you're just a low-life bloodsucker."

"What a bizarre, absurd thought. Nevertheless, we'll see how he fairs against my guard." Another vampire entered the room. The new arrival was over seven feet tall and packed with muscle. "Magnus, prepare for our friend's entrance."

Meanwhile, in the hallway, Dante soared through the corridor. He reached Goth Vamp, who was running at full speed. Dante slammed into him, sending him into the door at the end of the hallway. The vampire bounced off the shield and crumpled to the ground.

Dante landed and grabbed the vampire by his jacket. Angrily, Dante hoisted him up in the air. "What are you doing here?"

The vampire snarled in response. Dante slammed him again against the force field.

"I said, what are you doing here?" The vampire said nothing. Dante narrowed his eyes. "Just tell me what I want to know. I don't want to hurt you."

"That's a laugh," Goth Vamp said. "You Royals are always hunting us."

"I'm not a Royal," Dante replied. "I'm an Ancient."

"That's bullshit. The Ancients are all dead."

"Yeah, I get that a lot. I'm the first one in a long time."

"Well, good luck to you, asshole."

"Listen. My friends are on the other side of that door," Dante replied. "I need to get through there and help them.

You can either shut the shield down, or you can get the hell out of my way."

"You're not going to kill me?" Goth Vamp asked.

"You haven't given me a reason to." Dante set him down. "You can just walk away if you want."

Goth Vamp looked at him with a confused expression. "You are definitely not a Royal Lord, or a knight."

"Correct," Dante answered. "I'm not your enemy."

"I can't shut the shield down, but I can tell you this: Dmitri plans to hand some of the rebels over to Lucien, and the rest he's going to turn into vampires."

"Shit," Dante replied.

"Yeah, I'm not too keen on it either. Dmitri may be the leader of the coven, but this shit's gotta stop. He's 'take over the world' all the damn time."

"Thanks for the info," Dante said. "It might be good for you to get out of here. It's going to get ugly real quick."

"My name's Donovan, and the next time I see you, I'm going to break your face. You want a rematch, come to Bloodlines. Until then, I owe you one."

"Looking forward to it," Dante replied.

The vampire headed back down the hall, out of sight, towards the main entrance.

Dante slammed into the outer door. The door dented and shimmered with the vampire generated force field. He cursed and tried again, this time flinging himself from across the hall with all his strength.

Inside, Dmitri observed the shield's impeding collapse. "It appears that your friend is attempting to break in, trying to save you. Do you think he will be able to defeat all of us? You will all make very fine additions to our coven."

"Dmitri, I have to say your monologue is stirring and all that, but there's one thing your high and mighty coven doesn't know." Max smirked at the master vampire. "And that's just how powerful Ancients can be."

The shield collapsed around the doorway and Dante burst in, flying through like a superhero. He hovered for a moment before landing steadily on his feet.

"This man is an Ancient, the Truthsayer, as a matter of fact," Max commented. "I'm not completely sure of how that's possible, but there it is." The looks in the eyes of the vampires answered the question of their reaction. There was shock, and a twinge of fear.

"Impossible!" Dmitri responded, his fingers elongating into talons. "The Ancients are long dead. The Massacre of Rome destroyed them all." Magnus, standing to the rear, moved to action following the outburst from Dmitri.

With long, thunderous strides Magnus closed the distance. Dante stepped out of the way and brought up his leg in a roundhouse kick. The impact echoed throughout the room. Magnus doubled over at the waist. With a second strike, Dante brought his knee up into Magnus' face. The beast fell onto his back, dazed. The ground beneath the vampire shattered and crunched, splintering wood in all directions.

"How is this possible?" Dmitri spat.

Dante ignored him, as he looked over at Sophia. "Are you okay?"

"I'm peachy. Don't worry about me, get back into the fight!"

He kept Sophia and Max at the edges of his vision, but stared directly at Dmitri.

"We're here to free the rebels," Dante said.

Dmitri remained stoic and unmoved. "I am surprised that an *Ancient* would serve the cause of the Ardent Rebellion," Dmitri replied, positioning himself between Dante and the back room, where the rebels kept their shield.

Max gestured to Dante. Dmitri cleared his throat and continued. "Weren't your kind exterminated by their former masters?"

"That's what I'm told." He looked over at Sophia, who winked at him. "You think that aligning yourself will save you from Lucien when he decides that he's had enough of you?"

"We will have many more soldiers in our army," Dmitri answered. "Starting with you, your friends and the rebels themselves."

"If you want to fight Lucien," Dante said, "why not ally with the rebels? You have a shared enemy."

"Impossible," Dmitri replied.

"Only because you are convinced it is," Dante stated.

"The rebels hide like cowards in the service room aside the stage. They are not worthy allies," Dmitri spat. "When they are turned, they will be powerful and fearless."

"You will lose many of your own securing the rebels," Max piped up. "Many of them would rather die then be bound to the cycle of the sun the way you are."

"Only having their Ardent powers at night is a small price to pay for freedom from death and fear."

"Perhaps so," Dante said, "but couldn't you have better luck with allies that can use their powers during the day?"

"Your kind, however, would never make a truce with our people. Although the stories are limited, our history is clear that the Ancients considered the vampire race to be a blight to be extinguished."

"Not from my perspective. Though I have to admit I don't like the blood-drinking thing," Dante said.

"You speak as if you don't mean us harm. Could your claims be true? Are you only here for these people?"

"That is correct," Dante replied. "Only for them, and my friends. I don't want to fight you."

"You are an interesting one, Ancient. Your kind has been told to us in legends and myths. You are a story to scare new vampires into obedience to their coven masters. And now you are here and tell us that these stories are lies?"

"I can't speak for your stories, but if that's what they say…" He could see the other vampires closing on him, sealing any avenue of escape. "It doesn't matter. My people, the Ancients, are dead. Whatever their views were, they're not mine. Binding ourselves to the past doesn't change anything. I'm not here to start a war, Dmitri. I'm here to stop one."

"While you speak in mercy, Truthsayer, what you fail to understand is that if we do not deliver proof that the rebels have been dealt with, then our safe haven in this territory will be gone and we will be hunted down as your ancestors hunted us, by torch and pitchfork."

Magnus stood up and the four vampires circled Dante. "But if you are indeed an Ancient, and we deliver your blood to Lucien, he will have no choice but to acknowledge our claims and leave us in peace. We will then take the rebels and make them into soldiers for our triumph over the Lords."

Dante sensed the lie. It was a lie of desperation. Dmitri was a proud being, and to be consistently brought to heel by the likes of Lucien would be an insult he couldn't bear. Still, Dmitri was trying to protect his people, such as they were.

The vampires closed in. Dante looked back at Max and Sophia. They had pulled their weapons up to point them at Carmen and Magnus' backs, who had rejoined the others after shaking off Dante's attack.

The monsters' eyes were beseeching and confused, and Dante smiled slowly. Sensing that his time was running short, Dante needed to capitalize on the fear that the vampires seemed to have towards him.

"Max! Find the rebels and get them out!" Dante shouted, and called his gifts. He made a small half-circle gesture with his arms, and the power flowed through him. He vaulted upwards and spun in a circle, kicking Magnus with a sidekick square in the chest. The force of the impact flung Magnus backward into the theater wall, as if he was tied to a cable from behind and yanked back at lightning speed. Unfazed, the vampire jumped back up and with only two steps on the ground, he launched himself back towards Dante.

Out of the corner of his left eye, Dante saw Max and Sophia run towards the service door. His perceptions were distracted as Dmitri landed a solid punch on his jaw. Dante's world shook and rattled.

Dante swung back in defense. His hand swung wildly in an arc like a tennis backswing, missing Dmitri's head by inches. As Dante tried to retract his arm, he found that it was stuck. The arm had been snatched by Adelai with both of her hands, in an attempt to pin him down.

Dante struggled, waving his captured arm in an attempt to get his hand free. Magnus grabbed his other arm and yanked it back. The Truthsayer's arms were spread all the way in an iron cross, holding him still.

On the other side, Carmen lined up in front of him with a predatory grace. She gestured her hand outward and pointed at him in a gentle caress. Her long, red-tipped fingers lit up with green light, and the glow soon became a fire. He continued to struggle against his captors as the fire leapt from Carmen's hand and raced towards him.

In panic, with all the desperate strength Dante could muster, he flexed his legs and vaulted vertically, sending himself towards the chandelier. Magnus' hold slipped, and the fireball which was meant for Dante missed him by a scant few inches.

Adelai remained latched on for a few moments longer, coming off the ground for an instant before returning to the earth with a heavy thud.

Still floating in the air, Dante was out of hand-to-hand range of his attackers. That fact alone was keeping him from being overwhelmed. He bent down in a diving position and launched himself towards Carmen.

Her long hair spun in realization of the threat, and her long legs tried to pull her out of the way. Dante's speed caught her before she even had time to react with a snarl. He slammed into her fist first, and the vampire shot backwards and slumped against the wall.

Dante landed and checked Carmen. She had been knocked unconscious. He turned around to face the other three.

Adelai roared and cursed at Dante. Her delicate hands grew long and wicked. Seven inch claws snapped out of her fingers where once there were just short pink nails. Her speed escalated to inhuman levels.

She engaged Dante before he could react. Her first rake dug deep into his side, ripping blood free and causing it to seep out onto the floor. Dante struggled to get his bearings, and focused long enough to block a series of strikes from the furious teenage vampire.

When an opening presented itself, Dante managed to grab Adelai around the neck. He used the leverage to steady her as he slammed his open palm into her solar plexus. She gasped and quickly slumped over. Dante grabbed her by the collar of her jacket and flung her onto the stage. She skidded sideways and bounced off the edge. The journey ended with Adelai slamming into a wall. Lights and stage equipment crashed down on the stage, as well as the curtain, which fell over top of her.

With two of the vampires down, Dante stepped up and broke into a run towards the service door. He was only able to get a few steps before Magnus grabbed him in a bear hug from behind. Dante was pulled away from the stage. The much larger vampire pulled him up off the ground so he couldn't run away.

Dante brought his flight up. The two of them began to slowly float off the ground. Magnus panicked and dropped his weight, trying with everything he had to resist the pull. After a moment, Dante and Magnus were several feet in the air, well above arm's reach for any of the others to help the wayward vampire.

Thinking of a pinwheel, Dante spun in the same motion, like the hands of a stopwatch. Magnus was dragged along with him at first, but the centrifugal force sent the vampire sailing off into the air. Magnus slammed into the center of the stage, wood chips splintering off of his impacted chin.

Still aloft, the scene below did not bode well for Dante. Magnus had jumped back to his feet the instant he hit the stage. Carmen staggered back out and Dmitri unsheathed a wicked looking sword which had more in common with a serrated fishing knife then a martial weapon.

Dante found a spot to land on the stage. As his boots hit the surface, Adelai stepped around to circle him. Dante noticed that her claws were still tinted red from the wound on his side.

Staying still meant certain death in a four-on-one contest. Dante began to circle, keeping his legs shoulder width apart. Lacking patience, Adelai dove at Dante with a downward slash of her claws. He managed to block her strike double handed, trapping her talons above his head.

Roaring with indignation, she retaliated with a kick to his midsection. The impact forced Dante to release her. He flipped around and skidded to the ground on his side.

Seeing victory, Adelai marched towards him. A long jump saw Dmitri land on the stage to stand shoulder-to-shoulder with Adelai as they both advanced on the Truthsayer.

As Dante rolled up to his feet, a bolt of jade fire slammed into his gut, knocking him back down. Through the smoke, Carmen stepped onto the stage as well. She smiled seductively at him.

As he stumbled to get back up, Magnus grabbed him by the scruff of his neck and hoisted him up. Dante struggled, but the beating he had already taken had weakened him severely. Magnus was easily able to keep him under control.

Dmitri bared his fangs and smiled. "You have fought well, Ancient, you should be honored that your blood will serve to fuel our rise to exaltation." Dante struggled again, but to no avail.

His strength turned desperate. Dante closed his eyes and called to his gifts. They were slow to respond.

"Dmitri, wait," Sophia said, walking away from the service door and out onto the stage. "When we met in Bloodlines, I thought you were a being of power. Now I see you differently. I'm terribly disappointed."

The vampire snarled. "And what are you basing that on, girl?"

"You never defeated him, Dmitri. You had your entire coven hold him down so you beat him up like some little school yard bully. You think that Lucien will take you seriously after this? That you've scored points with the Lords? You're a joke, Dmitri," Sophia announced, putting the pressure on.

"You know Lucien, Dmitri. What would satisfy him? A cowardly attack when your foe is outnumbered four to one? *Hardly.* If you want Lucien to consider you a worthy ally, what better way then for you to defeat an Ancient in single combat? It would be impressive, wouldn't it? Lucien was able to do it. Why can't you? You're not afraid… are you?"

Dmitri growled, pausing. "Release him." Dante slumped to the ground. Carmen and Adelai walked down from the stage on the right, and Magnus walked down from the left.

Dante was surprised at how quickly they acquiesced. Sophia walked down from the stage. She sat in the front row, a center seat to the spectacle. Dante dragged himself up to his feet and found himself alone on the stage with Dmitri.

The master vampire raised his sword after scratching a small half circle on the ground. The extra time was a blessing. Dante could feel his wounds healing, as well as his strength returning.

Dmitri wasted no other time to slash downward in a left-sided arc. Dante barely had enough warning to avoid the sinister blade. The second strike came forward, in a thrust to the midsection. Dante evaded with a quick sidestep. He swung around with a kick. Dante's foot slammed into Dmitri's face. The sword clanked free and the vampire fell to the ground in a roll.

Dante saw the service door that housed the rebels open, and the group was watching the fight. Max and Sophia were in front of them, preparing to jump into the fray. Dante waved them back.

He dove over to the edge of the stage and picked up the sword. Bringing it up to strike, Dmitri intercepted the pommel of the blade and pressed it down, creeping the metal death towards Dante's head.

The two them remained locked in a contest of strength over the blade. The light of the chandelier danced back and forth, reflecting in the light of the sword. The blade careened closer to Dante's head. At the current rate of descent, Dante only had seconds to live before the blade's journey was complete.

He allowed his feet to slip from the force Dmitri was placing on the blade. Dante shifted over to the left, the power of flight keeping him upright. The blade slammed into the floor of the theater stage, chipping the hard wood finish.

Dante reached to the side and slammed his fist into the ribs of the vampire. The ribs shattered and the vampire howled in surprised pain. Dmitri released the blade and slumped over to the side. Dante scooped up the blade and placed it firmly to the neck of the coven master.

"So what are you waiting for, Ancient?" Dmitri spat. "Are you weak? Finish this."

"I have no interest in your death, Dmitri," Dante said. He pulled the blade back, placing the tip of the blade down. He leaned on it like a walking stick. "Nor do I care about your wars." He tossed down the sword on the stage causing the room to echo with the clattering.

Dmitri pushed his legs up and moved to stand. Several of the rebels came out over the edge of the seats into Dante's view. "I will give you two commands in exchange for your life. Do you see these people?" He gestured to the rebels. Dmitri, perhaps sensing what was coming, nodded.

"You will leave them be. You will not hunt them, sell them to Lucien or turn them." Dante walked over to him and offered his hand. "You won't kill the normal people either. You'll stay out of the world's sight, and live in peace." Dante pulled Dmitri up. "Do we have an understanding?"

Dmitri snarled. "Yes." He barked a short burst of language. Carmen nodded and gestured to the wall. A shimmering red portal appeared, and she stepped through. Magnus waited by the door for Adelai to pass, and then followed.

Dmitri started towards the portal, his boots clicking finally on the stage. "We will not stay silent forever. The twilight of the Ardent is upon us all. We will return then."

"I hope we can be on the same side, when you return." Dante said.

Dmitri seemed to contemplate that. Without a look in the direction of the rebels standing in the rows, he stepped forward into the red glow. "Perhaps," The portal shimmered for a moment as he passed through, and then vanished in a wisp of fog.

Max and Sophia walked up to the stage. Dante turned around and walked over to the edge.

"Hey man, you really saved our backsides down there." A voice came out from near the service room. "My name's McCray. I'm the leader of this little group of misanthropes."

The owner of the voice hopped up out to the audience seats, where several others started to move their way around to encircle Dante and Sophia. "We owe you big time." He saw Max and hopped over to grab him in a strong handshake. "Max, you old bastard. I didn't know you were still alive. I figured Lucien would have caught up to you by now."

"He did McCray, but thanks to these two, I made it out in one piece."

McCray regarded Dante and Sophia with a bemused expression. "That's quite a feat. Sophia, it's very good to finally meet you in person, and who's this?"

"This is Seraph." Sophia's clear voice sounded right past Dante. "He's the one you've been waiting for." Dante's eyes got big, and he made a shushing gesture to Sophia, who completely ignored it and grinned.

"Are your people safe? I hope Dmitri will keep his word." Dante said.

McCray nodded. "Dmitri is many things, but he's pretty honorable. I think we can trust that he'll stay away from us."

"We don't have much time," Sophia spoke up. "Lucien's moving into position. It's not going to be long before the whole city gets burned up."

"Another Ardent war, here in Louisville… that bites," Max said.

"There's not a lot we can do while we're being tracked," McCray said. "We keep running, never taking the offensive. So far, we've set ourselves up in public places. They're the only protection we have right now."

"It's that damn Ardent scanner. We seriously have to take it out," Sophia said.

"You know, the entire city block that Bloodlines happens to be on is shielded from the scanner," Max stated. "If you hold out there, you could at least get some peace while we're working out the details."

"That's a good thought," McCray said. "It will give us time to heal. I would imagine now that you've put Dmitri in his place, he'll be less likely to screw with us."

"Do you think the other Lords know about the scanner?" Dante asked. "They can't love the idea that Lucien has such an edge. Maybe we can reason with them."

"It's a thought. I remember some of the Lords rated far lower on the asshole-a-meter than Lucien," Max commented.

"Max, are you off your rocker? They don't see us as people. We're slaves, remember? If they kill Lucien, they'll just be stronger when they come to exterminate us."

"Things are different now, McCray, we have a unified voice. They will have to listen," Sophia piped up.

"Girl, there's no way. We're outnumbered and outgunned. On top of that, they can track our every move."

Dante sighed. It was the same song that Janet sang. "Hiding clearly isn't working," Dante spoke. "We need a new strategy, one that will give us some chance at survival."

McCray scratched his stubbly chin. "What do you propose?"

"When the scanner is destroyed, we fight."

McCray's eyes got big. "Is he serious?" Max nodded.

"I know how powerful Lucien is. I fought him and he nearly killed me," Dante said. "But there comes a time when you just have to make a stand. Tell Lucien, all of his allies, and your other enemies that you won't go quietly."

"Your little friend is quite the leader, Max," McCray said.

Max looked at Sophia, who nodded. "There's a lot to him. He's the Truthsayer."

"An Ancient? I thought that they were a myth."

"He's the real thing, truth sense and everything," Sophia replied. "The world's changing. We need to change with it."

"If the Ancients have returned, perhaps we really do have a chance to finally be free," McCray said with a smile. "Seraph, consider yourself a member of the Ardent Rebellion. Destroy the scanner, and we'll come out of hiding and stand with you."

"Well, champ," Max stated, "looks like we've got ourselves a quest."

"Let's get to it," Dante answered.

"But first, dinner," Sophia said. "Kicking ass makes me hungry."

McCray nodded. "We'll be in touch."

SEVEN

Max decided to drive back without the benefit of a teleportation circle. The passage was quiet. The heavy traffic had died down as the evening went on. Dante and Sophia were in the back seat in their usual places, as Max drove the car.

"Where are we eating?" Dante wanted to know.

"What about the diner right next to campus?" Sophia asked.

"Yeah, it's open for the next couple of hours," Max answered.

"Let's just get something to go," Dante said. "It's been quite a night."

"Don't let us keep you up, baby," Sophia teased. "You need to rest up. I believe you owe me another sunset tomorrow."

"Will you two get a room?" Max groaned.

"Why? We have a back seat right here," Sophia answered. She made a face as she looked at Max through the rear view mirror.

"Max, lighten up, will you?" Dante asked.

"Hell no, I don't want your loving going on in my car." He pouted. "I rather like this car."

Several loud beeps jumped out from Max's armlet.

"Is your microwave popcorn done?"

"Not exactly, I set my tech to scan the school for any hostiles. It took several hours to break through the encryption and access the Ardent scanner to that specificity, but it finally completed."

A holographic image of the school appeared on the windshield. There were little colored dots all around, moving from place to place.

Max looked smug. "Brilliant, huh? Here's all the people on the campus, color coded by focusing cues based on Ardent empowerment."

"Mind translating for us, Max?" Dante interjected.

"Speak for yourself, I understand him just fine... go on, Max," Sophia deadpanned. Dante made a face.

"Each dot represents an energy signature of a person. The color represents what kind of person. A white one is an ordinary person. A blue one is a knight, Ardent Lord, or rebel, like me and Sophia. See? Here we are." He pointed at the outline of the car the road going up to the diner. It contained two blue dots and a gold one.

"Wait a second, Max, my dot is gold?" He pointed to the screen.

"It sure is. Your Ardent energy frequency is different. You're an Ancient," Max said.

"What's a red dot mean?"

"What do you mean a red one?" Max wanted to know.

Dante nodded. "There are a bunch of red dots here."

"I'm not sure what those are, but they have a decidedly different frequency in their signatures. "

"Max, there are at least ten of these red dots," Sophia said, her forefinger counting one by one. Dante looked over as well. Max craned his head over, the car sliding off to the right."

"Keep your eyes on the damn road!" Dante snapped.

"Easy there, tiger. Live a little," Sophia chuckled. "You just went up against a coven of vampires, and you're worried about a little reckless driving?"

"Damn, that doesn't make sense." Max looked a little more closely. "I wonder if this is what Lucien meant."

Sophia was curious. "What do you mean?"

"When he caught us in his warehouse, he asked me if I knew anything about the new race of Ardent," Max said. "He was pretty pissed when I didn't know anything either."

"Why are their dots so much fainter than ours?" Dante asked, narrowing his eyes.

"The energy signatures are really, really weak. It means they are probably just latent talents at this point."

"Perfect," Dante said. "What do we do?"

"We need to tell them," Sophia said. "They need to be warned."

"We can't just start a student club." Dante paused, moving his hands so that he was holding an imaginary microphone. "Set your dorm on fire? Find yourself flying? Sign up for the Ardent club, first meeting right after intramural ping pong in the student activities center."

Sophia rolled her eyes. "No, smartass, but we need to keep an eye on them, make sure that when their powers manifest, we can be nearby to deal with the effects."

"They won't believe it, and how could they be expected to?" Max said, gripping the steering wheel tight.

"They'll get used to it. I'm more worried about Lucien's reaction, honestly," Sophia commented.

"I take it he'll be pissed?" Dante said.

Sophia nodded emphatically. "Lucien is all about control. This is prime recruitment material here."

"He'll put knights on campus in order to deliver the sales pitch. Lucien may even take some by force or arrange for an accident if they don't agree," Max said, still paying far too much attention to the map of the school, rather than the road.

"So we better figure out who these new Ardent are, really quickly or we're going to start seeing more knights come calling."

"I'll start cross referencing the information overnight. Tomorrow I should be able give you more information on the names."

"So are we good for the evening?" Dante said. "I'd love a little time to relax."

"Don't get too comfortable," Max answered. "The world just got a whole lot more complicated."

∴

"Fancy meeting you here, Seraph," Sophia said as she sat down next to Dante in the cafeteria. It was not terribly crowded for the early morning, but the row of tables next to the glass wall were full, so Dante chose a seat in the corner.

"Yeah, almost like I was waiting for you," Dante answered.

"Did you sleep okay?" Sophia asked.

"It was all right. Surprisingly, I had trouble powering down," Dante answered. "What about you?"

"Like the dead," Sophia replied, threading her fingers through his. She leaned her head on his shoulder for a moment before resuming eating her breakfast.

Sophia sighed, "This is nice."

"Yeah," Dante answered, "very normal."

"Is this strange for you?" Sophia asked, not exactly facing Dante, toying with her food like a cat with yarn.

"Being here with you like this?"

"No, your haircut," Sophia groaned. "Yes, I meant you and me. Seriously Dante, sometimes I wonder what's going on in that head of yours."

"You can be a brat. Do you know that?"

"I have heard that, yes." Sophia tapped his nose. "It's part of my multi-faceted charm."

"Anyway, to answer your question," Dante replied, "yes, it's very strange sometimes. It's been a long time since I've been with someone." He turned the conversation. "What about you?" She didn't reply. Instead she looked out forward, like she was staring through the plain grey cafeteria wall. Dante nodded. "I take it that means yes as well."

Sophia shook her head, stretching out and threading her other hand in his. "Sorry, I was thinking about the last guy I was with."

"Something the new guy wants to hear."

"Don't be an ass," Sophia answered. "It was complicated."

"It usually is. Do you want to tell me about it?"

"Not really, but since you asked," Sophia replied. "The guy's name was Byron. He was the drummer in a heavy metal goth band."

"Always the drummers, isn't it?" Dante smirked.

"Not always, but it does help. We started dating right before I got my powers," Sophia said. "About a month later, I got recruited by Lucien, went from goth to preppy, and kind of ignored Byron. It wasn't intentional, but I had to make my work my number one priority. On top of that, I couldn't tell Byron about all this Ardent stuff, so he was kept in the dark."

"I take it Byron didn't like that too much."

"Totally not. He freaked out and called me a poser and a whore."

"Ouch," Dante said.

"For him, I suspect. I think I broke his jaw." Sophia grinned. "It still hurt though."

"That sounds like you."

"Yeah, but you know what? It gets really tiring trying to be something you're not, or trying to live in a way that is contrary to yourself."

"Is that the Ardent stuff, or the preppy, non-goth stuff?"

"Both, actually, I'm not thrilled I haven't been able to start that retirement I earned, especially with Lucien breathing down our necks. I've said it before and I meant it: I want my normal life, and the sooner this scanner is destroyed and we stop Lucien, the better. At least then I'll be able to change my wardrobe at the very least."

Dante nodded, absorbing the words.

"Your expression is a little too thoughtful for comments about my wardrobe," Sophia said. "Come on, *Seraph,* out with it."

"I was just thinking. I don't think I can have a normal life."

"Why do you say that?" Sophia wanted to know.

"For one, I can always tell when people are lying," Dante said.

"We knew that. I don't think that's an insurmountable obstacle. You just need to surround yourself with habitually honest people, like yours truly," she answered with a grin. "What else do you have?"

"I'm the first Ancient in a thousand years. The Ardent Rebellion is looking to me to be some sort of leader, right?"

"Kinda," Sophia replied. "So?"

"So, that means I'm not going anywhere. I'm in this life now whether I like it or not." Dante looked away. "I took on this responsibility. Now I'm kind of stuck with it."

Sophia's mouth wrung up in a odd expression. "You're concerned that your duty is going to be a problem for us, aren't you?"

"A little, yes," Dante replied. "How can you have your retirement and hang around me?"

"I'm sure we can figure it out."

"If you say so," Dante answered, not really convinced.

Her face scrunched up a little. "Don't think too hard about it, Dante... I'm not unhappy." She leaned in closer. "At least, not with you."

"That's good to hear."

"It's the truth."

"I know," Dante replied. "Truthsayer, remember?"

"How could I forget?" Sophia said. "Okay, off of me, onto you. What about you?"

"What about me?"

"You've been pretty quiet about how you're doing with the whole Truthsayer thing, and our brave new world," Sophia replied. "You try to be the strong, silent type, Dante, but I know you've got to be a little freaked out."

"You know me so well," Dante answered. "Yeah, I guess it's a little overwhelming."

Sophia waited for him to continue. She spoke when he didn't. "But?"

"It's strange, but there's a part of me who feels very at peace with the whole thing. It's like I was meant to be here, to be like this," Dante said.

"Are you creeped out that you're not creeped out?"

"Yeah, that's exactly it."

"Well, maybe that's because you are supposed to be here. You are an Ancient, after all." Sophia smiled. "They just don't give that to anyone."

"They are definitely busy," Dante said with a smirk. "Any idea who *they* are?"

"That's getting into philosophy or religion. Neither of which is my department."

"Oh, hey, Sophia!" A voice shook the pair out of their musings. Dante looked up at the edge of the table.

The owner of the voice looked very girly, almost adolescent. Dark eyes, which were nearly black, radiated under a head of nearly platinum blonde hair. She had an athletic build; her upper arms were toned with youthful muscle. The make-up she wore was heavy, more so than would have been appropriate outside of a formal dinner, and a sweet scent of winter breeze perfume filled the air. She was dressed in simple running clothes, and her delicate features shined with energy.

"Oh, hey, Naomi," Sophia said.

"Didn't expect you to be here this early," Naomi said, eyes darting back between Sophia and Dante. "Don't you work on Saturdays?"

"I used to, now I typically just work out," Sophia said. "Sometimes, I even let this guy work out with me." She gestured to Dante. "Naomi, this is Dante. Dante, this is Naomi."

"This is *the* Dante? It's great to meet you," Naomi said, taking Dante's hand and shaking it. "Sophia's told me *so* much about you."

"Has she now?" Dante raised an eyebrow.

"Naomi's my roommate," Sophia said. "I may have mentioned you once or twice." Dante flinched at the lie.

"More like *all the time*, but frequency is relative, I suppose," Naomi grinned. Sophia glared at her.

"You're going to get it," Sophia said lightheartedly.

"I'm not scared of you, missy," Naomi said. "But I have to split. I'm meeting my freshman seminar sisters in a few minutes."

"Have a good one, bitch," Sophia smiled.

"You too, slut," Naomi answered. "It's nice to finally meet you, Dante."

"Nice to meet you too," Dante said.

"See you!" Naomi said and rushed off to the other side of the cafeteria, where two freshman girls welcomed her to their table.

Dante shifted his attention back to Sophia, whose face was slowly turning red. "I'm surprised you'd have a freshman for a roommate, considering that you're a senior."

"Rachel set up my roommate assignment," Sophia replied. "She said it was Lucien's order. I've got no idea. It didn't really make sense to me either."

"Naomi seems nice," Dante stated.

"As far as roommates go, she's not too bad. A little too sunshine and puppies for my tastes though."

"You really miss being goth, don't you?"

"I do. I really, really do." Sophia pouted.

Max stormed into the cafeteria a few minutes later. His appearance was a little haggard, like he hadn't slept, and his armlet was beeping loudly. He scanned the room quickly and, upon seeing Dante and Sophia, made a beeline for their seats. He slouched down next to Dante.

"We've got a real problem," Max said.

"What is it?" Dante wanted to know.

"I was finalizing the analysis of the scanner data. I discovered we have a latent who's about to pop."

"Where?"

"Right here. She's in the cafeteria with us."

"She? Who is it?"

Max pointed directly at Naomi.

"Are you kidding me?" Sophia spat. "My roommate?"

"Depending on what her power is, she could kill everyone in this room," Max replied. "We need to get her out of here."

Sophia ran a hand through her hair in frustration. "We're too conspicuous this way, we can't just go running in, there'll be too many questions. Plus we'll scare the hell out of Naomi before we can get her out of here."

Max continued to run the analysis with his armlet computer, looking up every so often.

"Oh, bloody hell." Max spat, barely covering his mouth before clipping the words out loud for the entire cafeteria to hear. Sophia glared at him and Dante looked up to him quizzically. The three of them huddled together. "Another surge," Max whispered, looking grim.

"So what do we do?" Dante said. "Do we have any time?" Max continued to run his analysis when Sophia started pulling frantically at Dante's sleeve.

"I'll try to talk her out of here," said Sophia. "How much time do we have?"

Max called back, "Three minutes, maybe?"

"Shit," Sophia jumped up and rushed towards Naomi. Dante followed quickly. Sophia came and stood in front of Naomi's friends.

"Hey Naomi," Sophia said.

"Oh, hey," Naomi said with a little confusion. "Did you need something?"

"Um… yes, I do," Sophia stammered. She looked at Dante, who shrugged. She glared at him. "I need some help with something back in the room." It was true enough.

Naomi looked up, amongst papers and pencils. "I'm kinda busy here. Can we chat about this later?"

"Come on, Naomi," Sophia replied. "I'm on a timeframe here."

"I'll come by later on, okay?"

"Naomi, you need to come with me now," Sophia commanded.

"Sorry, I just can't leave. We're not done with our project."

"Naomi, just come on."

"I *said* I'm not done," Naomi said, slamming her hand down on the table. Fire began to seep out from her fingers.

"Oh shit! What the hell?" Naomi yanked her hands back from the table. They were still smoldering. Small wisps of smoke appeared in her hands, dancing around her fingers like a charmed set of snakes, curling up towards the ceiling. Tiny sparks appeared next, jumping off the sides of her fingernails.

"Oh my God, fire!" One of the freshmen screamed. Naomi threw her arms around in an attempt to put the fire out.

"Dante," Max yelled as he ran forward towards the group, "get them back!" Dante grabbed the other two girls at the table and yanked them backwards, just in the nick of time. Naomi's body erupted in flames. Fire spread up the curtains and across the floor.

In under a minute, fire began to crawl throughout the entire cafeteria.

EIGHT

"Sophia!" Dante screamed as the fire's blast wave struck him. The two freshman girls, whom he had just saved, were thankfully out of range of the impact. The force slammed Dante to the ground. The tile floor cracked under the pressure.

"Damn it!" Sophia snapped. As the smoke was making everything hard to see and the air harder to breathe, Dante barely made out Sophia's form, standing behind a bluish shield.

Students rushed to the door, piling out of the cafeteria with such ferocity and desperation as to make the glass doors groan and buckle. The metal frame of the doors held, but the loud snaps of the flexing metal could be heard throughout the room, over the roar of the fire.

"Max?" Dante crawled on the floor, eager to stay out of the smoke. He scanned what little view he had, and saw Max standing behind a force field very similar to Sophia's.

"Dante, the kitchen," Max shouted. "Close the service door." He pointed up. There was a heavy duty flexible door that came down from the ceiling when the cafeteria wasn't open. It looked like a silvery garage door. "Take this, it's a portable shield emitter. It will keep the service door from melting." Max tossed a small square device to Dante.

The kitchen was filled with cooking implements, oils and a ton of flammable substances. There was a gas stove used to cook hamburgers and other baseball stadium food.

"What about your shields?"

"We can't move them once we put them up. The emitter is the only way," Max said. "It's up to you."

"Max, it's getting hot in here," Dante said. Even at his distance, the pain from the fire was overwhelming. "I don't want to get char-broiled in the damn fire!"

"There isn't any choice," Max said. "If you don't close that door and get the shield up, we'll lose the building and everyone inside. Don't think, champ. Just do it."

Dante moved slowly towards the kitchen, the heat beginning to sear his arms as he attempted to shield his face. The smell of burning flesh mixed in with the smoke, making Dante gag as he pulled himself forward.

He didn't see the unlock lever for the door. The flames started to dance within a few feet of the kitchen. Hisses from the fire were screaming right near his ears.

Dante crouched down and leapt up at the top of the doorway, slamming both his hands into the concrete surface. Two swift cracks greeted him. Twisting his hands within the rubble of the concrete, he could feel the cool surface of the steel door. He yanked it down with all his strength and the chains holding the door moaned and ripped. The service door slammed down unceremoniously, just as the fire brushed against it. Dante quickly placed the shield emitter on the door, and a bluish shimmer covered it.

Dante pulled the fire alarm, causing the area to be blanketed in water. Once removed from the searing flames, Dante's arms began to heal. He vaulted over to Max, who was considerably farther away from Naomi than Sophia was.

"Is there anyone else in here?" Dante shouted over the fire.

"Negative. It's just you, me, Sophia and Ms. Nuclear over there."

"Is Sophia all right?"

"She seems to be, her shield is strong."

"What do we do now?"

"Can you get to Naomi?" Max asked, typing on his armlet's keypad.

"You're kidding, right?" Dante asked. The path to her was nothing but a sea of flames.

"No," Max answered, "If she loses consciousness, her power should shut off."

"This is a bad idea," Dante snapped.

"Hang on, champ," Max said. "Take a couple more of these emitters. They may help."

Dante grabbed one of the tables next to him and swung it forward as a shield. He slapped on the emitter, and the entire length glowed with a faint blue shimmer.

"Here goes nothing," Dante said as he slowly walked towards the ball of fire that was Sophia's roommate.

Naomi now appeared to be completely enveloped in the fire. Only a vague humanoid outline was visible to Dante through the heat and steam from the fire suppression devices. Her hands were still waving spastically, every so often a softball size white flame would hurl itself out of her grip, smashing into a wall or table around her.

Even with the shield emitter diffusing the fire, the table started to crack immediately. When Dante reached the halfway point in his journey, the table exploded from an ejection of plasma. He noticed that it looked like a solar flare. The wave pierced right through the table and struck Dante in the chest, tossing him away into the back wall.

"Any bright ideas, Max?" Dante said. He had sunk nearly a half an inch into the concrete.

"Don't you think you should scrape yourself out of the wall before you say that?" Max said with an ill-timed chuckle.

"Not funny, asshole. I told you that was a bad idea."

Sophia yelled, "I've got an idea! Dante, can you get to me?"

"Sure, why not?" Dante growled. He pried himself out of the wall and started the path towards Sophia. Dante took this journey in a crawl, which helped him avoid the plasma, fire and flash-frying a little bit.

He snaked up behind Sophia. The force field was shielding them both. Dante's burns started to close.

"I always do enjoy when my man is on his knees." Sophia smirked.

"I'm your man now, huh?" Dante replied.

"We can discuss that later," Sophia said. "Right now we have to take that bitch out."

"Can't you just zap her with your lightning thing?"

"Nope. The shield prevents any other powers from leaving, I'd just cook myself."

"What's your idea then?" Dante wanted to know.

"You are going to be my shield," Sophia answered. "You still have a shield emitter, right?"

"You have *got* to be kidding."

"No, grab one of the tables and hold it in front of you. Between you, the table, and the emitter, I should have enough time to shut my shield down and then hit Naomi with a lightning bolt."

Dante shook his head. "This is crazy. Even with Max's gadget, the tables only last about a minute. If that fire hits you…"

"I know. I'll be cooked alive. We don't have a choice."

"All right, but if this goes south, stay behind me, I'll try to stand grounded to give you time to put up your force field again."

Dante snatched up one of the tables. He positioned it in front, and activated the last emitter.

"Okay, I'm dropping my shield." The bluish light faded away and Sophia immediately started coughing from the smoke.

"Sophia!"

"Damn it!" She pulled herself up and threw a bolt of lightning from her gauntlet. The electricity bounced off the dome of fire encasing Naomi.

The table began to crack. "We just can't get close!" Sophia snapped. "We can't cross the distance!"

"That's it!" Dante said, the table creaking. "Can you teleport me to her?"

"Maybe," Sophia said. "Can you take the heat?"

"I guess we're going to find out. Take this." He handed her the edge of the table. She held onto it, using her back to keep it in place.

"Dante, I don't like this," Sophia said.

"We don't have a choice," Dante answered. "I'm ready, kick it on."

Sophia looked scared. She pulled Dante to her and kissed him. "If you die, I'll kick your ass."

"I'll try not to disappoint."

A blue flash enveloped Dante. He landed in front of Naomi. He only saw her for an instant before the pain enshrouded him. It was unbearable. He shielded his face immediately, hoping he would *have* a face by the time this was over. He swung. He felt something hard against the edge of his blistering fist. It felt like a jaw. Hopefully it was. Dante crumpled to the ground from the attempt.

Several moments later the fire started to fade. The white flames slowly churned into a more reddish hue. An instant after that, they blinked out, much like the flashbulb of an old style camera.

Dante opened his eyes to see Sophia's face. She grimaced. There was soot and redness reflected there. "You asshole," Sophia said sweetly.

"Are you all right?"

"You looked like you went five rounds with a volcano, and you're asking me if I'm all right?"

"Yeah, I guess I am," Dante answered.

"I'm fine," Sophia said, "thanks to you."

"We can celebrate the success when I look a little less like beef jerky."

"You're healing pretty fast. You *almost* look like a human being."

"How sweet," Dante answered. "Is Naomi okay?"

"She'll have a hell of a shiner, but she'll be fine."

Max leaned over into Dante's field of vision. "That was some brave shit, champ."

"Hey, I'm the Seraph, right? I've got a reputation to uphold." Dante smirked. "Could someone help me?"

Sophia took his hand and pulled him up. He was a little wobbly on his feet, but an examination of his arms showed that he was nearly completely healed.

Max looked around. "We really need to be somewhere else right now."

Dante scooped up Naomi in his arms. "So, where are we going?"

"Back to our room," Sophia answered. "It's the least conspicuous place we could go. I'd imagine Naomi's going to assault us with questions."

"Works for me," Max replied. "Stand by for the teleport."

"Couldn't we just walk?" Dante wanted to know. "I think I'd rather be done with teleports today."

"We need stealth on our side," Max answered. "Ready?"

"Sure," Sophia said. "Don't be a baby, Dante."

The bluish light swept them all up before he could answer.

．＋．

"Love the Hello Fluffy poster, Sophia. Is that yours?"

"That's very nice, asshole. No. That's her bed, the one with the pink lacey border."

"Sophia wishes she had my mad talents in interior décor," Naomi said groggily. "Damn, Dante, you pack a pretty mean hook."

"I'm sorry about that," Dante answered.

"It's okay," Naomi said. "I was burning down the cafeteria, after all."

Max smiled. "We all went through it, kid."

"Went through what, exactly?" Naomi wanted to know.

"The manifestation, the power is really overwhelming the first time. It gets easier to control as time goes on. When I got my power, I leveled a city block."

"Really?" Naomi said.

"Are you sure?" Dante said skeptically.

"Well, maybe not the entire block." Max shrugged. "The point is we all learn control."

"What are *we* exactly?"

"Ardent," Sophia answered. "That's the term for our condition. It's people with special powers."

"I saw you with the blue thingie." Naomi pointed at Sophia.

"It was a shield," Sophia commented. She made a hand gesture of a dome.

"I can't believe I've been your roommate for all this time and I never knew."

"Seems like a real coincidence that Lucien had you room with a latent." Dante said.

"That can't be a coincidence," Max said. "He's definitely up to something."

"Lucien?" Naomi said. "I think we need to impose a moratorium on references I don't know." She paused, looking at Sophia. "Hey, wasn't your boss' name Lucien?"

"Ex-boss, and yes, he's the one we're talking about."

"Was he some kind of mobster or something?"

"Something like that," Max answered. "When did he set the two of you up as roomies?"

"At the beginning of last semester," Sophia answered.

"Do you think he had the Ardent scanner the entire time?"

"Scanner?" Naomi said in confusion.

"It's a device Lucien built that can find Ardent anywhere in the city."

"Like radar?" Naomi suggested.

"Exactly," Max replied. "He could have had the scanner for months or years. There's no way to know. It probably was awhile though."

"He always said that he had the gift of prophecy," Sophia said. "It's just another reason to hate him. He's a liar."

"He tried to kill me," Dante said.

"And enslaved my friends," Max added.

"I get it. Lucien equals bad," Naomi interjected, a little flustered. "Can we move on?"

"She'll need to be trained," Sophia said. "She doesn't use an armlet, or a focus that I can see."

"I'll help," Max replied. "I have several devices that I can use to catalogue her power. We should be able to use that information to help her control it."

"Get started, Max," Dante said. "We may not have much time."

"What do you mean?" Max raised an eyebrow. "You know something that we don't?"

"He's coming. I don't know how I know, but I do," Dante said. "We need to be ready."

Nine

One week later

"Well, well. Look who decided to grace the gym with his presence," Sophia said with her arms folded, hip cocked, adorned with a smirk. "You're late."

"Sorry. I got held up," Dante said as he slipped into Sophia's embrace.

"Max showing off his latest tech, no doubt," Naomi said, powering down a fireball spinning in her hand.

"That's really good," Dante observed. "You've improved a lot this week."

"Thanks, Seraph," Naomi beamed. "It comes totally easy now."

Sophia nodded. "I still don't recognize her power. She's got nothing like anything I've ever seen before."

Dante smiled. "It's the time for that."

"What do you mean?" Naomi wanted to know.

"Kind of hard to explain, but I can feel it."

"Whatever floats your boat." Sophia smirked. "We're pretty much done here, anyhow." Sophia stepped away from Dante, who immediately missed the contact. She stepped over to her workout bag and started putting her training gear away.

"We should stick around," Dante said. "Max is supposed to meet me here in a few minutes."

"Max is coming by?" Naomi said. Her face took on an excited smile. "Oh crap. I look horrible." She frantically smoothed down her rumpled hair. An amused look passed between Dante and Sophia.

"Looks like someone has a crush," Sophia smirked.

"You bitch. I don't want to hear it," Naomi said smiling. "Not after dealing with your Dante fixation all year."

"Slut, watch your mouth," Sophia warned.

"Fixation, huh?" Dante raised an eyebrow. "You never told me about that."

"And I never will. Can it, shorty."

"Oh, please, I can SO kick your ass."

"This kitten has claws, watch out," Sophia answered. She brought her hands forward like the paws of a tiger.

"Watch out for what?" Max said as he entered the room.

"Naomi's antics," Dante answered diplomatically. "Did you get what you needed?"

"Yes, I did. You're not going to believe this. Seriously, this is some crazy shit."

"That sounds juicy," Naomi said with a hint of the sly. "What did you find Max?"

Max raised an eyebrow, but continued. "I got the energy analysis of your power activation. The vibrations of transference coincided with a most peculiar event."

"English, please, Max," Dante requested, "or get me a phrase book."

"When Naomi blew up the cafeteria," Max answered.

Naomi groaned, "Gee, thanks."

"My pleasure," Max answered with a grin. "Anyway, I was able to track the moment when her powers began to activate."

"Well, don't keep us in suspense," Sophia said, taking a swig of water from her bottle.

"The moment Naomi shook Dante's hand, her powers flared to life."

"Excuse me?" Dante was surprised.

"You were the catalyst, Dante," Max completed. "Maybe it's because you're an Ancient. That would imply that there's some sort of connection there."

"Reminds me of something August said. We need to figure out what that connection is," Dante said.

"It's no big deal," Sophia chuckled. "Just don't touch any more freshman girls, and you should be all right."

"I don't make a habit of it, actually."

"You better not, or you and I are going to have words," Sophia said sweetly.

"If the lovebirds are done," Max interrupted. "We have to decode this interaction. If Dante can create Ardent, then perhaps we have some allies against Lucien."

"Even if I could, we can't seriously be considering just awakening Ardent," Dante countered "That's just inhuman. I mean, think about it, they're just kids, Max."

"Sophia was about their age when she awakened, Dante, as was I," Max replied. "It's the way of things, and we need to make sure we can control the manifestations. If we don't, we could lose half the school in a single Ardent eruption."

"Do you think Lucien has more information on this in his databases?" Dante wondered.

"I doubt it," Sophia answered. "He doesn't know jack about you. He admitted as much when he ordered us to harvest you."

"He would never ask a traitor anything unless he had no recourse," Max said. "He definitely is missing information."

"Someone's coming," Dante said.

"How can you tell?" Naomi said. "I don't see anyone."

"There's someone teleporting in," Dante looked around. "No, I don't know how I know. Just be ready."

Three men appeared in a circle directly to Naomi's left. Each one of them was dressed in the traditional black suit with gold armlet of Lucien's knights. Sophia scanned between them, nodding to them as they bowed. Her armlet flashed into existence. "Well, well," Sophia said. "Byron, I certainly didn't expect to see you here."

"Ah, Sophia, my lovely fallen angel."

"You were always the charmer, Byron, before I cracked your jaw, of course. I take it that it healed all right?"

"It did. I really ought to thank you. Without you, I would have never met our master."

"You work for Lucien now. How did I not know about this?"

"It's a recent occurrence. My powers manifested only a short while ago." Byron smiled and blew Sophia a kiss. She responded by rolling her eyes. Dante chuckled morbidly.

"Isn't it fun when the ex shows up?" Dante said.

Sophia returned a glare. "Not one more word, *Seraph.*"

"Oh, I don't know what you're all bent out of shape about. He seems nice."

"You are impossible," Sophia replied. She walked over to stand with Naomi. "Byron, I suppose you're here to deliver the sales pitch." He made a face.

"She's not interested," Max said, moving between Naomi and the knight. "Piss off."

"The traitor is here. I should have known. I am not concerned with the words of someone who defies his god," one of the other knights spat.

"Jason, you will behave," Byron said evenly. "Ryan, please make sure we're not disturbed." The third knight walked over to the door and locked it.

"You should be concerned with *my* words then, Byron," Dante said. "Maybe you haven't heard, but the Ancients have returned to the world. We're pretty angry with what you've done to it."

"I have heard of your existence, Ancient. You are of little consequence."

"Try something, and see for yourself how inconsequential I am." Dante raised his arms, tightening his hands into fists. "You game, Max?"

"Sure, I don't have anything else going on." His armlet flashed blue, electricity cascading up and down his arm. "Sophia, would you be a dear and escort Naomi out of here?"

"Screw that, I'm not leaving," Naomi interrupted. She closed her eyes for a moment. As they opened she was wreathed in white fire. "Let's dance, you irredeemable bastards."

"Come on Naomi, let the boys play," Sophia said. "Don't worry, your time will come." Sophia bowed with a smirk.

"This sucks," Naomi snapped. Her fire went out and she stepped back next to Sophia.

"We'll take our leave now," Sophia said. "Good luck, *Seraph.*" Her gaze on him was intense, and said far more than her words did.

Her gauntlet shined for a moment, then a teleport energy wave spirited both Naomi and Sophia away.

"You the new boyfriend?" Byron asked in the still moment following their departure.

Dante nodded. "Yes I am. Is that a problem?"

"No, not for long." Byron looked at Jason. "Kill him."

Jason attacked Dante immediately. The spear on his gauntlet appeared as he rushed into range. The blade arched in a wide crescent, going for a head shot. Dante blocked the shot with his forearm. The blade stopped with a dull thud.

Dante reached over and grabbed the knight's gauntlet. He yanked with all his strength. Jason flew towards him, his feet leaving the ground. The flight was stopped by Dante's knee when he raised it into the knight's face. There was a sickening crunch. Dante released the wounded soldier to slump over on the floor.

Ryan squared off with Max while Byron circled around Dante. A long bolt of lightning flew out of the knight's armlet and struck Max's chest. He was carried off the ground by the impact, spinning and crashing into one of the bleachers. Ryan pressed on, walking toward Max with his blade.

"Max!" Dante shouted, turning to run over to his fallen friend. Byron body-checked Dante as he moved to intercept. He tripped and skidded across the ground, sliding a couple of feet short of Max's location. As Dante stood up, Byron let a bolt of lightning fly. The impact slammed Dante into the outer wall of the gym, causing the concrete around him to quake and crack.

"Not so fast, you bloody bastard," Max snapped as he threw a lightning bolt of his own. Ryan ducked out of the path of the bolt. The lightning cracked the outer wall, causing rubble to trickle down on the ground. The knight hurled another salvo of lightning. Max raised his armlet as a shield, but the impact propelled him back onto the gym mat.

"You will have to do better than that, traitor," Ryan said. He raised his armlet back up to throw another lightning bolt. Dante grabbed the knight's armlet and squeezed. The gauntlet and the forearm beneath it shattered. He screamed.

"Is that good enough for you?" Dante asked.

"Screw you," Ryan spat.

"Now, that isn't very nice," Dante commented. He threw a punch into the knight's face, knocking him unconscious.

Byron raised his blade and pointed it out towards Dante. "Stay back, monster!"

"I'm not the monster. That would be your boss," Dante said as he moved toward the knight. "Just get out of here."

"Wait, what?" Byron said, his blade lowering slightly.

"I said get out of here, all of you," Dante answered. "Pick up your shit and get out of here. I don't want to see you on campus again."

"You're letting us leave?"

Max stepped up. "You're a sharp one. That's the deal. Just leave Naomi alone."

Dante nodded. "We're not looking to fight, just to protect."

Byron shrugged. The blade on his arm faded into vapor. He dragged Jason and Ryan into the center of the gym floor. "Lucien will come for you, regardless of what you do to us."

"Or *not* do to you, I'm sure," Dante answered. "It wouldn't be anything new, Byron. I hope you understand what world you've stumbled into. If you come after us again, we may not be so nice about it."

The knights vanished in a circle of blue light, teleporting away in an instant.

Max powered down his armlet. "He's not wrong, you know. Lucien won't stop coming until he gets what he wants."

Dante shook his head. "We can't watch Naomi all the time. Two quick teleports and she's gone."

"Maybe not," Max answered. "There could be a way to protect her, and the rest of us, for that matter."

"What are you thinking?" Dante asked. The look on Max's face showed promise.

"A jammer, champ," Max replied. "I have a few things to work out, but it may be possible for us to set up a broadcast device." Max rubbed his eyes, then began to type away on his armlet computer. "Maybe we can turn the tables on those bastards."

"I hope so," Dante said as they walked out of the gym into the light. He saw Sophia, who wasted no time in making her way over to him. Naomi followed quietly behind.

"Leave any of them alive?" asked Sophia.

"All three, I'm afraid." Dante shrugged.

"That's too bad, especially with Byron. You did kick their asses, though, right?"

Max chuckled and slapped Dante on the back. "He certainly did some of that."

"You weren't so bad, yourself," Dante answered. "You just have to love the lightning."

"You're too kind," Max replied.

"Can we skip the bromance?" Naomi groaned. "What the hell happened in there?"

"They attacked us. We beat them. We let them go," Dante replied, stepping into Sophia's arms for an embrace.

"But what if they come back?" Naomi wanted to know.

"They *will* come back," Sophia said. "Lucien will keep coming. There are so many Ardent waiting to awaken, it's too appetizing a target for him. If he could secure even half of the latents on this campus, and each of them is as powerful as you, he'd be able to turn the tables on the other Lords."

"So what do we do?" Dante asked.

"The latents have to be told of what they are," Max answered.

"Do you have any idea on how to do that without coming off like a bunch of lunatics?" Dante asked. "They're not going to believe this."

Sophia shook her head. "No, they won't. There's also the police to consider."

"I have an idea," Naomi said. Her eyes got big and bright. "Sophia, I'm going to need a little help with this."

"Sure," Sophia smirked. "Should we leave it a surprise for the boys?"

Max and Dante looked at each other. Both of them tried and failed to hide the hint of fear just below the surface.

TEN

"This is a crazy idea," Max said, looking over Naomi's shoulder. The four had returned to Sophia and Naomi's room. Naomi was busy typing on her computer. Dante and Sophia were sitting on the adjacent bed.

"I think the cops finally left," Dante said, looking out the window. The gym had swarmed with police after the explosions inside shook the school. "How do they just glide past this crazy shit?"

"Before the carnival, would you have believed that someone could smash through two feet of concrete?" Sophia questioned.

"I wouldn't have ignored what was right in front of my eyes."

"Sure you would have," Sophia said. "It's what we do. Perceptions are completely a product of the mind." She tapped the end of his nose. "Have you ever lost your sunglasses when they were on the top of your head?"

"Well, yeah, but that's not the same thing."

"Sure it is. You didn't expect them to be there, so you couldn't tell that they were there. Your mind overrode your eyes."

"Are you saying people do that with the Ardent stuff?"

"*Especially* with the Ardent stuff. Not all of it, but most of it," Sophia said, ruffling Dante's hair. "Take a look out there, Dante. The news will report that there was some kind of earthquake or gas line breach at the gym that was responsible for the damage to the inner walls."

"People don't *want* to know, do they?" Dante asked. "Is that it?"

"No, they truly don't want to know," Sophia answered. She leaned her head on Dante's shoulder. Dante wrapped an arm around her.

"How's the invitation coming, Naomi?" Sophia asked.

"Not bad," Naomi answered. "I got the list of names from Max's scans, and snatched up their email addresses. I crafted a message asking them if they want to be a part of a new student club."

"What's the club about?" Sophia asked, "Wait, wait, don't tell me. It's a pole-dancing aerobics club."

"Ha, ha." Naomi leaned back from the keyboard. "Actually, since the majority of latents are freshmen, it's a social networking club. A meeting group, you know, for dating, meeting new friends or whatever."

"Very cute," Dante said. "Does your club have a name?"

"I thought about this one for a long time. I decided to call it *Ardent Rising*," Naomi answered. "After all, we're the new generation right? We're rising from the old."

"Hear that, Dante?" Sophia said, slapping his arm. "You're old."

"You're no spring chicken either," Dante replied sweetly.

Sophia's eyes narrowed, though they remained amused. "You are so lucky that I like you. Men have been killed for less."

"I don't want to bloody hear about being old," Max said. "I was born before the three of you were twinkles in your *grandmothers'* eyes.

"You gotta love older men, right Naomi?" Sophia smirked.

"I've got no idea what you're talking about," Naomi answered.

"Shit," Dante said, pain shooting through his head from Naomi's lie. "Anyway, when are you having this meeting?"

"Not me, you, Seraph." Naomi grinned, nearly hopping up and down on her chair. Sophia chuckled. Max rolled his eyes.

Dante was not quite as amused. "What do you mean, me?"

"I'm not going to try to explain this. They'll just think I'm crazy." Naomi waved dismissively.

Dante threw up his hands. "What happens when they think I'm crazy?"

"The damage to your reputation is not my concern," Naomi answered. "I have three more years in this place. You're graduating in the spring. A little laughter is good for the soul."

"That's great. My rep at this place is *so* stellar anyway."

"You poor baby. Don't worry, I think you can handle it." Sophia patted Dante on the thigh.

"You two make me sick," Naomi said, making a face. "Are we good to send this note or not?" Her finger danced over the face of the keyboard, the nail tapping on the top of the enter key.

"Go ahead," Max answered. "It's a good plan. It might even work, eh?"

The computer made a happy noise. "It's sent," Naomi said. "So what happens now?" She stood up from her chair and plopped down on her bed. She glanced at the clock. "Crap, it's almost one in the morning."

"Okay boys, that's your cue to leave," Sophia said. "We can't have you both getting written up for breaking curfew." She rested her chin on Dante's shoulder.

"I can tell when I'm unwelcome," Max said with a smirk. "Dante, you ready?"

"Yeah, we've had a long day. Are you going to be all right?" Dante said to Sophia as he brushed his hand through her hair.

"As if I need you to protect me," Sophia said with a smile. "I'm fine, Dante."

"Meet me for breakfast tomorrow?"

"Sure. How about in the café, since my roommate decided to go all nuclear on the cafeteria?"

"Are you ever going to shut up about that?" Naomi made a face.

"No, probably not," Sophia replied. She kissed Dante on the cheek, provoking yet another disgusted look from Naomi.

"Good night," Dante said as he and Max left the room.

∴

"We're in a lot of trouble now, Dante. I wouldn't be surprised if Lucien sent more knights after little Naomi straight away," Max stated as they walked back to their dorms.

"What are you saying?"

"I'm just saying that Lucien isn't going to be swayed easily," Max said. "When it comes to Royal Lords, force is the only action that they understand."

"Then we shouldn't be leaving them alone," Dante snapped.

Max put a glove on Dante's arm. "Easy champ, Sophia's there with her."

"That's what I'm worried about, Max. What happens if Lucien teleports more knights in tonight? We need to get back there and guard them."

"Dante, you can't just hover over them every minute of every day. Sophia will call us if there is a problem. She's a big girl. She can take care of herself. If any of the nasty buggers come calling, she'll just teleport the both of them to the nearest mocha shop and contact us from there. You need to relax."

Dante sighed. It was a little ridiculous. Sophia had trained *him* after all. "I guess you're right."

"Guess, nothing. You're a regular firecracker right now," Max said sternly. His amusement showed through, a light hint of a teasing tone entered his voice. "It's nice to see you both getting along so well. You two are good for each other."

Dante shrugged. "I'm not so sure."

Max looked confused. "What do you mean?"

"She won her freedom."

"That's true," Max responded uncertainly.

"Every second she spends with me, she runs the risk that Lucien will come after her," Dante answered. "I mean, shit, Max, you and I are members of the Ardent Rebellion, and we just beat the crap out of his knights."

"Something that was very fun, I might add," Max said with a grin.

"No doubt, but what happens when Lucien decides to come after her for being a turncoat?"

"He could have done it already," Max answered. "Dante, there are *no* rules to what is going on here. Lucien considers himself a *god*. That's quite a massive ego. With that ego comes the assurance that he can do whatever he wants."

"So she dates me until Lucien has had enough and tries to kill her?"

"What did she say about it?"

"She told me not to worry about it."

"It's good advice," Max said. "You can't know what will happen, and Sophia understands the risks very well."

"Is it fair for me to let her take those risks?"

"I hate to break it to you," Max said, "but you're in just as much danger as she is."

"Yeah, but aside from avenging Rachel, she's risking her life to be with me," Dante replied. "It weighs on my mind."

"If I know Sophia at all by now, she'd be pretty pissed off if she knew you were thinking like this."

"Perhaps," Dante agreed.

"Look champ, there are no guarantees. I wish I could tell you it will work out all great with nothing but happiness and bliss for you two. I can't do that. What I can do, however, is tell you something that I had to learn over the past eighty years."

"What's that?"

"Carpe diem, my friend. Seize the day."

"Do you have a greeting card to go with that?"

"Ha ha. Seriously, life is pretty fleeting and happiness is very fragile, so if you have both right now with her, as I assume you do, then shut the hell up and enjoy it," Max said.

"I'm trying, but there's something else."

"You really think too much, don't you, Dante?"

"I was thinking about something that Sophia said to me once, she said that she didn't really like living this way." He gulped. "She wanted to have a normal life, complete with all the normal stuff. She didn't want to live in fear of Lucien, nor have to contend with all of this craziness. Sometimes I think she really feels like she's missing out."

Max interjected. "Well, yeah, but that doesn't really mean anything for you, does it?"

"What do you mean?" Dante looked confused. "I'm part of all of this… gifts and everything, right?"

"Well, yeah, but that's not the point. Even though you're both Ardent, what you have is really pretty simple. It's not about a superhero and a damsel in distress. It's about two people who care about each other, and want to be together, right?"

"I guess, but it's kind of like the elephant in the room, isn't it? I mean, how can you ignore something like this?"

"When you two talk, do you talk about your gifts? Or do you talk about the normal stuff that a couple of kids dating talk about?"

"Aside from the training, I'd say the latter, I guess. It's still pretty new," Dante replied.

"Then don't worry about it. Sounds to me, like in the right circumstances, you two would still be dating, despite all this hokum and nonsense."

Dante nodded. He was a little relieved, just a little. "I didn't really think about it that way. Thanks, man."

"Don't mention it. Now come on, we've got some work to do. Well, actually I've got some work to do, and you're on your own."

Dante made a face. "What do you have going on at one in the morning?"

"While you were going on about your sweetie-pie, I had an inspiration."

"It's nice to see that you were paying attention," Dante frowned.

"I can multi-task," Max answered. "We need to cut teleportation to the campus."

"You mentioned this idea earlier. We need to lock things down in order to keep Lucien from sending his goons in, taking Naomi and the others, and teleporting away without a sound." Dante nodded, considering the idea. It would at least afford them a chance to intervene if the knights came looking to kidnap someone.

"You got it. We could embed the device in the spire. There's an old radio antenna that would help the broadcast."

The administration building had a very tall central spire that extended forty feet skyward. It was the highest point at the school and could be seen from anywhere on the campus.

"How big of a radius are we talking about?" Dante wanted to know.

"A mile or two, I'd guess," Max answered. "I won't know until I actually set up the device. It won't stop a Royal Lord from teleporting, but it will stop any of his goons from getting in."

"I can help with the spire," Dante said. "You can't quite reach the top like I can."

"I will need to be on the *inside* of the spire." Max chuckled. "But if you're so intent on helping." An alarm suddenly went off on Max's armlet.

"What is that?"

"It was an Ardent energy spike," Max said. "I'd guess a teleportation."

Dante jumped, already prepping for action. "Where?"

"It came from Naomi's room," Max answered.

"In or out?"

"In," Max replied. "One person with a very high energy output."

"We need to get moving."

"Correction: You need to get moving, I need to get that teleport jammer activated to prevent any additional incursions. I'll set it up so that Sophia will still be able to teleport out with Naomi.

"How long do you need?" Dante wanted to know.

"I need fifteen minutes to get the device set and calibrated."

"That may be too long. I'll head back. If they're still there, I'll grab the girls and get them to safety," Dante said as he began to lift off the ground. "If not, I'll make the bastard sorry that he came to Salvatore tonight. Hurry back as soon as you can. If we trap someone here, we may need the backup."

"You got it, champ," Max said. "Be careful."

Dante nodded his agreement. Max disappeared into the darkness as Dante quickly gained altitude.

The lights began to blur as he moved. It wasn't more than a quarter of a mile to the residence halls, but he used the altitude to mask his approach above the unfurled pine trees surrounding the dorms. He landed lightly on the gray back of the dorm and hopped down in front of Sophia's window, standing on the air.

The lights were still on, but there wasn't much sound coming from inside. He looked around. Luckily, this part of the building was hidden from most vantage points by the pine trees.

There was a man inside the room, standing between Sophia and Naomi. The cut of his suit and the manner of his poise was obvious.

Dante pulled up the window and stepped into the room, coming face to face with Lucien.

"Ah, the Ancient comes back to play," Lucien snickered with contempt. "You're just in time. Naomi and I are leaving. Aren't we dear?"

"No freaking way," Naomi spat. "There isn't a chance in hell I'm going anywhere with you."

"You don't have a choice, my dear child."

"I say she has a choice, asshole," Dante said as he stepped forward into the room.

"Do you wish to die, Ancient?"

"Do you think you're man enough to kill me?"

"Sophia, take Naomi back to my office, while I deal with this impudent child."

"My lord?" Sophia said in confusion. "You released me. I'm not a part of this anymore."

"Leave her out of this," Dante spat.

"Sophia, you can't remove the gifts I have given you, any more than you can remove one of your hands from your body. I am, and ever shall be, your *god*. Now do what I say."

Dante moved forward into the small room, bringing up his guard, readying himself to fight.

"If you take one step closer, Ancient, I will bring down this entire building and kill everyone inside. How would you like that on your conscience?"

Dante backed off, "You're not going to get away with this."

"There is no one of higher authority, Truthsayer," Lucien replied. "Now, come on Sophia. We are leaving."

"No," Sophia said, her armlet shimmering into existence.

"What do you mean, no?" Lucien's hand launched out and grabbed Sophia around the neck. "You are mine."

"Not anymore," Sophia croaked out. Lucien raised her off the ground.

"Sophia!" Dante lunged at the Royal Lord. Instead of reaching him, Lucien's sword materialized out of nowhere, faster than the eye could see, and impaled Dante.

Sophia was dropped unceremoniously on the ground. "You bastard!" she snapped.

Casually, Lucien yanked the sword from Dante's chest, flinging him into a dresser. Dante clutched at the wound and slowly stood back up. "You would be my enemy, Sophia?" Lucien said. "After all I have done for you?"

Sophia's hands were shaking, but despite that, a blade formed out of her armlet. "You made me your slave," she spat.

"I gave you power."

"Power? You took my entire life from me."

"I *gave* you a life," Lucien answered coolly.

"Being your property isn't a life. I never wanted this!"

"Yes, you did. How quickly you forget."

"Go to hell," Sophia said.

Lucien sighed. "You've made your choice, then, haven't you?"

"My choice?" Sophia answered. "Well, this is a first. You're actually *giving* me a choice?" She pointed her blade at him. "Here's a news flash: My choice puts me on the side of the Truthsayer, not your demented ass."

"Then you will share his grave."

"Excuse me?" Naomi said. "I think you forgot about me." She leaned forward and swept her arms in two wide arcs. Fire seeped from them and coalesced into a single bolt. The projectile startled Lucien, who barely had enough time to look surprised. The blast launched Lucien through the window. On the way down towards the street below, Lucien vanished in a teleport.

"At least I left the window open," Dante said as he struggled to stay on his feet. "I wouldn't want you guys to lose your security deposit."

Sophia rushed over to him. "Give yourself a little time to heal. This is pretty bad."

"No it isn't. I've been hurt worse."

"Lucien cut you with an Ardent blade, genius."

"It burns," Dante grimaced.

"Let me see," Sophia said, pulling on Dante's shirt.

"If you wanted to undress me, you could've just asked," Dante said with a strained smirk.

"You wish," Sophia replied. The wound was dark, nearly black, with wisps of reddish smoke seeping out. "You're healing, but a lot slower than you usually do. That's not surprising, considering."

"What do you mean?"

"Ardent blades kill," Sophia answered. "Most people die in seconds. The weapons are infused with Ardent power, hence the name."

"Lucky thing I'm an Ancient, huh?"

"What you are is a dumbass, Dante," Sophia snapped. "You just don't get it, do you?" She took a moment and dressed the wound with gauze and antibiotics from a small first aid kit she had retrieved from under her bed.

"Hey guys," Naomi chimed in. "If you're going to fight, at least take it outside so no more blood gets on my rug, okay?"

"Shut up," Sophia said. "You guys think this is just a big damn joke, don't you?"

"No, not really," Dante answered. He glanced at Naomi, who wore the same confused look.

"Yes, you do. You're not taking this seriously. Goddamn it, Dante, he could have *killed* you."

"I know," Dante answered. "Naomi, would you mind giving us a minute?"

"Sure, I'll head to the break room and grab a soda. I'll be back in a few." Naomi slipped out of the room quietly.

Sophia walked over to her dresser and snatched up a plain white shirt. She tossed it to Dante, who pulled it over his head.

"He scares you, doesn't he?" Dante whispered. "Lucien. You're terrified of him."

"What do you think?" Sophia said, spinning on her heel and turning her back to him. "He wouldn't think twice about it, either, you know."

"What, killing me?" Dante asked.

"Yeah," Sophia said, folding her arms. "He wouldn't lose a single night's sleep. You didn't see the look in his eyes when he killed Rachel."

"For what it's worth," Dante said, as he dared to approach her. "I was trying to defend you."

"I know," Sophia said, "and you were stupid."

"Maybe, but he was choking you," Dante answered. "I couldn't just stand there and watch you die."

"What would have happened if Lucien had aimed a little higher and hit your heart? What would your damn chivalrous nature have earned you if his sword burned you to death from the inside?"

"It wasn't me being chivalrous," Dante said as he touched her shoulders. She relaxed slightly.

Dante gently pressed on her shoulder, urging her to face him. She did. Her eyes were a little bright, as unshed tears lined them. Sophia took her hand and pressed her palm to his cheek. "Do you have any idea what it would do to me if something happened to you?"

"I'm sorry," Dante answered. He closed his eyes for a moment to gather his thoughts. "I can't lose you, either."

Sophia's expression became startled with her eyes growing wide. She quickly recovered. "Oh, come on, Dante," Sophia said. She wiped her eyes quickly and forcefully. She stepped back, out of arms reach. "Don't get all gushy on me. You don't need me anymore. I've taught you everything you need to know."

"That's not what I meant. It's more than that, and you know it."

"You mean this… *thing* between us?" Sophia chuckled bitterly. "You really are a rookie at the whole dating thing, aren't you, *Seraph*?"

"Maybe, but it doesn't make me any less sure," Dante answered.

"A few years from now, you'll barely remember my name. You'll move on, become a detective or something. I'll be a little memory from your college days. You'll have your little perfect wife, with your little perfect kids with your little perfect house with your little perfect dog. That's just how these things go. Don't make this more than it is."

"That's not true. That's not even possible."

"Why not?" Sophia challenged. Her eyes dared him to answer. "What makes you *so* sure?"

"It's a simple truth," Dante said. "I love you."

Sophia pushed him back into the wall. "Do you have *any* idea what you're saying?" Her hands danced from his shoulders around his chest to grab his head. "You can't just say that, and not mean it."

"I'm the Truthsayer, remember?" Dante said with a small smile, bringing his hands up to mirror hers. "I mean it with everything in me."

Sophia took a moment and just looked at him. Her eyes were almost astonished, and a stray tear slipped free. "I love you too," she said softly. She brushed a lock of his hair away from his eyes. "I'm scared."

"I am too," Dante replied, rubbing his thumb on her cheek, "but you make me feel like I can do anything."

Sophia smiled. It was a good smile. She then launched herself at Dante with an unbridled passion. She grabbed at him, pulling him close, like even the scant inches that separated them was far too much distance. Dante responded in kind, stroking her hair gently.

"Shit," Naomi said as she opened the door. Surprisingly, Sophia didn't let go of Dante, merely turning her head and looking at the intruder. Dante smiled, though his cheeks turned a little red. Naomi shook her head and closed the door behind her. "I take it you two made up?"

"Not at all, but this beats pistols at twenty paces," Sophia replied.

"That's good. Gunfire would definitely get the residence assistant's attention," Naomi said, sipping on her soda as she plopped down on her bed.

"We can't have that now, can we?" Dante answered. "It would be the height of the problems that plague us right now."

"Damn," Sophia said. "You just abuse sarcasm. You know that?" She released him, and wandered over to her bed and sat down opposite to Naomi.

"I try," Dante chuckled.

"You succeed," Sophia answered.

"So, if you two are done with your little banter and your making out," Naomi said with a frown. "What's next?"

"I would have expected Lucien to teleport right back here with a legion of his knights," Sophia said. "What kind of crazy world do we live in where Lucien doesn't go all homicidal at the drop of a hat?"

Dante grinned. "It's interesting that you mentioned his knights. Max placed a jammer in the school spire. He said it wouldn't stop Lucien, but any of his flunkies would be powerless to teleport in or out."

"Clever," Sophia said, "but if Lucien can't get at us with his conventional troops, he'll go after us with his backups."

"Backups? What do you mean?" Naomi asked.

Sophia shook her head. "Lucien will send the vampires again."

"Real vampires?" Naomi yelped.

"Yeah," Dante nodded.

"That is insane, but the sun will be coming up in a couple of hours," Naomi questioned. "Won't they burn or something?"

"Not quite, unfortunately," Sophia said. "They don't burn, instead they lose all their Ardent powers. In essence, they're normal people when the sunlight hits them. He'll wait until tomorrow night. Without teleportation, Lucien won't risk the exposure that a knight could cause. The other Lords would move against him if he was discovered."

"I thought he was out to kill them all," Dante said.

"He is, but he's not ready yet."

"So, what do we do?" Naomi wanted to know. She yawned. "I don't know about you guys, but I'm tired."

"Yeah, some rest isn't a bad idea. I would imagine you guys are safe for the moment. You guys sleep, I should go." Dante turned around and opened the window. "I'll have Max monitor the teleport traffic in case Lucien returns for round two."

"Are you sure you don't want to stay?" Sophia asked very seriously.

"No," Dante smiled. "I do want to stay, but I don't want to break your roommate's mind."

"No joke," Naomi said. "Seeing you two making out is like watching my parents kiss. Gross." Naomi made a sick expression. The mood broken, Sophia turned around to face her roommate.

"Remind me to come barging in the next time *you* have a guy in here," Sophia said sweetly. "I'm sure Max would appreciate that."

"Come off it, Sophia," Naomi warned. "Knock it off."

"Or what, short-stuff?" Sophia replied. "You wanna go?"

"Ok, as much fun as watching a chick fight would be, I'm heading back," Dante said. "So no fighting after I leave, okay?"

"You're no fun," Sophia pouted. "I was going to snatch her bald."

"You behave," Dante said. He stepped through the window. His power kept him floating on the other side, nothing beneath him but darkness.

"See you tomorrow for breakfast?" Sophia asked. "Ten o'clock at the café?"

"I can't wait," Dante said with a smile. "Good night, Sophia."

"Good night, my Seraph," she answered. Their eyes locked. Naomi's eyes rolled.

Dante chuckled and flew off into the night.

ELEVEN

As Dante reached a good cruising altitude, the cool air of the night blasted him. Instead of flying the entire way back to his dorm room, Dante landed on the scenic path behind Sullivan Hall. The entire journey would take just a bit longer, but it afforded Dante the time to relax before heading to sleep.

There was a rustling in the woods on the side of the dirt road. At first Dante paid no attention, but there was a familiar presence in there. He could tell who.

"August," Dante said.

"Your senses are improving, Truthsayer," August answered, stepping onto the path next to Dante. "Your teacher should be pleased. You have progressed nicely."

"I'm glad you think so," Dante answered. "I take it you're not here just to compliment me."

"There is much work to be done." August reached within his coat and pulled out a sword and scabbard. "I understand that your skin has met the metal of an Ardent blade tonight."

"You know, if you were watching, you could have helped," Dante said as he rubbed the site of his fading wound instinctively. "Maybe we could have taken care of Lucien for good."

"I was very far away," August answered quietly, "and besides, would you help kill your own child?"

"I thought he was your lieutenant."

"He was my son first. I gave him the power that he now wields."

"If you don't mind me saying, you could use some lessons on parenting if that's how *your child* turned out."

"He was a good soldier," August said, "and a good friend."

"Did he fall to the dark side or something?"

"Darkness did consume him, yes, but from what source, I do not know," August answered. "In light of that tragedy, I have something to give you." He handed the sword over.

"What is this?" Dante wanted to know.

"This is the *Ardent Vow,*" August replied. "The ancestral sword of the Truthsayer, and my ally for over a thousand years."

"It's an Ardent blade?" Dante admired the scabbard. It was well used, but still in good repair. The leather was lighter on the edge, but all the weaves were still as tight as they were on the day it was made. The cross-guard of the sword's hilt was rather nondescript, save for the lines of gold spiraling up to the bright white crystal at the center of the pommel.

"Yes, *Ardent Vow* was forged by the Empyrial Council in the elder days."

"Why would you give this to me?"

"It is time. You must learn much for the light to prevail. It begins when you take the blade."

"Um… all right," Dante said as he grasped the scabbard. The weapon felt familiar in his hands. It was as if it had been there a hundred times before.

Then there was the flight. Dante felt yanked up, as if invisible springs bounced him up towards the heavens. Out of reflex, he closed his eyes in defense against the wind blowing upwards through the ascent.

When he opened them again, he was somewhere else.

The room was huge, almost the size of a football field, and circular. Dante was standing on a platform overlooking the entire area in the center. The walls were stone. A large cauldron of fire rested beneath him. A skylight of pure sun shined down upon the fire.

"What the hell?" Dante looked around, and small flashes of light jumped on the floor of the room.

August walked up beside him. "Welcome to the Empyrial Amphitheater."

"The what?" Dante snapped.

"The connection we all share."

"Can you *try* to be more cryptic? How did I get here?"

"You have not moved physically. The movement is solely of the spirit."

"So we're still standing on the path to the dorms?"

"That is correct. What you are witnessing in front of you is a spiritual recreation of the birthplace of the Ardent people. This place is our refuge from any of the others. Only Ancients may travel here. You were here once before, as your power awakened."

Dante drew the *Ardent Vow*. The blade shined in the reflected sunlight. The edge was as flawless as a diamond. "The sword was forged here, wasn't it?"

"Very good," August said. "Look below."

Dante scanned the empty area below the platform. "What am I supposed to see?"

"Narrow your focus, think about your friends."

Dante complied. Tiny pin pricks of light appeared in the space below. Soon the motes changed into images. They shifted and whirled around until he saw Sophia. He was standing right next to her. She was sitting on her bed, chatting with Naomi. He sat down on the bed, though neither of them seemed to notice him. August was still there, standing in the doorway of the room.

"You are connected to them, Truthsayer."

"Naomi and Sophia?" Dante asked.

August nodded. "Not just them. You are joined to the entire Ardent race."

"You mean everyone? Lucien included?"

"This is the greatest secret of our people. We are everywhere within our progeny."

"Sophia is just going to love this," Dante smirked. Surprisingly, Sophia started looking around with a confused expression.

Naomi narrowed her eyes. "What is it?"

"It was odd, I could have sworn I heard Dante." Sophia looked out the window and shrugged when she didn't see anything there.

"You've got it bad, girl," said Naomi.

Dante stood up and walked over to August. "She can hear me?"

"Not exactly, she can feel your presence, much like you can feel hers."

"How deep does the connection go?"

"In time, you will be able to sense her thoughts as well."

"Oh shit," Dante said. "She's *really* going to love that."

"Come, it's time to go," August said, walking through the door. The portal was closed and he passed through it like a ghost.

"Here we go again," Dante answered and walked through as well. On the other side of the door was the Amphitheater. From his vantage point, he could still see Sophia, but she returned to her place as a small but vibrant light in a sea of other lights.

"Look out into the night, Truthsayer. See all the latents as they sleep." August made a sweeping gesture and nine lights flashed into view. Simultaneously, Dante was seeing all of them. Some were up late watching movies. A couple of others were grabbing a late night snack from the vending machines. In every way, the group of them was completely normal. *Just like Naomi was.*

"They aren't asleep," Dante said.

"On the contrary, they are, and now they are all about to wake up," August said. He raised his hands towards the images on the other end of the Amphitheater. The latent lights began to flash colors, glowing red and white.

Fear radiated from their images. Dante faced August. "You're turning them into Ardent, aren't you?"

"They will be my new children in this millennial time. They are born a thousand years after the line of Empyrial burned in Rome." August clenched his fists and the colors flashed gold. Waves of golden fire were thrown up in the air, nearly touching the top of the Amphitheater dome.

Dante panicked. "August, they're in the dorms. If they blow up like Naomi did, hundreds of people are going to die."

"You are here to stop the destruction, Dante. I cannot halt the power once I've summoned it."

"Are you serious?" Dante scanned the images. One guy had accidentally smashed a soda machine. A girl's couch was quickly freezing. Another girl was throwing lightning all over the place, her TV picture froze in place right before it exploded.

"Reach out through the connection and calm them."

"What are you talking about?"

"Tell them. Use your power to slow theirs."

Dante shook his head. At least two of the students were in Sophia's dorm. That made up his mind for him.

"Hey! Listen to me!" Dante shouted. Surprisingly, the latents turned to face him, though some of them looked around for him before he spoke. He must have been a disembodied voice to them. "I'm going to help you all through this."

"Oh, God," a girl said as a bolt of force shot out from her hands and smashed her microwave. "Please help me."

"I'm going to," Dante said as he looked down on each of them.

"Who are you?" another girl looked up. "I can't really see you, but I can hear you. Who are you?"

"Seraph," Dante answered. "I'm Seraph. I've been sent to help."

"I can't take this. I just can't!" one guy said as he staggered in the common room.

"Hang on. All of you." Dante disconnected and looked at August. "How do I turn this off?"

"The Amphitheater will respond to your commands," August said. "Tell her to make their powers rest. Use your blade."

"Great, so I have to threaten a room with a sword." Dante looked down at the fire in the center of the Amphitheater. He raised the *Ardent Vow*. The Amphitheater hummed at the sight of the blade. A sudden rush of air accompanied the sound. Interlocking joints moved as stones creaked around. The flashes of gold light began to slow. The power seeped out of them, and nearly in unison, the group fell to the ground in exhaustion.

Dante stepped out of the Amphitheater again and walked into the rooms with the now empowered Ardent. They all looked up at him. The questions they couldn't find the voices to ask were radiating from their minds. He could sense that now. "I'm connected to each of you," Dante said.

"I know all of you have questions. If you want answers, go to the *Ardent Rising* meeting. I'll be there."

"Thank you. You're the nicest hallucination I've ever had," the girl said, looking at the twisted remains of her dorm room. "Think this will come out of my security deposit?"

"You're welcome. Don't worry, it gets easier to control," Dante answered.

"You better be right about that," the guy said. "This really sucks."

"I'll see you tomorrow. We'll talk in person then." Each of them waved goodbye and went back to the delicate task of fixing up whatever they damaged in their eruption.

"Well, that was eventful," Dante said. He looked over at August, who had finally completed whatever-it-was that he was doing. "You know, a warning would be nice next time."

"I'll keep that in mind, the next time that the situation presents itself," August said with a light smirk.

"Wait, was that a joke?" Dante pointed at the elder Ancient.

"Perhaps, but there is much still to do, Truthsayer," August answered. "The Royals will still come after the Millennial children. You will need to protect them."

"Speaking of assholes, is Lucien in here?" Dante looked around again, this time attempting to find Lucien. It didn't take long, and he saw the light of his enemy. Connected to Lucien's image was a wisp of reddish mist, leading off towards another light.

"What is that smoke?"

"I do not know. I have never seen it before," August answered. He drew up his hands, and coaxed the images forth. The lights in the room re-organized so that Lucien's form and the dark image connected by the wisp of smoke landed right in front of Dante. "It has an overwhelming presence. It is connected not only to Lucien, but to every other Ardent in Louisville."

"What about the vampire coven out of Bloodlines?"

"No, they are not connected," August answered. "None of the Ardent near the nightclub are joined."

"It's the Ardent scanner," Dante jumped. "You found it! How can you tell where it is?"

"The Caroline Warehouse, near the Old City. Wait, something is wrong," August said. A mass of darkness emerged from eminent shadow.

"Brother," the dark image said, "you have sought me out, and now you have found me." It coalesced into a human form, and landed gently onto the platform. After a moment, a familiar face stared back at Dante.

"Sophia?" Dante said as his jaw hit the ground.

"No," the image said, "I took the form of one whom you would find pleasing. In the elder days, I was known as Hope."

"Hope," August repeated. "You call me brother, are you of the Empyrial as well?"

"Yes, of the council, many years ago, before the second war."

"How did you come to be here?"

"During the conflict," Hope answered. "I found this to be a safe haven amidst the torment the Royals were placing on our people."

"How is it that I have not been able to sense you?"

"I have masked myself, so that I may observe securely." Dante felt the pain of deception.

"August," Dante said, unconsciously bringing the *Ardent Vow* to readiness. "She's not on the level."

"You are the reborn Truthsayer," Hope said. "Your power must be impressive to sense truth in even my words."

"And what makes you so special?" Dante replied.

"Every puppet needs a puppeteer," Hope answered. She drew a sword of her own. The sword dripped black venom, the blade was a dark red metal. "I am the beginning and the end of chaos on this miserable rock you call a home."

"You are Morte-Veras," August summarized, he drew a two-handed sword, far larger than *Ardent Vow,* out of nowhere.

"I am the first Morte-Veras," Hope said. "August, you and your pathetic masters thought you could crush the mantle of chaos in the world. We merely injected our power into your children."

"Lucien," August said, gripping his sword tightly. "What did you do to them?"

"I gave them the *ego* to resist your domination. It took many years to slowly break their duty and loyalty. On Lucien, it was impossible. I had to completely possess him in order to corrupt his thoughts."

"Monster!" August exclaimed. "You will pay for your crimes."

Hope laughed in a way that made Dante's skin crawl. "Know that every moment of every day, your child screams for the tender release of death."

August launched himself at Hope, lunging with his sword at the monster's heart. Hope delicately danced her blade in a half circle, which parried August's strike. The impact of the blades clashing, drove August down to one knee. The elder Ancient returned to his feet quickly, pressing the attack. "Dante, get out of here, return to the world."

"What about you?" Dante stood ready, though Hope showed no interest in going after him. Instead, the creature chased August and began a series of wild attacks, each one knocking August around like a rag doll. The last one hit August in the side. Wet snaps and blood greeted them.

"My time is over. You have to live on, or this was all for nothing."

"I am not leaving you," Dante said, moving closer.

"No, we're the last of the line." August dislodged the blade from his ribs and leapt forward, lunging again. This time his blade steered true, impaling Hope in the chest. "The line must survive."

The creature looked down, unfazed. It retaliated with a strike of its own, running August through the sternum.

Dante screamed and swung his sword at Hope. She yanked the sword from August's chest, causing him to crumple down. Hope moved with incredible speed as she parried Dante's strike. Her sword shattered and she skidded back.

"August," Dante said.

"Dante, be their Seraph. Lead them." He slammed Dante with fading strength, and Dante felt the world leave him.

Dante's eyes opened and he was once again on the path to his dorm. August was gone. He looked down at *Ardent Vow,* still in his hand. He stumbled his way to his dorm.

Robotically, he unlocked the door to his room, and entered, nearly bumping into Sophia.

∴

"I hope you don't mind," Sophia said. "I thought I saw you outside my window, earlier. With all the commotion tonight, when I called your room and you didn't answer, I came to check on you."

"I'm glad you're here," Dante said. He took *Ardent Vow,* and placed it on his desk.

"Were you outside this whole time?" Sophia wanted to know.

Dante shrugged. "Not exactly, but I wasn't in the dorms."

Sophia stripped off her jacket and tossed it on the back of Dante's chair. "You missed the fireworks. A bunch of the latents popped."

"I know, I was there… well, kinda," Dante answered. "It's a long story. Were you hurt?" He tossed his jacket off as well. It landed on top of Sophia's.

"Nah, Max called and we made it to the basement. We just waited out the storm, as it were." She ruffled his hair. "To be honest, I expected it to be a lot worse, considering what Naomi did."

"It would have been. We got lucky."

"Hey, you're not looking so hot," Sophia said. Dante's eyes were bloodshot and he was shaking slightly.

"I don't think I can do this, Sophia," Dante said in a very quiet voice.

Sophia's expression became serious. "Do what?"

"Be the Seraph, lead the new Ardent, all that shit." Dante waved his hands dismissively. "It's too freaking much."

Sophia regarded him critically. He felt small from her gaze. "You don't sound like yourself, Dante. Did something happen to you? Were you attacked?" She rose slightly, as if to meet whatever enemy he faced.

"Not directly," Dante replied. "August was."

"That's the other Ancient, right?"

"Yeah, as I was walking back to my dorm room, he came up to me," Dante said. "Something killed him."

"How did it happen?" Sophia wanted to know. She stroked his hand gently.

"August took me to this place. He called it the Empyrial Amphitheater. It was some kind of mindscape where the Ancients could connect to all the Ardent. Since the Ancients, or the Empyrial as they called themselves, were the ones who created the other Ardent, this place served as a way for them to see their creations."

"Like a giant radar or GPS."

"Exactly. When we were inside, he asked me to focus on one of my friends, to see the potential of the connection. I chose you, and got to see you talking to Naomi in your dorm room."

"How much did you see?" Sophia said in mock terror. "Sorry. Trying to lighten the mood here."

"It's okay. I saw you notice my presence. I was actually there, just not physically."

"Oh good, for a moment there, I thought I was losing it." Sophia put his hand to her face. "Then what happened?"

"August awakened the latents."

"Excuse me?" Sophia said. "All of them?"

"Yeah, he brought me there to calm their power, so they didn't kill anyone when they exploded."

"So you stopped them? How?" Sophia asked. Her eyes were alive with interest.

"It's one of the Ancient powers, I think," Dante answered. "It got really crazy after that."

"What do you mean?"

"We met another Ancient. August called her a Morte-Veras."

Sophia shrugged. "That's not a term I'm familiar with."

"I think it's a dark Ancient. August saw that it was connected to all the Ardent in the city, except for the ones in Bloodlines."

"That sounds an awful lot like what Max said about the Ardent scanner."

"My thoughts exactly," Dante said. "We also noticed that this thing was heavily connected to Lucien, more so than with everyone else. When the creature was discovered, it said that it had possessed Lucien long ago."

"Wait a second," Sophia said. "*How long ago?*"

"A thousand years," Dante answered. "The creature has been puppeting Lucien for a long freaking time."

"You're saying Lucien isn't the enemy, it's this monster inhabiting him?" Sophia concluded. "I don't know how Max is going to take this one."

"Yeah, we'll have to be careful telling him about that," Dante answered. "Max has dedicated most of his life to hunting Lucien. What is it going to be like for him when he discovers Lucien is just a pawn?"

"We can worry about Max tomorrow," Sophia replied. She pulled Dante close, resting his head on her heart. "Now, tell me what happened next."

"August attacked the Morte-Veras. He was completely outmatched. I tried to help, but I didn't have any more luck. The monster ran him through the heart with a sword. He sent me to safety as he was dying right in front of me."

"Oh shit," Sophia said, cradling his head. "I'm sorry, Dante."

Dante pulled back slightly, so he could look Sophia in the eyes. "I can't stop this thing. I couldn't even hurt it. I'm supposed to be this big leader, right? What kind of leader can I be if I can't even face our enemy?"

Sophia's eyes got intense. She put her hands over his. "You are not going to face this thing alone. Do you understand me?" He turned his face away, and she took his head and forced it back to look at her. "I am going to be right there by your side when we kill this bitch, okay?"

"What happens if this thing kills you in the process?"

"Careful, Dante. You're starting to sound like you actually care," she said sweetly.

"I do care. I seem to recall I told you I loved you earlier tonight."

"And that, love, never gets old." She kissed him, and then continued. "If we go against this Morte-Veras and the Lucien-puppet, there is major risk, but that's what we do."

"I thought this wasn't your fight," Dante said. "Didn't you want to be out of all of this?"

"I did, but things change," Sophia replied. "Now I want to be very into it, with you."

"I just don't want you to get hurt."

"I don't want to get hurt, either. You're not going in alone, and, Dante, you're the *Seraph*. It's not a job. It's who you are. Most likely, in less than a month, this campus will be jumping with Ardent, they need us to be leaders for them. They will need guidance and temperance. I figure you can provide the temperance, because I'm fresh out."

"You sell yourself short," Dante said. "I'm surprised you haven't kicked my ass yet for whining."

"Oh, an ass kicking is a-coming, but for right now, I'm willing to let it slide." She kissed his cheek.

"That's good to know. Hell, the meeting of Naomi's *Ardent Rising* club-thing is tomorrow," Dante said.

"Yes it is. You better get some sleep. Freshmen have been known to eat people alive, you know."

"What do I tell them?"

"You're the Truthsayer. It might be good to start with the truth," Sophia said.

"I don't know what I'd do without you."

"I hope you never find out."

TWELVE

"Did he just go in?" Sophia said as she walked up the next evening to the meeting room. The *Ardent Rising* kick-off meeting had been scheduled in one of the school's smaller lecture halls and had just begun a few minutes before. The campus was mostly quiet, as classes had ended hours earlier. Max was leaning against one of the pillars by the door, tapping on his armlet absently.

"He went in a few minutes ago," Max said, not really looking up. "Naomi's in there with him. Dante's been filling the Millennials in."

"Millennials?" Sophia made a face. "What a terrible name. It sounds like something you'd come up with, Max."

The older man chuckled. "Nope, that one came from your boy. He claims that August called them that, but I think it's a smoke screen for Dante's complete lack of cleverness." Sophia sat down on one of the couches outside, near a school telephone in an alcove across the hall.

"How do you think they'll take it?" Sophia asked.

Max shrugged in response, "Hopefully better than I did. I signed up with the first bloke I saw, and he just happened to be a homicidal maniac."

"Yeah," Sophia answered. She looked all around the room, as if she was trying to find something missing. She rubbed her arms to stave off the cold. "I made the same mistake. I wonder what my life would be like if I hadn't."

"It's a paradox," Max replied. "We cling to the past, yet are powerless to change it. We know we should drive forward, but we always return to those things we have no control over."

"That's quite poetic. Is that from some old British poet from the 12th century?" Sophia asked.

Max blushed slightly. "Not exactly. Naomi wrote it for an editorial class she's in. I find that it resonates with me."

"So you're reading her papers now. That doesn't seem very fair." Sophia smirked. She shook her finger back and forth at him. "There's a rule or two against that, isn't there?"

"I wasn't grading them," Max retorted. "She just wanted to get my thoughts."

"So you obliged her."

"Yes, is that so wrong?"

"I disagree, you didn't oblige her," Sophia said. She crossed her arms over her chest.

"What are you talking about?" Max said. He imitated her pose, though the bulk of his armlet and gloves made the motion a little comical.

"If you would have obliged her, you would have stuck your tongue down her throat. Then you would have read her paper," Sophia said as she waved her arm dismissively.

Max was speechless. His mouth opened and closed like a trout, without a sound.

Sophia rolled her eyes in an exaggerated expression. "Damn, you really *are* blind, aren't you?"

"I beg your pardon?" Max answered. His eyes glared at the obvious insult.

She patted Max's face. "British-boy, you *do* realize that little Naomi has a ten megaton crush on you, right?"

"I am not bloody talking about this," Max snapped. "Seriously, that borders on insanity."

"Hey, hey, don't get mad. I'm not one to judge. I fell in love with the Truthsayer after all."

Max was seriously bothered. "I'm telling you that's not something I want to discuss. I'm sorry."

"All right, but I'd say you're missing out."

"With Lucien out there still hunting me, I'll just have to keep missing out and live vicariously through you and my main man in there."

"That reminds me of something. Since you're being a wimp about Naomi, we might as well move on to a different subject," Sophia said. She walked over to the window of the meeting room. Naomi was sitting cross-legged on the stage. Dante was standing at a podium. He was answering questions like a professor during a lecture. The students in the audience were very engaged. They looked as though their continued existences hung on each and every one of his words. Sophia smiled. He had come a very long way in a very short time.

"Dante told me something about Lucien," Sophia said. "Honestly, he was pretty worried about how you'd take it. I thought I'd spare him the trouble and piss you off myself."

"That's quite a lead up, isn't it?" Max replied. "Well, don't leave me in suspense. Out with it." He leaned back to get comfortable. He tapped a key on his armlet which caused it to whirl and whine softly in the background.

"All right then. You've asked for it." Sophia squared her shoulders and spoke. "Lucien is possessed by some sort of Ancient. Dante called it a Morte-Veras. Does that ring any bells for you?"

Cocking his head to the side, Max's face scrunched up in thought. "It sounds familiar, though I'd have to check my databases to be sure. How did he find out?"

"I'm not sure. It sounded like the creature told him. With the Truthsaying, it must make ferreting out the truth a lot easier." Sophia clapped her hands together, then brought them up to her lips in contemplation. "Dante said this thing killed August. If it all aligns, this thing is the actual monster behind Lucien's badness. It claimed to be in control of Lucien for at least a thousand years."

"That's not possible," Max snapped back. "So, you're saying Lucien is some sort of innocent bystander?" He glared at Sophia. "You don't really believe that, do you?"

Sophia exhaled. "I don't know." She rubbed her eyes. "I just don't know. I do know that Dante believes it, and I believe in him. I guess my question is, do you?"

"Of course I do," Max replied quickly. "This is different though. Whether I believe in him or not, the boy is pretty green. How do we know that this thing didn't twist its words or use some power to mask the truth?"

"I guess we really don't," Sophia responded. "If it is true, however, we have a different task then just getting the Ardent scanner."

"What do you mean?"

"Dante thinks that this Morte-Veras has some sort of link to the Ardent scanner. So we need to kill it in order to save the rebels. He even knows where it is."

"Where's that?"

"It's in a warehouse on Bardstown road, near the Old City. The place has been bought as historical property, no doubt by Lucien, and set up as a safe house for the care and feeding of his knights."

"Is this the part where we go in there and bust it up?"

"As much as I would like to, I think that might be a mistake. The Ardent scanner would let Lucien know we were coming from a mile away. We saw how well your masks worked last time," Sophia said with a frown.

"What about if we could approach undetected?" Max snapped his fingers. "We do know of a staging area that is invisible to the scanner."

"You're thinking about Bloodlines, aren't you?" Sophia's eyes got big. "We'd have to fight our way in. Dmitri isn't going to be very welcoming after we kicked the crap out of him."

"Unless they can be reasoned with," Max said. "Perhaps you can provide the necessary incentive."

"Have you met my boyfriend? He's totally not going to go along with this. He's a worrier as it is. Sending me into the vampires' lair, as fun as it would be for me to mash up Dmitri's face again, isn't going to work."

"We'll have to convince him," Max replied. "Surely he'll see that your delicate touch is required to soothe the savage beast."

"We could always send Naomi in. I'm sure that nubile eighteen year olds would get the appropriate attention of the vampires there."

"She stays out of it," Max snapped, before he realized that he'd been baited.

"So you *do* like her?" Sophia blinked innocently. "Admit it."

"Bloody hell," Max blushed again. "Do you ever stop?"

"Not really. Dante has mentioned that I have remarkable determination."

"I heard him differently. He said you were stubborn," Max retorted.

Sophia laughed. "That's all semantics. It's six one way, half dozen the other."

Unceremoniously, the door to the meeting room popped open and the students spilled out into the hallway. A couple waved to Naomi before leaving, but the majority kept their heads low and walked directly back to their dorms.

Naomi hopped out of the room with a grin on her face. "That was awesome," she said proudly.

Dante followed, immediately stepping into Sophia's waiting arms as he arrived. "I think so too."

"Do they understand?" Max wanted to know. "Think they'll listen?"

Dante nodded. "I gave them the low-down on the entire Ardent thing. They wanted to stay together afterward. I think they believed me."

"It was mystical," Naomi said. "You know that whole connection with the Ancients thing? I totally believe it now. They were totally into you. *Ardent Rising* is a complete success. I am a freaking god."

"Maybe they just thought I was hot," Dante answered with a smirk. Sophia had the good courtesy to roll her eyes at him.

"No way, there was definitely something supernatural at work there."

"I guess you're not as cute as you thought, Dante," Sophia said. She kissed him full on the lips to take the sting away.

"I don't need to be," Dante replied with a smile. He looked back over at Max. "We're going to meet again next week to follow up, then we'll get them started on some training. A lot of them have been trying to get their gifts under control since last night and having a hell of a time. They could use all the help they can get."

"I thought you turned them off," Sophia questioned. "How are they able to do anything?"

"It takes a lot of effort to keep them disconnected," Dante said. "I lost control after a couple of minutes. They had already calmed down, and I was too weak anyway." The image of August's dying body floated in front of Dante's eyes. He shook his head in an attempt to escape the visual.

"What happened?" Naomi said, though the look on Dante's face told her to drop it. She turned to Max. "Um, okay, what do we do now? We're still not safe with the Ardent scanner in place."

"We need to take it out, but we're going to need some help," Max answered. He flipped a switch on his armlet and a small screen lit up. "There's one place in the city that is invisible to the scanner."

"Bloodlines," Dante said. "Though the entire city block around it should be shielded, also."

Max shook his head. "I think Lucien knows something is up. The suppression is now localized to the Bloodlines club and the hotel next to it. McCray and the rebels have been notified. They're staying inside the hotel now."

"I'm sure Dmitri loves that," Sophia said. She stepped out of Dante's arms. "He owns that hotel; that's where his coven lives. Nothing happens in that hotel without his knowledge. He's making McCray pay an arm and a leg for the privilege, no doubt."

"Any chance he'll break his word?" Dante said. "While the rebels are asleep, it wouldn't be hard for the vampires to get a little snack."

"He may need to be reminded," Sophia said. "Also, if we're going to take a shot at the scanner, we'll need Dmitri's help."

"What are you suggesting?" Dante wanted to know. "Are we going in?"

"No, stud, I'm going in. You're staying outside." Sophia looked at Max. He nodded in agreement.

Dante shook his head. His shoulders tightened. "That's ridiculous. Last time you met with him, he tried to turn you into a vampire."

"He'll be more agreeable to me this time," Sophia said defiantly. Dante's resolve didn't weaken. He shook his head in response. Sophia's eyes darkened. "If you think you're going to get away with telling me what to do, Dante, you better stop right now. Despite the fact that I love you, I will kick your ass."

"I'm not scared of you," Dante snapped. "If it keeps you from turning into one of the children of the freaking night, then I'll take the ass kicking."

"How about a compromise," Max said, "before blood is spilled?"

"Wow, Sophia, the claws come out, don't they?" Naomi laughed. "I'm staying back here."

"I know where you sleep, bitch."

"As I was saying," Max interrupted, "you go in. We wait in one of the stores on the street. Any sign of trouble, we swoop in for a rescue."

"I still don't like it," Dante said as he folded his arms. "It's too risky without an escort."

"If you go in, people are going to die," Sophia said. She placed her hand over Dante's heart. "You don't want to live with that, Dante. I'll be fine. I've been going to Bloodlines for years. I'll be safe there. I'll be safe enough to get us what we need."

"Dmitri won't be awake for at least another two hours, Dante. I've got a few things to take care of before then. How about we all meet at your room at eight?" Max said.

"I'm good with that," Dante said. "I'll try to get a nap in."

"That's fine," Sophia said. "I'll need the time to change. I certainly can't go into Bloodlines looking like I just stepped out of a preppy catalog." She made a gesture towards her khaki and sweater outfit.

"This should be interesting," Naomi said. "I'll be sure to take pictures for the Internet."

"If you want to live through your freshman year, you'd be wise to rethink that decision," Sophia retorted with a glare.

"Why must everything resort to violence?" Max said sarcastically.

"Where have you been?" Dante answered.

.˙.

Dante woke up groggy. The nap didn't really help all that much. Every time he tried to sleep, the image of August being run through flashed before his eyes. Dante hopped down from bed and went through the steps of getting cleaned up and dressed. By the time he got out of the shower, there was a knock at his door. As he pulled on his shirt, he heard Sophia's familiar voice coming from outside. He hurried up, finished getting ready, and walked out of the bathroom, meeting Sophia's eyes with a self deprecating smile.

"I should just give you a key," Dante said as he opened his arms for her. "I'm getting used to you just popping in."

She stepped into them. "I figured you'd like some privacy in the shower, at least, with the others around. I don't know if you're into the whole public nudity thing."

"You are *so* wrong," Dante said.

"And you *so* love it," Sophia answered. Her hair had been done up, exposing her neck. Her eye makeup had a black tint to it. Her outfit was obscured by the long green coat she was wearing.

"So now that all of the official minutes are out of the way…" Max said as he stepped into the room. Naomi walked in behind him, dressed in a huge puffy coat. "You girls want two strapping men to escort you to dinner?"

"Why thank you, kind sir." Naomi faked a curtsey. Dante coughed, trying to stifle a laugh. Sophia walked over to Dante and put her arm around him.

"Absolutely, but you two slugs will have to do." She patted Dante on the shoulder. He rolled his eyes and Max just winced in fake anguish. "Come on, you two. Get the lead out."

"Where are we going to go for the food?" Max said as he looked at Naomi. "*Someone* saw the need to burn the cafeteria down."

Naomi's eyes got big. "For the love of God, that is ancient history. Will you *ever* stop bringing that up?"

"Destiny Café," Sophia replied, ignoring the banter. "It's the one right across the street from Bloodlines. It's very discreet. It'll be a good place for the three of you to wait while I go inside to see Dmitri. Also, I need to take my own car. If someone is watching me, they may suspect a trap if we all go together. I definitely can't be seen coming up there with the likes of you."

"If I didn't know you better, I'd figure you were insulting me," Max chimed in, spinning his BMW keys on his right hand. His gloves weren't on, which was unusual for him. Instead he had on heavy looking sunglasses that were more like a visor with two lenses. A faint trace of wiring danced behind his ear.

The look in Sophia's eyes indicated that her fear trumped his joke. Max muttered uncomfortably, "Okay... two cars it is. I assume the love birds will want to ride together?"

Dante nodded. Sophia smiled. The four of them parted in the school parking lot and went to their cars.

"This is a nice ride, Sophia," Dante said as he opened the jade passenger side door. It was a sedan, a couple of years old, but kept with care and was immaculate both inside and out. On a side thought, he wondered how she kept it so clean when it was parked outside. He concluded it wasn't important.

"Thanks," she muttered as she backed the car out of the spot and headed for the main drive in the front of the school. The ride over to the restaurant was made mostly in silence.

Dante put his hand on her arm. "I'm here for you."

Sophia covered his hand with hers. "I know you are, but I'm fine. I'm not stressing about this."

"Knock, knock," Dante said.

"Oh, this ought to be good. Who's there?"

"Truthsayer," he answered. "Lies hurt, remember?"

Sophia rolled her eyes, but her skin reddened slightly. "How clever. I get it, I get it."

"I won't let anything happen to you," Dante said with determination.

"Oh my dashing prince," Sophia said putting her hand over her heart. "What if he tries to take me away in the club? You can't just blast your way in to rescue me."

"Why not?" Dante said, only half joking.

"You're getting pretty used to all this, aren't you?" she replied. "You're getting pretty smug. I think I need to kick your ass again."

"Be nice, Sophia, I have my very own superhero name now." He winked at her.

"You're such a smartass."

"Better than being a dumbass."

Sophia's laugh was a sweet respite. They pulled into the parking spot of the café and Max maneuvered his car right next to Sophia's. Dante looked behind them and saw the Bloodlines nightclub. People had already amassed outside and were waiting in line to get in.

Sophia turned him back around. "One thing at a time, okay?" Dante nodded as they entered the café.

The bohemian style of the restaurant served their purposes well. The loud colors and multi-leveled organization of the tables gave them a good vantage point as well as the privacy they were looking for.

"I got some news that I think we should discuss," Max said after they ordered. "Before you go into the lion's den, that is."

Sophia nodded. "All right, Max, hit me. What do we have?" Dante's hand crept up and intertwined with hers. Naomi rolled her eyes. Sophia glared back at her roommate.

"When I checked in with McCray in order to let him know about the little party we have in store for Dmitri, he told me something that made my blood run cold."

Naomi pushed a mug of hot chocolate to him. "Drink this."

"I meant that figuratively, but if you insist." He smiled at her and took a sip. "Lucien attacked the other two city Lords last night with his army. We suspected that he would use the vampires in the attack, as he's done before, but he changed his strategy at the last moment in order to maintain the element of surprise."

"What happened?" Dante wanted to know. This could have been a good thing or a very, very, bad thing.

"He made two strikes against the other two Lords sequentially. The reports say that in both cases when Lucien entered the scene, the opposing knights just surrendered. Both Raphael and Uriel were harvested for their power without a single drop of blood being spilled."

"Let me get this straight," Dante said, "he's got the army of three Royal Lords with the Ardent power to match?" He rubbed his eyes. "Can this get any worse?"

"Not really sure. We're talking epic levels of bad," Max said. "We're seriously humped."

Naomi snatched back her hot chocolate. "What will Lucien do now? He's got no one else to conquer."

"I'd assume he'd go after the vamps and the rebels. They're all that's left of the Ardent who could mount a resistance. He'll probably go after the Millennials at the school too."

Naomi snapped her fingers. Her face lit up with thought. "The vampires and the rebels know that, don't they?"

"Yeah, I suppose so," Dante said as Max and Sophia nodded.

"So they'll have to see reason," Naomi said. "If they don't join forces, we're all history."

"Dmitri has a pretty enormous ego, but he's not stupid. It might be enough."

"All the more reason for me to go in there," Sophia said. "Speaking of that, it's time for me to go." Dante took her hand, and she replied in silence by squeezing it.

"We'll stay in here until you give us the all clear," Max said.

"If you need help, send us a signal and I'll cook the bastards," Naomi said supportively.

Sophia smiled. She leaned down and kissed Dante. "I'll be back soon," she said. Her eyes were determined, though her hands shook slightly.

"I'm holding you to that," Dante replied. With a nod and a wave, she was gone. The bell rang on the door as she exited with a note of finality. Dante took a moment to be proud of her courage. The fear set in a moment later.

THIRTEEN

"I don't like this, Max," Dante stated. Max rolled his eyes. Sophia's red head, slightly covered by a ski-cap, could be seen in front of the heavy oak door at the entrance of Bloodlines. Despite their best intentions, Dante, Max and Naomi remained glued to the window watching Sophia enter the building. "We should have gone in there."

Max inspected at his armlet. "Calm down. She's fine; she's just walking in." Dante scowled, looking down. Naomi's eyes darted back and forth between them. The waitress went by, handing Naomi another hot chocolate. She took it in both hands and started to sip.

"Just how long have the gods, or lords, or whatever," Naomi waved dismissively, "been around, Max?"

"They claim forever." He made an exaggerated roll of his eyes. "They forbid seeking knowledge of the old times, something about their ancient enemies."

Dante looked up. "Do you think they were talking about my people?" It was obvious the feud between the Royals and the Ancients was very deeply rooted. Even the lowly servant knights knew the stories and feared Dante because of them.

"I don't think so. The Ancients were mentioned separately in the stories." Max kept his eyes on the armlet. "Your people were said to be the insane, twisted enemies of the Lords. Cursed with clarity and paranoia, their wars dropped the world into a thousand years of darkness, until the Lords destroyed their Roman stronghold and drove the Ancients to extinction. The enemies referenced here are a different set. They weren't mad, just evil to the core; a plague to be wiped from the earth."

Dante nodded. Didn't Dmitri say something about a massacre in Rome? August would have certainly told the story differently. He said as much when they travelled to the Amphitheater.

The Amphitheater.

"Of course," Dante said sharply. "I can't believe I didn't think of it before."

"What are you going on about?"

"A little spying," Dante said with a grin.

∴

Sophia walked to the front door of Bloodlines. There was a new bouncer there, but he had apparently been told the score when it came to the armlet that Sophia was wearing.

"Official business?" The giant bouncer, who was clearly a vampire, asked.

"Yes, I need to see Dmitri," Sophia said. She pulled off her ski cap and unzipped her coat revealing her goth attire. She was dressed in a blood red halter corset and black leather pants.

"Go inside, and wait at a table."

"Thanks," Sophia said as she entered the club. She tossed her jacket on the back of one of the chairs and sat down. She scanned the room. There were a few faces that she recognized. Carmen, Dmitri's coven mate, saw Sophia immediately and sauntered over to her table.

"What an unexpected pleasure," Carmen said. The room's lighting was dim, but the grin on her face was apparent, even in the darkness. "How are you this evening, my dear sweet Sophia?"

"What a greeting," Sophia said. "I'm honored. Thank you, Carmen. It's so good to see that your wounds have healed. My man went a little rough on you," Sophia replied. "I didn't realize you were so soft."

Carmen looked up for a moment with a dismissive expression. "Ah, yes, the Ancient. He's a little inexperienced for you, isn't he?"

"There's something to be said for breaking them in, isn't there?" Sophia responded.

"Too true, I remember doing the same to Max, many years ago," Carmen chuckled.

"Oh, wow, that's too much information for me. If you don't mind, I'll just let Max know that you're thinking about him."

"Please see that you do. He broke my heart, you know." Carmen pouted slightly, but the smirk on her lips was a giveaway. "Now, let's move beyond the chit-chat. You're here because you want something."

Sophia stirred her drink with a straw. "Why would you think that? Maybe I just wanted to enjoy a drink in this great atmosphere."

"Not very likely, and I'd imagine you're not representing Lucien's concerns anymore. If you were, you'd come in with a battalion, not just by yourself." Carmen reached out and brushed a stray lock of Sophia's hair out of her face. "So, my dear, why don't you enlighten me as to what you want?"

"How about you run along and get your boss, so I don't have to repeat myself?" Sophia waved her hand in dismissal. She looked around the room again. The crowd had grown significantly.

"He should be here in a moment. He's dealing with a pest control problem in the hotel." Carmen smirked. "It seems that the Ardent Rebellion decided to set up shop in our coven."

The tone made Sophia nervous. "Have they started any trouble? If not, I don't see why there's this hostility. Dmitri did give his word to the Ancient to leave them alone."

"Times have changed, my dear Sophia," Dmitri said. He walked down a flight of stairs towards the main club area. McCray was behind him, chained up with his hands behind his back as he was dragged down the stairs. "Lucien's men have changed the rules for all of us."

"I thought you were an honorable man, Dmitri," Sophia said with a sneer. "Clearly you're nothing but a coward."

Carmen snarled, but a shake of Dmitri's head silenced the attractive vampire. Dmitri shoved McCray so that he landed on his knees in the center of the floor. Sophia ran over to him.

"I'm fine," McCray said. "Twenty minutes ago, the shielding around this area went down. Bloodlines is no longer protected from Lucien."

"So this is why you deny your vow to the Ancient? Neither Seraph nor the Ardent Rebellion has broken any vows. It is Lucien who broke his word. Why would you punish them instead of the true culprit?"

"You mistake my intentions, Sophia," Dmitri said. "I will merely complete the task I began when last we met. If Lucien will have war, then I will have an army to fight him with."

"You're going to turn the rebels into vampires? How completely stupid are you?" Sophia said. She activated her armlet, which crackled with bluish lightning. She sighed inwardly. So much for a polite conversation. "Lucien will just evade you until the sun comes up, and while you roll around in your sleep with none of your Ardent powers, *he will murder each and every one of you.*"

"I disagree," Dmitri said, "and you're being extremely rude. I was debating turning you as well, but now I think I'll just kill you, instead."

"You want to take a shot, big guy? I'm sure your regular customers won't have a problem with an Ardent fight in the middle of this nice club." The blade of her gauntlet grew to its full length. "And it will be a fight."

"I'm not sure I'd agree," Dante said, as he walked up to Sophia's side. "It won't be a fight at all." Max followed right behind, shoulder-to-shoulder with Naomi.

"You've grown arrogant since we last met, Ancient. I have been wondering what your blood tastes like."

"Keep wondering," Dante said. "You know what's going on, Dmitri. The war is here. Lucien started it. We need to work together or all of us are dead."

"You are not worthy allies to the coven," Dmitri said. He roared as his claws emerged along with his fangs. Horrified club patrons screamed and ran for the door.

Max looked around at the fast-emptying establishment. "Well, so much for your rep as a place of family entertainment."

"You will all die, starting with you, Truthsayer." Dmitri rushed toward Dante, who remained still. The vampire's claws were poised for Dante's heart, and his face reflected insane aggression.

Sophia grabbed Dante's arm. "Move!"

Dante held fast. "It's okay, Sophia, trust me."

Dmitri's body began to convulse within a foot of Dante. Another roar sprang from his lips with a look of astonishment and horror. He stopped his forward movement like a puppet whose strings were cut. Dmitri slumped to his knees as the rest of the coven and the rebels looked on in astonishment.

"What have you done to me?" Dmitri screamed. His claws reverted back to normal human nails. The fangs retracted back to normal. "This isn't possible!"

"I call it *banishment*," Dante said. A line of sweat formed on his brow. "Thanks to an old friend, I figured out how to turn off Ardent powers." Dante shoved Dmitri back.

"Guess what, Dmitri? Now you see the true blessing of the Ancient people. We gave you your powers, and we can take them away. Moral of the story is: don't mess with us."

Sophia raised her blade to Dmitri's throat. "Does anyone else want to be dropped like your leader? Release the rebels."

The other coven members complied. McCray's chains were unlocked. He shoved the vampire back, drawing his own armlet into existence.

"I think we've made our point," Dante said. Dmitri stood back up, his power restored.

"What are you doing?" McCray said. "The vamps were going to turn us! Finish them off." Dmitri snarled at this.

"He meant what he said," Max answered, stepping into the light. "Without all of us, we don't stand a chance against Lucien. McCray, we need them."

"How do you expect me to trust them after this betrayal?" McCray spat. "They swore an oath and broke their word."

"Don't trust them," Naomi said, still at Max's side. "Trust *him*, trust the Seraph. There's no other way."

Sophia looked at Dmitri. "What about it, big D? Think you can fight alongside the Ardent Rebellion?"

"Do I have a choice?" Dmitri said.

"Yes, you do," Dante answered. "You can leave this city and never come back. Maybe you can keep moving ahead of Lucien, but with the Ardent scanner in place, you'll be running forever."

Sophia smiled. She released her blade back into the armlet. "You always said you wanted to bring Lucien to heel, Dmitri. This is your chance."

Donavan stepped out of the crowd. "Listen to them, Dmitri. The Seraph had the opportunity to kill me and he spared my life. He's spared yours twice now."

Carmen sauntered up to Dmitri. "I agree with them, my lord. I hunger for the blood of the Royal. We should go and retrieve it for our pleasures."

Dmitri looked around. He locked his gaze on McCray. "We fight together. We destroy the scanner. We kill Lucien. Then we go our separate ways, no truce given or expected."

"Fine," McCray answered. "If we see any deception, you won't have time to die by Lucien's hand, you'll die from mine. Are we in agreement?"

"Know that the same applies to you, McCray," Dmitri answered. "Yes, on those terms, we will stand with you."

"We need to strike quickly," Max stated. "We don't have much time. With the scanner active and Lucien's other enemies dead, he won't wait to hunt."

"We will attack tomorrow at dusk. We have the location of the Ardent scanner. The rebels will scout the location during the day. We will teleport into the fray just as the sun goes down," Sophia said. There were nods of assent among the group.

"It's settled then," Dante said. "Tomorrow, the scanner dies, and the fight against Lucien will truly begin."

⁘

"This has to be the longest day in history," Naomi said. She was sipping an espresso at the campus café between classes the next morning.

Max was sitting at one of the couches with his feet up, reading a newspaper. "Technically each day is the same, Naomi."

Naomi made a face. "You know what I mean. How can you be so damn calm about it?" She sat down next to him and swatted his legs off the coffee table.

Max kept on reading. "This isn't my first gig, Naomi. I've found that the best thing to do is to try to do anything but think about the impending terror."

"You're not scared, are you?" Naomi said with a smirk. "With the rebels and the vampires, we've got a good force to take on Lucien, right?"

When Max didn't answer right away, Naomi's smirk faltered. He folded up the newspaper. "It's a good plan, but it isn't foolproof. Estimates state that our two forces will be pretty evenly matched. It could go either way."

"What about the Millennials?" Naomi said, now visibly shaken. "If they joined us, would that make a difference?"

"They've only had their powers for a couple days, Naomi. They're simply not ready."

"I guess we'll have to take our chances," Naomi replied. She snatched Max's coffee and took a sip. "Where is our favorite Seraph and his girlfriend?"

"I'm not sure." Max tapped her nose. "Where do *you* think they could be?" Max wagged his eyebrows suggestively.

Naomi made a face. "Seriously, never speak of that again."

"I'm kidding. They're doing their early morning gym workout. You know the one."

"You mean the kind in which Sophia punts Dante around like a soccer ball?" Naomi said.

"That's the one, except he ends up cracking the walls most of the time." Max said, snatching back his coffee. "In a weird way, I think it's normal for them. It's a way for them to take their minds off of things, and try to act like real people."

"You think that they try to act like real people, as opposed to warriors of the Ardent Rebellion?" Naomi said. "Why do they do the sparring? They could just go on a date. They could go to the theme park, get breakfast off campus, heck, they could go ice skating for all I care."

"Careful, you sound a little envious," Max said.

"I *am* envious, you jerk," Naomi answered. "It's been *months* since I've been on a date, and they have the chance and they waste it on duking it out in the freaking gym."

"Why do you think that is?"

"Well, like you said, they like to sweat together…"

Max interrupted, "No, I mean why haven't you been on a date. There must be half a dozen guys that are interested in you."

"Just not the one I want," Naomi said with uncharacteristic courage. She looked at Max with intensity. "My tastes are more… exotic than your normal Kentucky boys."

Max's eyes got big for a moment, but he played it cool. "I see. You're looking for a foreigner, are you?"

"I found one. He hasn't asked me out yet," she said with a small, shy smile.

"Maybe he thinks he's too old for you."

"Then he'd be mistaken."

"Well, maybe he's waiting for the right moment."

"There's no time like the present," Naomi said. "I might just say yes." She smiled.

"Well, in that case…" Max began to say.

He was interrupted by the sound of someone gagging. It took him a moment to realize the sound was coming from Naomi. She leapt up and tripped over the coffee table. As she staggered, she grasped at her throat, as if she couldn't breathe.

He vaulted over the table to reach her. "Naomi? Naomi!" Max said. She couldn't get a sound out. "It's okay, sweetie. I'm calling emergency services." He reached for a cell phone, only to have Naomi swat it out of his hand.

"That won't be necessary," Naomi replied. "I'm all better, just a little momentary discomfort." She smiled, but it wasn't Naomi's sunshine smile, it was a dark expression, full of malice. "These little girls are such tricky creatures, aren't they Max?"

Max was stunned. Naomi struck him in the chest, catapulting him into one of the café walls. Two students were thrown in opposing directions from his velocity.

"You're not Naomi," Max said, readying his armlet. "What the hell are you?"

"Don't you recognize your god?" Naomi said.

"Lucien, you son of a bitch, let her go!" Max pointed his armlet at her.

"Oh please, I beg you, try to be more original. You're going to fire that thing in here? Who are you trying to deceive, Max? Besides, if you strike me, won't you hurt your little whore?"

"Bastard," Max spat.

"This body will give me what I need. Don't worry, Max, I'll deal with you, *very* soon." Naomi walked into the stairwell leading to the basement.

Max could hear the faint snap of a teleportation. Looking at his scanner, he saw Naomi's reading vanish from the campus. "Shit, shit!" he snapped. Max threw up his hands. "Welcome to the land of the buggered. Population: me."

∴

"I thought you said no one could teleport on this campus, Max," Sophia said as Max materialized inside the gym.

Sophia was taking a sip from her water bottle, and Dante had floated down next to her from his vantage point above.

"Naomi's been possessed. Lucien's got her," Max said, panting. He was shaking in anger. His voice was barely controlled.

"When?" Sophia asked. She zipped up her bag without another word.

"About four minutes ago, it took me that long to exploit the back door protocol in the jammer in order to teleport up here."

"Lucien's making his move," Sophia said. "Do you have any idea where he'd go?"

"He's going for the rebels," Dante said. "I can feel it."

"We've got to go to them," Max said. "They won't stand a chance."

"The group is hiding in Janet's Martial Arts school," Dante answered. "What's the fastest way there?"

"Teleportation," Max said. "We need to warn McCray. I'm sending him a message now." He began to type furiously on his keypad.

Sophia looked between them. "Someone has to got to get the Millennials to safety. If Lucien goes for a two-pronged attack, they'll be plucked up without a fight. I'll go take care of them, you go after Naomi."

Dante nodded. He pulled on his gloves and donned his coat. "All right, but make sure you signal us if there's any trouble."

"I got it, Dante," Sophia answered. She grabbed the back of his head and pulled him to her. After a quick, but intense kiss, she spoke. "Now go bring my roommate home."

"I will, I promise," Dante said.

"I can't reach McCray," Max spoke as he walked towards the couple. "We need to go now."

"Get us over there, Max," Dante commanded.

Max tapped several keys on his armlet, and a blue circle formed. Sophia stepped back away from the circle. Her intense gaze was the last image in Dante's eyes before they landed.

An instant later they were in the parking lot of Free Crane Martial Arts.

The familiar roadside image in Dante's mind was quickly replaced with the terrible vision of the entire marketing board, blackened and charred. The entryway into the school was blocked by the mass of two fire trucks. Firemen scattered everywhere desperately tried to put out the angry flames, or at the very least, contain the fire so it wouldn't spread to the other buildings.

Max ran towards the entrance. Dante rushed to try to keep up with him, and was a few steps back when Max reached the front. When Dante reached Max, his mouth was agape with horror. The entire storefront, the main room and the doorway were all covered in fire. Max stood stunned for a moment and then started to tap furiously on his armlet keyboard. "The bloody entrance is already over 300 degrees," Max spat gruffly. "There are several life signs in the basement. All the other exits are blocked, there isn't any way out." Dante looked around. They were getting looks from the emergency personnel. A couple of the perimeter firefighters yelled at Max and Dante to stay away. They stepped back to a discrete distance.

"Max, can't you throw up a shield and rush through the fire?" Dante coughed. The blaze was getting worse, and the support beams around the front of the school were fast eroding.

Max appeared to ponder the suggestion for a moment and then shook his head. "It won't work, mate, I can't move a shield once I create it. I can't use it to breach the perimeter."

"What about the little shield emitter devices?" Dante wanted to know.

"They're too weak to make any difference over such a large area," Max replied.

Dante looked around. The fire was obscuring everything surrounding the building. He fixed his eyes to the roof. "Max, how hot is the roof right now?"

Max clicked on his keys. "About 120 degrees… but the smoke mixed with the paint chemicals is toxic… what are you thinking?"

Dante didn't answer. He ducked behind a parked car and concentrated, starting to float slightly off of the ground. "If we can't get in by the sides, I'll go in through the top. I should be able to get through with a quick jaunt."

Max looked incredulous. "What about getting them out? You can't just smash through the back of the building?"

"Why not?"

"What do you mean why not? Did you see the number of people out here? If you fly through the top of the building, and then smash your way through to escape, don't you think that people are going to notice? You're completely outing us, mate."

"I thought people wouldn't believe what they see," Dante asked. "People were getting all manner of crazy last night at Bloodlines."

"There are limits, Dante. I'm not sure this is the best time to test them."

"People are going to die, Max, it's just that simple. I have to risk it."

"You're not just risking yourself, Dante. You're risking the whole lot of us if you get exposed. Without being hidden, we're all targets."

"Why can't they just teleport out?" Dante throw up his hands in frustration.

"There has to be a jammer active in the area," Max responded.

"Why can't you just it shut down?" Dante asked. "Then the rebels can get out on their own."

Max made a face. "I can't find it with my sensors. It will take too long for me to track it down. Everyone inside will be dead from smoke inhalation by then."

"We can't just let them die," Dante said, nearly stomping. "Do you have another idea?"

"Well, actually…no, but maybe I can help you. Instead of flying onto the top of the building, there's another building directly behind the school that is still clear of the fire. If you make it look like you're jumping from the other structure, and use the smoke to mask your approach… it's still too far for a normal person to jump, but it's a lot more plausible than actually explaining away your typical defiance of gravity thing."

"Okay, okay. What about the fire alarms, did they activate when the fire started?"

Max's tech whirled in query and response. "Good question. Um… no, they did not. Janet installed a pretty advanced halon system into the building a couple of years ago. It should have automatically fired up, no pun intended. As soon as smoke hit the area, it was programmed to kick on the fire suppression system and notify the fire department of an incident." He winced. "Before fire started, it must have been disabled."

"They can do that?"

"Yup. The exits to the basement have been sealed from the inside… means that when the attackers teleported in, Janet must have barricaded the rebels inside. Because of that, it probably means that Lucien's flunkies set up a jammer to prevent teleportation. Then Lucien sent Naomi in to start the fire."

"So, do I need to activate the fire extinguisher system? Is it enough to put out the fire?"

"That's the idea, champ. It won't get all of it, but it should slow down the fire enough for the fire crews to get in there and pull the people out." Max's tech beeped. "For this to work, you're going to have to stay hidden, moving through the rubble without alerting anyone to your presence. You'll also need to free Naomi."

"If I can get close enough to her, I should be able to disable her powers." Logic said this should work, but he'd never tried to banish the power of a Royal Lord before. There's a first time for everything.

"That should do it," Max replied. "At the very least, she'd be easier to subdue."

"So I need to get to the basement and activate the halon system," Dante said.

"Yeah, it's in a small room on the outside of the main basement area," Max replied.

Dante nodded. He folded his hands to keep them from shaking.

"Around the back of the building there is a service corridor. The smoke isn't getting in there. The compression of the system is keeping it free. Walk down that way. It's the only way to get there safely. At the end there is a service register, you'll have to smash it open."

Max looked around and put up a small projection of the area. Dante was immediately grateful. He wasn't exactly stellar with directions under the best of conditions, and this definitely didn't qualify as anything but a desperate plan.

"Focus, Dante. Next there is a small console with an emergency button. Hit it and that should take care of the fire. You'll be able to breathe in the halon, but be careful. It's not exactly the same thing as normal air.

"Once you do that, on the left side there is a small intermediary room to the main basement. You're going to need to get that outer door open as well. It's approximately two inches thick. The fire crews don't have anything strong enough to pierce it. Most likely, behind that outer door is where Naomi is."

"Shit." Although his anxiety about playing ninja was seeping through, Dante knew that Max was right. "All right, so which way do I go?"

Max tapped on some more keys. "There's a panic room in the back of the basement. It's where the rebels will most likely be."

"How will I keep in contact with you?"

"Take this." Max tossed Dante a little device that looked like a bud on an earpiece. "It's a two way radio. I'll wait for your signal." Dante nodded, looking back at the fire.

"You realize this entire plan is completely insane," Dante said. The smoke made gnarled fingers pointing towards the sky.

"Completely and utterly," Max replied. "You got a better idea?"

"Definitely not, so let's get on with this." Dante sprinted away from Max. He headed in the direction of the back of the building. He was mindful of the firefighters, making sure he was out of sight before beginning his flight up to the roof. The smoke gathered behind him as he passed between the burning building and the surrounding shopping center buildings, tracing around in a huge crescent arc.

There was plenty of smoke being carried both by the wind and by his speed. The building was an old bakery which had been closed a couple of years ago, but had not received a new owner. Thankfully the back of the building was equipped with a fire escape, which allowed more stealth in actually getting up to the roof. The vantage point made it very easy to be picked out by the firefighters and the gathered crowd if he flew all the way across. The fire escape was a better option.

Dante clattered up to the roof quickly. The back of the building had smooth concrete on the rooftop. The sound reverberated as Dante walked, but despite the fear of discovery, his gait remained determined. As he reached the edge of the building, his position let him see the entire school's topside, which was blanketed completely in smoke. "Max, can you hear me?"

"Speak up Dante... I can barely read you."

Dante nearly shouted, "I can't see the building, Max! It's covered in smoke!"

"Can you make the jump?"

"I don't know where to land!" Dante replied in fury.

"Its 43.2 feet from your current position, Dante, all you need to do is jump straight forward," Max answered. "You can't fly! If anyone sees you, we're all humped."

"All right, fantastic, what are the odds of me landing on my face?"

"Pretty good, but don't let that stop you."

Dante groaned. "Charming. Okay, here we go."

He imagined his jump as a perfect parabolic shape, depositing him on the school roof with barely a sound. The actual implementation was a little more awkward as he fell into the smoke bank. He braced himself to land and was met by the sounds of crunching glass and the smells of burnt wood. As he skidded and slammed to a stop, he realized that he must have undershot the landing and smashed into one of the windows on the back of the building. He stood up. Dante was on the main floor.

The fire was everywhere, and he had to float up to the ceiling to avoid the bulk of the flames. The heat of the flames stung him, but Dante noticed he didn't feel the fire nearly as much as the last time in the cafeteria.

Grabbing the edge, Dante crawled along the ceiling until he got to the back stairwell. The area around him was made of concrete, so it was not burning, though he could hear little pops as the concrete cracked from the heat. He vaulted around the room and bounced off the wall, hurling himself into the service conduit.

"All right, Max. I'm in the walkway. There's nothing but smoke in here." Covering his face and crouching down, he stayed below the smoke. Dante didn't exactly find it hard to breathe near the ground, but it still burned in his lungs.

Stumbling slightly, Dante followed the corridor in complete darkness. The swirls of smoke mingled with the sounds of the rushing fire and of cracking metal.

The end of the circuit was met with a small fan. The smoke pooled at the end. With a quick jab, the fan shattered into the open room. The smoke swirled out of the way. Dante flipped down and landed in a tiny control room. The smoke cleared enough to see.

The room was only big enough for Dante to turn around in, with a tiny chair facing a keyboard and a control panel. Dante screamed into the headset, "Max! I made it to the control panel. How do I turn this on?"

The ear piece crackled back at him. "The bloody button in the center. It's marked 'Halon,' genius."

"Oh, right." Dante shook his head and slammed the button. The casing on the console crackled open. The screens became blanketed in white smoke, and the fire started to go down.

Dante waited in the room, glued to the monitor. Shortly afterward, the fire began to rise again. It was a slow increase initially, but roared back with ferocity. "Max! It's not working. The fire's coming back up."

"Put the headset onto the console, champ. I can get a video feed of the interior of the building. I can see what's happening."

Dante pulled the headset off and placed it on the console. Small silver wires crawled out of the device and snaked under the panels. Max's image soon came up on one of the standing monitors. His eyes looked down at Dante. He waved, though Max didn't seem to notice.

"Dante! It's Naomi. She's attacking two of the rebels inside the main basement, you have to stop her. She's killing them!"

Dante didn't waste any time, but he picked up the earpiece before he slammed his fists into the exit door. The sound reverberated as the metal caved in. Dante pushed himself into a full run towards the basement doorway. He covered the corridor's distance in a matter of seconds.

Dante struggled for each gasp of air. He was taking smoke into his lungs. As Dante kept moving forward, he felt his skin start to burn. The corridor fast turned into a firestorm, the air and ground mixing in a strange ballet of fire and smoke.

Dante nearly collapsed, though he continued to struggle forward until he reached the end of the path. The rebels were screaming as they were being burned alive. Between Dante and them was a ten inch thick steel door.

Dante slammed his fists into the metal, which hung on defiantly. The screams were pleading. He heard voices, begging to be spared, calling out over the fire. He slammed into the door again, this time with his entire body. He felt something crack in his shoulder, but the door remained sealed.

Then he heard the screaming stop. Naomi's voice distorted into a hideous laugh replacing the screams. He hit the door again, this time with everything he had left. It broke in just enough to pry a passage open.

As he stepped through the damaged door, the room was completely saturated in fire. He couldn't make anything out in the area, save a small central core of bluish plasma in the center. The image was familiar.

He called out to Naomi, who seemed to regard him as of little consequence. He could see two tiny pin-pricks of light which must have been her eyes. As he approached, he could see her hands come up in front of her body, almost in a stance of prayer.

"Dante! I'm getting an energy spike, take cover!" Max screamed into the headset. Dante dove for the ground without regard, crashing into one of the main support beams.

The metal beam, already weakened by the heat, flexed and bent. The groaning metal nearly came completely undone.

A jet of bluish and crimson flame scorched over Dante's head, nearly lighting his hair in its wake. "Hot enough for you, Truthsayer?" Naomi's sweet voice rang over the roar of the fire.

"Let her go, Lucien or Hope or whatever the hell you are."

"I like this host, it fits well. It kills well. Did you enjoy their dying screams?"

Another wave of fire arced from Naomi's fingertips. This time the bulk of the blast landed in front of Dante, and he stumbled backwards to evade the impact. Banishing her power, even if it were possible, wasn't going to work. He needed time to prepare that ability, and this situation afforded none.

"I don't know what to freaking do, Max!"

"Knocking her out will break the connection, but you're going to have to get close to her," Max replied calmly.

"Are you sure that will work with a hell-spawned, bastard, evil Ancient?"

"You got a better idea?"

"That's turning into the catch phrase for this party." Dante staggered around, trying to stay out of the line of fire. Naomi was launching the flames at him much like hurling in a game of dodge ball. She would wind up the throw and let loose like a fiery pitcher and the flame would bounce around as if it were made of rubber.

After the third successful strike smashed Dante to the ground, he didn't have enough strength to get back up. Instead he crawled slowly over to the wall, trying to use one of the broken pillars for cover. The support beam was ensnared in broken concrete, with a two foot extension of rebar sticking out.

As he slumped over to it, he saw the pillar of blue fire that was Naomi stalk towards him. The heat became unbearable, the pain increasing to the point where it was blurring his vision. Dante staggered outward with his hand and grabbed the rebar, pulling on it to bring him to a standing position.

As Naomi loomed over him, Dante got a closer look at the rebar, wobbling in the concrete. Pieces of it were popping out and cracking, much like a splintering piece of glass.

The possessed Millennial walked around the pillar, the fire all but masking her features. In that instant, the answer popped into Dante's head. As she stood next to the pillar, he pulled on the rebar with all his remaining strength. The pillar exploded in a shroud of crumpled rock. The shards smashed into Naomi, penetrating the flames. One rock struck her in the head and she instantly fell to the ground. The fire vanished from her body.

The fire went out immediately. The halon system, which was having no success putting out the fire while Naomi was throwing plasma flame all over the room, was now choking out the fire.

"Max, can you tell if she's all right?"

"Put the headset on her. I'll run a bio-feedback routine."

Dante laid the headset down on her forehead, and a slight bluish glow covered her head. He then picked up the device again.

"She's okay, Dante, just knocked out. The connection has been severed."

"Is there someone out there?" A woman's voice shouted from behind another metal door on the far end of the basement.

"Hang on! I'm coming!" Dante yelled. Burning debris was scattered everywhere. Dante pushed through the rubble and falling support beams as he moved forward toward the sound of the shouting.

"Who's in there?" Dante roared.

"Dante, is that you?" The woman's voice called again.

"Yeah, it's me, who is this?" he responded.

"It's Janet," the voice said.

"It was Lucien. He possessed the girl and set her on you guys. He's been kicked out. You're safe now."

The door opened, Janet and five other rebels ran out into the main room. Their armlets were exposed and blades extended. "Find McCray," Janet said, walking past Dante as if he wasn't even there.

Dante spoke as she passed, "Wait, where's McCray?" the rebels scoured the main room looking. Dante picked up Naomi, who was completely unconscious.

"Tommy's over here," Janet said. The body was charred beyond any recognition. "Has anyone seen McCray?"

"I found him," one of the rebels said. Janet ran over to him. McCray was against a wall. His body must have impacted with enough heat and force to chip an outline of his body on the wall itself. There was a massive hole in his chest, like his heart had been surgically removed.

"Do you like what you see, *Seraph?*" Janet spat. She stalked over to Dante. He had been staring at McCray in horror. It took a moment but he turned around to face her. "This is what we get for believing in you. *This* is what McCray's faith has been rewarded with. Tell me, was it worth it?"

She started to cry. Tears flowed down her face freely. One of the other rebels tried to put an arm around her, only to have it thrown off angrily. "You and Max love to play the freaking heroes. Guess what, *hero,* this time you failed. You can forget about your little crusade against Lucien. You can go float back to the heavens or, better yet, crawl back under the rock you came from. We're done. We're leaving this hellhole of a city and never looking back. We should have left weeks ago, before you brought this down on us."

"I'm sorry," Dante said. His voice was broken.

"If I ever see you again, *Seraph*, I will kill you. Now, get out the hell of my place."

Dante didn't say another word. He took step after step, and carried Naomi outside. Max was waiting there.

A helpful EMT took Naomi from Dante's arms. Dante just sat down on the back of a parked car. Max walked over to him.

"Are you all right?" Max wanted to know. He had heard the entire exchange with Janet over the microphone he'd given Dante. "I have half a mind to rip that bitch a new one."

"She's not wrong, Max," Dante replied. His voice was very far away, almost catatonic in its sound. "We screwed up. We couldn't protect them, and now McCray's dead. The rebels are leaving the city."

"There was nothing you could do, Dante. You did your best," Max said, patting him on the shoulder.

"My best wasn't good enough."

Max sighed, not really knowing what else to say. "What happens now?"

Dante walked away. "Naomi can never know what happened here. Only one of us should have to live with this."

FOURTEEN

"Dmitri backed out for tonight, didn't he?" Naomi said, sitting on Max's bed. Her head was bandaged, and her voice was a little on the whimsical side. The pain medications she was given were very strong. Sophia was standing in front of the desk, arms folded and wearing an intense expression. Max was sitting in his study chair.

"Yep, as soon as they heard that the Martial Arts school had been hit," Max answered. "I'm wondering if he would have gone through it in the first place. He's such a chicken shit."

"He just knows a lost cause when he sees one," Naomi said, flopping back on the bed.

"Don't you start now," Max said. "The last thing we need right now is another negative voice."

"Have you seen Dante?" Sophia wanted to know. She rubbed her arms against the cold. "He hasn't returned my phone calls."

"All ten of them, I'm sure," Naomi smirked.

Sophia's glare stopped her cold. "What happened to him, Max? He didn't say anything."

"He failed," Max replied. "At least, that's how he feels. I tried to talk to him, but I didn't have any luck. He was almost in a trance. I didn't have a good visual for most of it, but the scene was crazy."

"This is bullshit," Sophia spat. "The last thing he needs is to be alone right now." She looked at Max and Naomi, who nodded. "Where the hell is he?"

Max tapped a few keys on his keypad. "He's standing on the balcony at the top of the spire."

Sophia nodded. She flung her coat on. "Can you deactivate the jammer for just a second so I can get out there?"

"Yep," He opened his armlet and typed several commands. "The shield is down, go get him back."

Sophia smiled. "See you later, bitches." A flash of blue light enveloped her and she was then standing on the balcony of the spire. The night air hit her immediately. It was an unseasonably warm night, but the air still hid the chill in the wind.

Dante was standing next to her, staring out into space.

"Hey, handsome," Sophia said, leaning over the balcony. Dante's face was pointed out towards the horizon, his dark hair obscuring his expression.

He didn't answer. He didn't even acknowledge that she was there. He didn't even move. Dante just kept his eyes forward, gazing out at the starlight.

"You going to talk to me about what happened?" Sophia said, still staying at his perimeter. "Max told me it screwed you up pretty good."

"Max has such a *charming* way with words, doesn't he?" Dante said. His voice was flat and dead. That more than anything startled Sophia. She'd never heard that kind of brittle emotion in him before.

"It doesn't mean that Max's wrong, either," Sophia challenged. "What happened?"

"Lucien got Naomi, and while he was in her body, he killed McCray and another one of the rebels."

"Oh shit. I'm sorry, Dante."

"It wasn't *your* fault. You weren't there."

"It wasn't yours either. You know that, right?"

"Sure," Dante replied. "Fine. Great. Are we done?"

"Not by a long shot." Sophia grabbed him by the shirt collar and twisted him around. She pushed him back into the wall of the spire with a quick thud. "Talk to me!"

Dante glared defiantly. He shoved her back. "Get your hands off of me. Who gave you the right?"

"You're going to fight *me* now?" Sophia spat. "You think that's going to make you feel better?"

"No, I just want to be left alone."

"I don't believe that, and you don't either. If you did, you wouldn't take the time to argue with me, you'd just fly off this damn tower we're standing on." She reached out to him, this time her touch was gentle. "I want to help you, but you *have* to tell me what's going on."

"It's no use."

"Dante, please," Sophia said. Her voice was tender, and she squeezed his shoulder reassuringly. Dante sighed audibly. "You've been there for me. Let me be here for you."

He seemed to mull it over in his mind for a moment, then he pulled her into his arms. He buried his head in her neck like he was trying to hide from the world.

"I let them die," Dante began. The words made Sophia flinch. "I heard their screams. I was just on the other side of the door. If I'd been a little faster, I could have stopped it."

"I see," Sophia said. "Keep going."

"Because of my mistake, now we're really screwed. Janet took the rebels away from the city. Dmitri backed out of the fight too. We're alone. There's no way we can win."

"Careful, Dante, you're rapidly reaching full bitch status," Sophia said in a voice with no venom. "You're the *Seraph* of the Ardent Rebellion. Since when did it become okay for you give up?"

Dante slid down the wall. "If it were just my life, I wouldn't be as worried." He eyed her knowingly.

"You're trying to protect me again? My charming prince, you just need to get that shit out of your head. I'm not some big busted damsel for you to save."

"I know, but what happens if we lose?" Dante asked.

"If we lose, others will take our places. The Ardent are rising. Shit, Naomi's little club is going to be the next Ardent Rebellion." Sophia knelt down in front of him. She took his hand in hers, holding it gently. "Listen to me. This fight isn't over. You're an Ancient. Kicking ass is part of who you are. You have to keep going. I need you to keep going."

"I haven't been a lot of help."

"I should smack you again for that, but I'm feeling generous at the moment. You are the *Seraph*. With all the Ardent, it doesn't matter. Rebels, vampires, knights, Royal Lords, all of them are scared shitless of your power and what you represent. You unite all the Ardent of every kind. That's your greatest gift. You are the bringer of unity."

"So what are you suggesting?"

"Let's give them something to think about. Screw it. Let's hit the warehouse, just the four of us. You go in the front, occupy the knights and try to draw Lucien out. Naomi will assist you while Max and I go after the scanner."

"How do we know Lucien won't possess Naomi again? She nearly killed me last time."

"Remind me to beat her ass. If you threw Lucien out of her tiny freshman brain, Naomi should be protected for at least a few days before Lucien can even make the attempt to inhabit her again."

"They'll be a lot of them," Dante said. "Max was saying at least dozen or so. That doesn't include Lucien, who has the strength of three Royal Lords now."

"I know you can take them," Sophia replied. "See? I'm telling the truth and everything."

"I know you believe it. Doesn't mean it's true."

"It's up to you to *make* it true, Dante. You're an Ancient who belongs to the Ardent Rebellion. Even if the *actual* rebellion is being a bunch of punk asses, it's up to you to be the hero."

"I can't exactly call myself a member of the Ardent Rebellion anymore," Dante chuckled critically. "Janet threatened to kill me if she ever saw me again."

"I'll put that bitch in a body bag," Sophia spat. "Fine, then you're the Seraph of *Ardent Rising* then. Those kids worship you. How can you give up?"

"From my perspective, I only need to be your hero," Dante said. He pulled her close.

"You already are," Sophia said. "You forget that sometimes, but it's a given. Now, let's go bag us an Ardent scanner."

∴

"This is even crazier than your last plan, Sophia," Max said as the group drove towards Lucien's warehouse. The area that served as the hiding place of the Ardent scanner wasn't terribly far from Waterfront park, the location where Dante was first abducted by Sophia.

They had indeed come full circle.

"Come on, Max," Sophia groaned from the back seat. "Aren't you ready to beat the shit out of Lucien?"

"Absolutely, Sophia. The beating part sounds like a truly delightful idea to me. It's getting the shit beaten out of us that I could live without. I would prefer my tactics to have a little more stealth and cunning."

"Stealth and cunning go right out of the window when your enemy can see you on his omni-present eyeball," Sophia retorted. "We go full bore straight ahead on this one."

"I'm glad. All this hiding is getting really old," Naomi said. She was sitting next to Max in the front passenger's seat. Earphones were plugged into in her ears and she rocked back and forth with the heavy techno music.

"When the fireworks start, make your way towards the foreman's office," Max stated. "While you two engage the main force, we'll go through the roof access doors and find the scanner. Once it's destroyed, we'll signal you to get the hell out. Is everyone ready with their headsets?"

"We're good here," Dante answered. Naomi and Sophia nodded as well.

"Remember, Dante, once the guards are disabled, draw Lucien out and then meet us on the roof to help with the search," Max answered. "Don't engage Lucien by yourself, not unless you absolutely have to. We just need to get him on the main floor. We will be hard pressed to make our way through the entire complex to get the scanner taken care of. Lucien is too powerful to take on single-handedly."

"I see," Dante replied. He folded his arms while his mind screamed for action. "We're putting a lot of faith in my ability to persuade the knights to leave. Hopefully Lucien won't call the cops."

"He won't," Max stated as the car skidded to a halt three blocks away from the warehouse. Max stepped out first and zipped up his long coat. A set of VR glasses slid on over his face, and his gauntlet began to crackle with blue lightning in the darkened night.

Sophia tapped her arm softly and her armlet appeared. The crystal embedded on the top burned bright white. "This is it."

Naomi hopped out and stood next to Max. Her eyes began to glow with the starting embers of a roaring fire. "Let's do this."

Dante walked around the car. "Naomi and I will walk up, but they'll expect an attack from you, Max, so be careful getting in."

"That's what teleporters are for, champ."

"Wait," Dante paused. "Why aren't there jammers here?"

"There is a jammer. It just so happens that it's turned off right now. I think we are expected, so be ready for anything." Max replied with determination.

Sophia took a quick step and locked her arms around Dante for a moment. "You come back safe, you hear me?"

"I'll do my best," Dante said as he leaned down for a quick embrace. "Be careful."

"Careful is my middle name," Sophia said with a smirk. A quiet flash of bluish light enshrouded Max and Sophia. A second later, they were gone.

Dante walked up to the door and knocked loudly. Naomi was at his side. The door creaked open, and a young, light haired man with a gleaming armlet was standing in the entrance. Two other guards were coming up the central path towards the door.

"Hi," Dante said. "My name is Seraph. I'm your friendly neighborhood Ancient. I wanted to talk to you about life insurance plans. Life insurance, as I mean, you get to keep your lives by running screaming from this building. May I come in?"

The guards looked at each other for a moment, completely confused. Dante answered their unspoken questions by striking the first guard in the face with his elbow. The young man fell to the ground as the two other guards came up to engage. Naomi stayed back, waiting. The guards stayed focused on Dante, and from the upper level of the warehouse, more of the guards were beginning to come out and rush towards the front door.

Dante fought his way through the opening into the center of the main area. It was a large room, several stories high with a catwalk crisscrossing the second level. It was a complete melee. Dante was set upon by four guards at once with more coming. One of the guards had the bright idea to fire a lightning bolt, only for Dante to use one of the others as a human shield. Each of them got closer.

"Naomi! Is that all of them?" Dante said as he dodged a blade coming high from one of the guards. Naomi was still standing at the doorway. She observed the fight in front of her like it was a professional wrestling match.

"Almost," she said back. "You're doing great!"

A strike rattled Dante's jaw as one of the guards landed a lucky hit. "Not good enough," Dante muttered. He grabbed the aggressor's armlet and crushed it. Eight enemies surrounded him, with four still coming. Two of the new arrivals, seeing Dante being swarmed by the others, decided to make a beeline for Naomi instead. They got a blast of fire for their trouble.

"That's it, Dante. They're all here! Do it!" Naomi shouted. Dante had been tackled by the group. He closed his eyes and sent his mind outward. A moment later he found himself in the Amphitheater again.

The place looked the same as last time. The scratches in the floor from August's sword were still present. Below him, he saw the knights swinging their fists at his unmoving body. Here there was no movement, and the image was fixed in place, like a video tape paused in mid scene.

"Let's see," Dante said. "I think I remember this one." He drew *Ardent Vow* in the air. The room shook and roared. A column of lightning flew from the skylight in the roof and struck the blade of the sword. On the instant of the impact, Dante was thrown back into the real world. The swinging impacts from the knights had stopped. They each had a matched expression of shock on their faces. Dante stood up and pushed himself out of the crowd. The knights, like their images within the Amphitheater, were frozen in place.

Naomi smirked and sauntered over to the frozen mass. "They're so cute when they're helpless." The knights' eyes darted back and forth. "All right, Dante, get up there." She walked over and stood behind Dante.

"You sure that you have them? I won't be able to hold them for long."

"Oh yeah, if they try anything, I'll flash fry them."

"Stay safe, Naomi," Dante said as he started his flight up to the second level.

"You too, Seraph." Naomi smiled as a wreath of white flame lined her form. The slowly recovering knights started to stagger back. They shielded their faces from the fire, and scurried to the perimeter of the blistering heat that was being generated by the young Millennial. Naomi stretched out her hands, and a perimeter of fire pushed the crowd back. A half-moon shaped area of fire slowly crept forward, carefully pressing the shaken knights through the doorway and out of the warehouse.

On the catwalk above, down the center of the warehouse, there was a long corridor suspended by cables. Dante landed there and walked forward, unsheathing *Ardent Vow* as he went. His eyes scanned the area. There was no sign of Sophia and Max, who were, if they were following the plan, waiting for Dante to draw Lucien out so that the scanner would be vulnerable.

The metal steps of the walkway abruptly gave way to plush red carpet. He continued forward towards an enclosure on the edge. Here the catwalk ceased and became an actual second floor to the warehouse. The hard concrete floor was covered up by the carpet, but Dante could feel the solidness of the cold stone below as he walked forward.

"Dante, this is Max, come in," his friend's voice chimed in through his earpiece.

"I hear you, Max. What's up?"

"We've landed on the roof. We're proceeding inside."

"Good. I'm standing on the catwalk in front of an office door."

"Is Naomi with you?" Max asked. His tone indicated he already knew the answer.

"No, she's tending to the knights below. I'll draw him out myself."

"Evasion only, right?"

"I'm afraid not, Max," Dante said.

"Are you going off plan, Dante?" Max wanted to know.

Dante gritted his teeth. "This has to end, Max, one and for all."

"Dante," Sophia cut into the broadcast, "are you sure that's a good idea?"

"Absolutely not, but scanner or not, we can't wait for him to kill anyone else." *Ardent Vow* glinted in the light like it agreed with Dante's perspective.

"Then stay put. I'm coming to you," Sophia said.

"No, you need to help Max. That scanner has to be found."

Sophia's voice cracked, just for a moment. "I don't like this."

"I can do this, Sophia, trust me," Dante answered.

"All right, be safe, *Seraph*. I love you."

"I'll do my best," Dante said as a ghost of a smile touched his face. "I love you too." The conversation ended and Dante resumed his movement towards the end of the hall.

At the end of the path there was a huge, ornate oak door. Singing tales from ages past, the door looked like it would have been more at home in a medieval castle than a warehouse. As he reached the door, it opened, revealing a young woman with long auburn hair. She scurried out through the door as fast as her high-heeled shoes would carry her.

"Come in, Truthsayer," Lucien's voice bellowed. "I've been expecting you."

Fifteen

The smug bastard didn't even have the decency to look intimidated. Lucien stayed at his desk, his legs outstretched and his arms folded behind his head. The room was tinted red, mostly from the silk fabrics covering several lamps scattered throughout the room. The night sky was barely visible through a small skylight, which had just enough of an opening for a sliver of the moon to peek through. The walls were lined with matching leather couches, a seeping red so deep that Dante wondered if they were actually dyed in blood. It was certainly within the realm of possibility that Lucien was enough of a monster to do that.

Lucien spoke first. "Thought I would redecorate, this drab color isn't much for my tastes." He put down the newspaper he was reading. Absently he reached for a small cylindrical object on the edge of his desk. "Well, so, you're here for me, Ancient?" he said confidently.

"Draw your weapon, asshole," Dante spat defiantly. "You and me, right here." He raised *Ardent Vow*.

"Are you sure you're not here for the Ardent scanner?" Lucien said. He kicked his legs down off the desk and rose to his full height. He absently wandered over to a long display case, where a thin blade rested on top of a pillow the color of molten brass. "Truthsayers can't lie, can they?"

"Have you enjoyed your party in Lucien's body, *Hope?*"

"So, you remember," Lucien answered. He drew the long blade, which turned black as soon as his hand grasped the handle. "Your mind is stronger than I gave you credit for. Nearly a thousand years I've lived in this body. It's a second flesh to me, now."

"How about you take a hike and go back to the Amphitheater?" Dante asked. "Are you afraid to face me there?"

"Considering your mentor died by my hand in your wretched Ancient construct, I would say no. I'm not afraid. In the Amphitheater, I have no flesh, and I so enjoy the sensation of spilling blood with human hands."

"You really are one sick bitch. Do you know that?"

"It is appalling how little you understand, Truthsayer. I will feast on your heart's blood."

To Dante's credit, he only flinched a little. "I will stop you, Morte-Veras."

The thing wearing Lucien's face replied with a chuckle, "You are no match for my powers, Truthsayer."

"We'll see about that," Dante replied.

"Do you truly understand what it is you face, Ancient?"

Dante nodded with a mocking expression. "Sure. An asshole coward who's far too afraid to step into the light."

"That is where you are mistaken, Truthsayer. I am not afraid. I have lived to see my enemies dead."

"There's one still left," Dante retorted.

"A situation I intend to remedy." Lucien readied his blade, and moved into an Asian martial stance. "Tonight will see the end of your line, now and forever."

"Oh, for the love of Heaven, would you just shut up and fight?" Dante said, bearing down with his heels with such force that the marble flooring cracked. His raised his arms in a martial stance, *Ardent Vow* raised above his head. The gesture was at once unfamiliar and second nature.

The sword drawn, Lucien slashed his blackened blade down, faster than the eye could see. A quick dive pushed Dante out of the path of the blade. The sword came down on the ground and sliced through the marble tile a scant number of inches away from Dante's head.

Lucien landed with an intense crunch. The tiles gave way and broke under his strength. He twisted the blade out of the marble and pulled it back into the air. Lucien smirked, and propped the blade forward, much like a fencer's stance.

The fallen Royal Lord rushed forward again, lunging for Dante's heart. Blades clashed three inches in front of the intended target. With a cavalier twirl from his sword, Lucien knocked *Ardent Vow* loose, spinning it away to lodge itself into the wall on the far side of the room. Dante retaliated with a quick punch to Lucien's face, forcing the beast into the center of the room.

Dante circled slowly. The room wasn't large enough for a complete evasion, but he could skim the wall to avoid the enemy sword's reach. As he wandered up the wall, he noticed that he had maneuvered himself within a short leap of *Ardent Vow*. Lucien's eyes darted between the two points, following Dante's eyes. He coiled up and launched again. A quick lean was the only evasion available. The attack missed his heart, but pierced deep into Dante's right leg. The sword wound was bad, red smoke seeped from the painful area. Something had cracked inside it but he could still put weight on the leg, though it was very wobbly and unsteady.

Lucien's face twisted into a sadistic chuckle. He raised his sword in front of him, clutching it two handed, and moved his legs shoulder-width apart. Dante circled again, jockeying for position, trying to get closer to the other sword. Lucien's movements kept the *Ardent Vow* out of reach with his own blade.

A wet snap and searing pain greeted Dante as his leg knit itself back together. The sound drew Lucien's attention, distracting the Royal Lord. Dante lunged forward at Lucien's midsection. Lucien went for a decapitation. His blade spun in a crescent swing similar to a clockwise twirl. Dante feinted left with his body and spun up and around. His momentum carried the same speed and movement Lucien's blade, taking a position in the wheel of its movement. As he passed below Lucien's arm, he veered away, flinging himself up in a neatly tucked flip. He landed on the other side of the desk. A half a moment later, *Ardent Vow* was again in Dante's hands.

Turning his body forward, Dante faced Lucien, who started walking around the desk toward the proper dueling distance. The Morte-Veras grunted. Anger betrayed the cavalier movement of Lucien's fighting style. A sliding slash flew out from Lucien. The desk, which was in the way of the slice, was torn asunder from the impact.

A full downward strike was the response. The blades clanged together as Lucien blocked the shot. He rushed forward, slamming Dante with the edge of his shoulder. Dante flew back into one of the concrete walls, plowing through it towards the stairwell. Dante, who activated his flight to stop, hovered above the second floor staircase, watching Lucien walk towards the hole between rooms.

Lucien came at Dante full force, his blade flashing in the darkened warehouse. The strike was parried, but the force of the impact sent *Ardent Vow* from Dante's hands again. The blade spun and landed in the center of the ground below, embedding itself into the floor like Excalibur.

Lucien slammed into Dante. As the impact came, Dante managed to grab Lucien's sword arm. The two of them fell from the sky like a meteor. The impact smashed through rock, stone and metal, landing on the first floor.

A halo of gray mist covered the area. Lucien walked out first, sword in hand. His eyes scanned for Dante only to meet the end of his fist as Dante let loose a strike with his little remaining strength.

Dante pulled *Ardent Vow* from its prison. Although his wounds were healing, he was drained. Dante propped himself up, using the sword to keep standing. Lucien walked gracefully towards Dante. "Cower in fear, Truthsayer."

"Go to hell," Dante said. He raised himself back into a fighting stance and walked forward. "You're a joke, Hope, you think that because you're stronger than me, that you can scare me?"

Lucien roared and came down with his sword. Dante's arm swung high, bringing *Ardent Vow* to meet his opponent's blade above Dante's head, then he grabbed Lucien's throat with his left hand. A gurgle was the response from the Royal Lord.

"You're a shadow from the past, Hope." Dante squeezed, and Lucien's throat cracked. His hand released, and Lucien fell to his knees. "Time for you to go back." Dante reared back and slashed Lucien's face with the tip of *Ardent Vow*. The wound put a diagonal scar between his eyes and across his nose. The impact site of the blade sizzled, and then a strange explosion went through him. Lucien flew back into the wall and smashed into the concrete. Pieces of rubble collapsed around him like a curtain falling down after a performance.

"Dante," Sophia called out through the headset. "Are you all right?"

"Yeah, I got him, Sophia. Lucien's down."

A quick flash revealed Sophia and Max. They walked towards Dante. Sophia was carrying a box in the shape of a trapezoid, with a large black crystal in it.

"Finish it, Dante," Max said as he looked down on his old master. "Send the bastard to hell."

Dante turned back towards his friend. "Max, it wasn't him." The Truthsayer walked over to Lucien's fallen form. "The creature has left him, Max. Check your scanners. I'm sure you'll find a difference in his Ardent signature."

Max grumbled, but complied. Several beeps from the armlet later, Max looked up. "A huge amount of energy fled Lucien and deposited itself inside the Ardent scanner device."

Sophia nodded encouragingly. "Which means?"

Max groaned, "Our Seraph is right. The creature has fled Lucien."

Dante shrugged. "I imagine he's more valuable to us alive than dead, especially since he controls the entire Royal army in the city."

Sophia chuckled. "I wouldn't mind him doing our bidding for a change."

Max smiled like a shark. "When Lucien wakes up, he and I are going to have a nice long chat."

After a couple of minutes Naomi ran up to Max and hurled herself into his arms.

"You idiot," Naomi said. "You could have been killed trying to sneak past Lucien."

"I'm fine, love, thanks to our Seraph. He took the monster down." Max gestured to Dante. "You did it, champ."

"Thanks, but we haven't won just yet." Dante shrugged.

"What's the situation with the scanner?" Naomi asked. "I managed to get the knights outside."

"It's right here. The central nexus is encased in some kind of crystal," Max answered.

"Shatter it," Dante commanded.

"Yes, your majesty," Sophia answered dryly. A long blade formed out of Sophia's gauntlet and was poised over the crystal. Her eyes narrowed and she lined up the shot like a cue stick on the eight ball.

"Wait!" A voice shouted from behind them, but it was too late. Sophia's weapon pierced the center of the crystal. The black shards shattered, scattering on the ground. The tiny flecks of crystal fell into smoke as they touched the earth. A flash of black light enveloped the scanner device. Max, Naomi and Dante were thrown back on the ground from the force of the discharged energy.

Dante rose to his feet with *Ardent Vow* still in his hand. The others were far slower. Past the smoke of the impact, Sophia walked out of the fog and into their view. Her clothes were slightly torn. Her face wore a sinister smile. On her fingers were talons instead of nails, and her eyes were completely encased in black.

"I so love the female form," Sophia said. "It has been so long since I've taken a woman as an actual vessel."

Dante stood in shock. "Sophia?"

"Yes and no. I must thank you for releasing my power from Lucien's little jewel. He was always a clever one. A trait which made him the perfect host. Perhaps he was a little bit too clever."

"*Hope?*" Dante stalled. "This can't be possible."

"Yes, Truthsayer," Sophia's voice said. "Welcome to your end."

Sophia's now reptilian claws struck Dante in his midsection. Three shattered ribs propelled him to the ground. Max didn't waste any time launched a lightning bolt at the possessed Sophia. With her other hand, extremely casually, she blocked the energy strike with a dismissive wave.

"Bloody hell," Max spat. "Any bright ideas?"

"Here's one," Naomi said. She arched her back and let loose a stream of fire into the air. The reddish white flame manifested into a teeming wall between Sophia and the others. The monster staggered back slightly, but its hoarse laugh could be heard over the flames. "That's not going to hold her long. We've got to get out of here!"

"You're not going anywhere," Byron said as the knights walked back towards the assembled group. The entire knight force that was recently dispersed was present, each wearing matching armlets and coal black eyes. "My mistress wishes you to stay."

"Ok, that's really creepy," Naomi commented.

"They're possessed," Dante said. "The Morte-Veras has them also." Dante raised his blade to the first knight, who he recognized. "I always knew we'd meet again, Byron. The ass kicking we gave you in the gym wasn't enough."

"That was a different time, Ancient, now you die." Byron raised his blade to strike, only to be stopped by movement faster than the eye could see. He was hoisted off the ground and thrown to the side. The other knights, standing there confused, were thrown away as well. It appeared that the group of them had stepped inside a tornado, and were thrown in all directions.

As the dust settled, Lucien was standing in the middle. The wound on his face had closed, and his blade shined gold in the reflected light. "There isn't much time, Truthsayer. We must leave."

"Are you out of your mind? How can we trust you?" Dante shouted.

"You have no choice. Your powers are not enough to pierce the shielding of this place. I will protect you."

The words rang true. "Max?" Dante yelled. The sound of huge wings resonated in the room. Through the smoke, Sophia's form moved closer.

"There's some kind of interference that just went up. He's right, Dante. We've got to move!"

"Get us out of here," Dante commanded.

"As you wish, my lord." A portal of blue smoke appeared behind them. "This will take us back. Hurry." Lucien shuttled Naomi first. She looked at Max, who took her hand and jumped through with her. Lucien through went next. Dante took a moment to see the raven eyes that used to belong to his girlfriend. She moved towards the perimeter on the other side of the fiery barrier. Two large bat-like wings were folded on her back.

"You cannot escape me, Truthsayer. I will come for you."

Dante said nothing and stepped through the portal, returning to the comforting quiet of college campus. They appeared behind the library, and Lucien wasted no time closing the portal. As he did, Dante punched him in the face. The impact forced the Lord down. Dante grabbed him by his shirt lapels and yanked him up. "What the hell did you do to her?"

"Dante!" Naomi yelled. She looked at Max, whose face was a mask of confusion, then her eyes shot back at Dante.

Lucien didn't seem fazed by the strike. He spoke, but his voice was devoid of the usual arrogance. "I am sorry, my lord. Hope, the Morte-Veras, has taken Sophia. Its darkness has spread to Sophia's entire Ardent line. All my followers, save Max, have been corrupted by its evil."

"How come it didn't do this when it controlled you?" Dante wanted to know.

"My power is far greater than Sophia's. The creature needed to exert far more energy in possessing me than it does now. It can now afford to extend its reach."

"Why am I not affected?" Max said. He took a few tentative steps towards his mortal enemy.

"It is difficult to explain, but I will endeavor to do so. My lord, would you release me?"

Dante dropped him. A scathing remark was on the tip of his tongue, but he clenched his teeth in anger instead. "Start talking."

"I have struggled against the Morte-Veras' possession for one thousand years. During certain moments, I have managed to gain enough control of my body's actions to steer events. One of those few times was when I recruited you, Max. I knew that you would be my salvation."

"Hold on now. I didn't sign up for the Second Coming."

"Your will is a powerful weapon. I knew that from the moment I met you. It is why I offered you the brand of immortality. It allowed you to stay young, to remain alive, so that when the time came and Hope could be defeated, you would be there to do so. Your strength makes you resistant to its evil. That is why you are immune to its possession."

"I didn't know you were *that* cool," Naomi said.

"The Morte-Veras will not rest. It will continue to possess any of the Royal Ardent that it can find and kill all it can not control," Lucien said. "We must get you to safety."

"No way," Dante replied. "I'm going after Sophia."

"That is suicide, my lord."

Dante held up his fingers. "Number one: I don't care, and number two: what's the deal with the whole 'my lord' thing?"

"I swore fealty to your bloodline. To the death, I remain loyal to the Empyrial."

"This is unreal," Dante replied.

"Dante, before you go run off to your doom, think about it," Max said. He walked over to him and placed his hand on Dante's shoulder. "You attack that thing when it's surrounded by possessed guards, and you're going to die before getting within a hundred paces of Sophia. You need a better plan than that."

"I'd love to hear one," Dante replied with a hint of frustration.

"Knowledges may be our salvation," Lucien answered. "I have been within the creature for a very long time."

Naomi spoke up. "Shouldn't we get out of here?"

Lucien shook his head. "This place is as safe as anywhere, and the new Ardent reside here. They will prove to be immune to the effects of the Morte-Veras' possession."

"I'm a Millennial," Naomi said. "You possessed me. Why did that work?"

"I took you, my child. I ask your forgiveness. The Morte-Veras was possessing me as I possessed you. The power that the creature uses now is more primitive than an Ardent Royal's power. It cannot be used on one of the newly born, or one of the Empyrial line. Sophia's body does not have the ability to perform a possession as I did."

"Oh, well, don't let it happen again," Naomi answered. She blushed slightly, obviously not expecting Lucien's response. "So, *Ardent Rising* is safe, at least."

"*Ardent Rising*?" Lucien said in confusion.

"It's a student club that we set up for the newly popped Ardent," Naomi said. "They worship Dante as their god."

Dante made a face. "That's a little exaggerated, don't you think?"

"Maybe a little bit." Naomi grinned. "But only a little bit."

Lucien nodded and continued. "The Morte-Veras will hunt them first. It will be able to sense them through the Empyrial Amphitheater."

"I can sense Sophia the same way, right?" Dante wanted to know.

"I would suspect so," Lucien answered. "We should stay with your *Ardent Rising*." He glanced up at the main library building. "There isn't much time."

"You're not kidding," Dante said. "They're coming."

"How long do we have?" Max said. His armlet shined to life, cascading the tell-tale blue lightning. Eight flashes of blue light surrounded the group. "I guess we don't have any," Max answered himself.

The possessed knights moved as one, closing the circle that enshrouded Dante, Max, Lucien and Naomi. Lucien drew his blade, raising it in defense. Naomi lit herself up in a blaze of fire. Max aimed his gauntlet. Dante raised the *Ardent Vow*.

"If I can incapacitate them, can you get out of here?" Dante asked.

The first knight, who happened to be Byron, made his move. Lucien blocked the strike from the enemy's blade and slammed him in the chest. "I can teleport the group to safety," Lucien answered as the other knights engaged. The circle became a complete melee. Between swings, Lucien spoke, "Where are your Millennial companions?"

"They're in the dorms," Max answered. "Bloody hell," he spat as he let a bolt of electricity fly at one of the knights attempting to sneak around. "We're screwed!"

There was no other choice. Dante closed his eyes a moment and was once again in the light of the Amphitheater. He saw the circle of knights and raised his blade again.

As before, the knights stopped in mid action. Their eyes were wide open in anger and shock as they slumped over on the ground. "Get them out of here, Lucien," Dante commanded. "Leave me."

"Wait, no freaking way we're leaving you!" Naomi said, launching a jet of white fire.

"I need to stay here to keep them down." Dante's left hand was out in a gesture of suppression. The knights growled like cowed animals. "I'll meet up with you. You've got to get the others out of the dorms."

"Dante," Byron said as he remained slumped over on the ground. "She's coming for you. Wherever you go, she'll follow you."

"Byron, is that you?"

Byron's response was to roar at him.

"He was able to momentarily throw off the control," Lucien said. "If what he said is true, then you will need to keep moving."

"All right, get going, I'll take off by the air."

"How will we get in touch with you?" Naomi said.

"Don't worry about the cell phone," Dante said grimly. "Call for me, and I'll hear you."

"That is completely nuts," Naomi spat. "What are you going on about?"

"He is Empyrial, Naomi," Lucien said. "Such is the nature of his power." He turned back to Dante. "I will protect them with my life."

Max waved. Naomi didn't look happy about it. Lucien raised his hand in the air and in a flash of blue light, Dante was alone with his enemies.

Not wasting any time, Dante leaped up at the stars, taking off towards the northeast.

Sixteen

"Are you bullshitting me?" Brett, one of the *Ardent Rising* members, snapped at Naomi. She didn't flinch, but Eve, another one, did. The ten members of *Ardent Rising*, including Naomi, were standing around the pool table in the dorm community center. "This monster took Sophia, and Dante's on the run?"

"That's about the size of it," Max said. Amanda, a third student, shook her head as she obsessively picked at the label of her root beer.

"Where's that Lucien character?" Eve wanted to know.

"He's standing watch in the hall," Naomi replied. "With the creature out of him, he's not a bad guy." She paused and gave Max a wink. "A little stuffy, much like a British guy I happen to adore."

"And, of course, you'd pick now to say something," he chuckled.

"I'm touched that you guys are having a moment, but can we focus on the impending doom, please?" Jon, one of the other Millennials, asked. "What do we need to do here?"

"Dante wanted us to stay out of sight," Naomi explained. "The Evil-Sophia thing is going after him. He stays away, he can buy us some time."

"Time to do what?" Eve asked. "We're sitting ducks in here."

"I don't like it any more than you do," Max replied. "I don't see what choice we have right now."

"So are we just leaving him to die?" Amanda snapped. "We got to do something!" She slammed her root beer bottle on the table, shooting a little of the foam out of the top.

"And what, pray tell, do you suggest?" Brett questioned. "You heard Naomi. This," he looked for the words, "Morte-Veras, is coming for him, and it possessed all of Lucien's old gang."

Jon raised an eyebrow. "We have powers, too. We could go after it, go all bug hunt on its evil ass."

Lucien entered the room. He answered Jon's words without missing a beat. "Even if you could defeat it, you could hurt Sophia. The Morte-Veras would just jump to another person." Jon nodded and slumped against the wall, defeated.

Naomi sighed, "I don't know what to do. I hope Dante is faring better."

∴

Dante was standing on the top of the Empire State Building. Earlier, he had lost track of time as he poured on the speed, trying desperately to outrun the tidal wave of horror rushing through him. When he had returned to his bearings, he was nearly face to face with the Statue of Liberty. Realizing that someone would eventually notice that there was a floating man in front of Lady Liberty's nose, he landed on the tallest building in the city.

The Morte-Veras was still in his perceptions. The sinister creeping feeling of its presence made him shiver far more than the cold. The sensation from the Amphitheater was palpable. Scores of Ardent were lost to the Morte-Veras. Moment by moment they were amassing. The location of their grouping was a little perplexing. The thing controlling Sophia commanded them to meet in a field outside of Dante's college. Perhaps it was trying to provoke him.

It was doing a good job.

"Hey there, *Seraph*," Sophia said as she stepped out from the shadows around the corner. "Don't worry, I come in peace."

"I assume you're a figment of my imagination," Dante replied. "I don't sense the Morte-Veras here."

Sophia chuckled, her form dancing around him. "It's nothing like that. I'm really Sophia. Since the monster has my body, my mind is floating around your Amphitheater. Your connection to it is why you can see me."

Dante smirked. "What do you think of it?"

She looked around. "It's kind of bland, actually. I was expecting something a little more grandiose."

"I'm going to get you back," Dante blurted out. His face blushed in embarrassment. "Sorry, that came out of nowhere."

"My dear silly Seraph," Sophia said. She touched his face and surprisingly, he felt her warm hand. "I'm sort of in your mind, so it's not a surprise. I'm grateful for that." Sophia stepped away and looked out towards the harbor. Dante smiled and took her hand.

"No one else would be able to see you, would they?"

"No, but then again, you're on the top of the Empire State Building in the middle of the night. No one could see you either," Sophia replied.

"Fair enough. I'm sorry. I had to get away from the others. You, well, really the Morte-Veras was tracking me. I need time to figure out how to free you."

"You aren't going to be able to free me, Dante," she said sadly. "You have to come to terms with that."

Dante shook his head. "No, there has to be a way to beat the thing."

"You can't risk yourself for me. The creature is truly powerful. As Max would say, a single, frontal assault would be a bloody fruitless endeavor. The creature has waves upon waves of knights to defend itself."

"So what do I do, Sophia?" Dante replied. He turned to face her. She was so real, it *nearly* felt normal. "Do I run forever?"

"No, you go back with Naomi's *Ardent Rising*, and you kill Hope."

"Won't that kill you too?"

"Uh, yeah," Sophia answered. "Not something I'm too happy about, but it's the only way."

"I don't care. I'll keep running if I have to, but you can't ask me to kill you."

"Dante, this thing is using my body to murder and control. I won't have that on my conscience. You have to do it. The creature fears your sword, so finish it off."

"I can't do it," Dante said. He turned away. "How can you expect me to?"

"Look at me, Dante," Sophia said, turning him around to face her again. "You have to understand. Even as this is the end, I do not regret this. If I'm going to die, then I'm going to die for a good reason."

"I'm so sorry, Sophia," Dante blurted out again. "If you'd left the fight when Lucien released you, this would never have happened."

"I wouldn't have fallen in love with you, either," she replied, "and I wouldn't give that up for anything in the world."

"I don't know how I'm supposed to go on without you."

"I think we've had this conversation before," Sophia said, and made a face. "You'll go on. You're the *Seraph*, that's why you're here. I just wish I could touch you again, for real. In the Amphitheater, I have no flesh."

"In the Amphitheater, I have no flesh," Dante whispered.

Sophia made a face, obviously a little annoyed at the loss of the tender moment. "Yes... what is it?"

"The Morte-Veras said that to me when I faced Lucien down in the warehouse. It still possessed him at the time."

"Yes, since the Amphitheater is only for the Ancients, and the Morte-Veras doesn't have an actual body, it can only be spirit here."

Dante looked out onto the city skyline. The lights of New York were inspiring, but he missed the familiar images of Louisville, from the air traffic lights on the buildings downtown, to the lamps surrounding the college. Lamps under which, August took him to the Amphitheater for the first time in order to help birth the Millennials.

"I've got it!" he shouted. He rushed to Sophia and pulled her close to him. "I know what to do!"

"You've lost it."

"Maybe. But this will work, it has to."

"Don't tell me, Dante," Sophia warned. "If you do, there's a chance the Morte-Veras will be able to read my mind to get the answer. I'm keeping it out as best I can right now."

"All right, I'm heading back. This is going to work, I promise." He stepped over the railing.

"Dante?" Sophia said softly.

He turned around. "Yes?"

"If this doesn't work..."

"It will work," Dante interrupted.

"Yes, but if it doesn't. I want you to know that I love you, and if I'm gone, wherever I go, I'll still be loving you."

"I love you too," Dante said hopping back down and touched the side of her face. "I'll never give up on you, not ever. I promise." She leaned into his touch, covering his hand in hers. Sophia closed her eyes.

"Now, you need to go," Sophia said. Several tears lined her eyes. "They need you. I need you. You're the Seraph, so get your ass in gear," she whispered, her voice was weighed down with emotion. "Don't keep me waiting."

Dante nodded and resumed his position on the railing. He jumped off the side of the skyscraper and turned his movement skyward. Speeding southwest, he accelerated towards Louisville.

"Max, can you hear me?" Using the Amphitheater, Dante's voice descended into the common room. To everyone there, it was a disembodied voice. Max responded with a start. Naomi looked around, but laughed at Max's reaction. The Millennials looked at each other in confusion. Lucien smiled.

"Bloody hell, Dante, can you use a cell phone like a normal person?" Max snapped. He shook the chill off.

"There's no way. I just broke the sound barrier, I think."

"Yo, Seraph," Brett said. "Heard you were hiding with your tail between your legs."

Naomi smacked him upside the head. "Asshole," she spat.

Dante chuckled, "Maybe I was, but screw that. I have an idea."

"Let's hear it, champ," Max said. Lucien nodded. The others gathered around the disembodied voice like it was a campfire.

"The Morte-Veras is gathering its army in the park up the street from you. I'm going to dive bomb Sophia. If I can grab her, I think I can yank the Morte-Veras into the Amphitheater with me."

"How do you expect to get close? They'll be watching for an aerial attack. All of them know that you can fly!" Naomi snapped. "That's just crazy!"

"I'm going in hot, as in full speed. They'll never see me coming."

Max spoke up, "I appreciate your determination, champ, but you're moving pretty damn quick. If you are even a little bit off, you'll face plant at six hundred miles per hour. I don't care how invulnerable you think you are, Dante, that will kill you."

Amanda spoke up. "Won't you need to slow down to grab Sophia? If you don't you'll hit her like a missile. She'll splat, won't she?"

"Yes, yes, I realize that I'll need to slow down at the last minute. Hopefully I can land right next to her," Dante answered in exasperation.

"You're going to need backup, champ," Max summarized. "We can distract them long enough for you to make your move. Lucien will take point, along with Brett and myself. Naomi, Jon and Amanda will go in next, along with the others."

"Max, there are at least forty of them now," Dante answered. "You'd get slaughtered."

"There may be salvation. The Morte-Veras would need to exert a great deal of willpower to control so many," Lucien said. "These servants are new, and still willful. The beast will need to force its way through their mental defenses in order to make them obey even the simplest of commands. They will be slow to act."

"That gives us a chance," Eve said. "We'll go in with our big guns and shake things up. All we have to do is get them to disperse a little in order to have them chase us. That should pave the way."

Lucien looked thoughtful. "We will not have to hold them very long. The hands of the clock do not turn on their own in the Amphitheater. To assure victory, all we need to do is make sure you have your chance to reach Sophia."

"No, Lucien, you need to stay out of it," Dante replied. "This isn't a game, guys. The Morte-Veras will kill anyone who gets in its way. I'm sorry, but you've haven't had enough training. You're brand new!"

"Hey, man, we're *Ardent Rising*," Brett said. "There's no time like the present. We stick together. You said we're a new race, right? Well, we might as well get started acting like it."

Eve spoke up next. "You helped us. You're one of us, so we're helping you, and you can shut the hell up and deal with it." Her face went a little red at the last comment.

Naomi looked like a proud mom. "What she said. You can't do it without us, Dante."

There was a pause. Dante pondered the words. "All right, but be careful. We'll need to time this perfectly."

Max smirked. "Hell yeah. Let's go save the world."

Dante made a face. "I'll see you in a few. I have one more call to make."

Seventeen

"We're in position," Max said. His armlet was alight and the other hand carried a short steel baton. To his right, Naomi was smoldering in a dancing swirl of fire. Jon, Amanda and the other Millennials stood behind. Each one of them flexed their powers for the first time in a real altercation. The expressions on their faces ranged from excited to horrified. Lucien stood in front of the group with a portal open.

"I see the clearing, Max," Dante whispered on the wind. "I'm beginning my descent."

"That's our cue, folks," Max summarized. "Is everyone ready?"

"Not by a freaking long shot," Brett said with a sardonic smirk. "Psyche. Let's go kick some monster ass." He rushed into the portal, running full speed. The portal shimmered for a moment, and then he was gone. Amanda rolled her eyes.

Max looked at Lucien, standing in position, checking his gear one more time for the fight ahead. "I never thought I would fight side by side with you, Lucien." He paused for a moment. "Well, not in my right mind, that is."

Lucien smiled sadly. "I committed atrocities upon you and the others that can never be repaid. One day I will ask for your forgiveness, but not before I have atoned for some of this horror."

Max shrugged. "Lucien, if it wasn't you, it wasn't you."

"Perhaps," Lucien pondered that for a moment. "For what it's worth, I am honored to be standing here side by side with you, Max."

"Surprisingly," Max answered. "Likewise."

Lucien nodded to Max. "For the Truthsayer," he said solemnly. He summoned a two handed war sword, the blade's edge so brilliant it looked blue in the portal's light.

"For the Truthsayer," Max replied.

Lucien went through next, followed by Naomi, Max and the rest of the Millennials.

The knights were arranged in a crescent moon shaped arc. Sophia's possessed form was not visible. She stood in the most easily defendable position at the back of the group. Suddenly the crowd parted, leaving a clear path for the monster possessing Sophia to see the new arrivals.

"Lucien, my love. It is so good to see you again."

Lucien gritted his teeth. "Tonight you die, creature."

"And would you sacrifice the Truthsayer's love to accomplish that task? You know how important she will become in the coming years."

"If need be," Lucien said. "You cannot be allowed to keep her."

"You can make this better for all of us and surrender," Max said. His armlet was poised and ready. "The Seraph is going to want his lady back. He gets cranky, you know."

Hope rolled her eyes, vaguely reminiscent of the person she was possessing. "To borrow a phrase in the vernacular tongue: you and what army?"

"This army," Brett said. The other Millennials amassed together behind Max. Naomi walked up, her smoldering form blazing into white fire.

"*Ardent Rising* is going to beat you down, you heinous bitch," Amanda spat. Electricity danced through her fingers.

Jon looked both concerned and enthralled. The other Millennials readied themselves as well.

Hope's eyes narrowed as she roared, "You misunderstand. Even with your little rabble, you are still outnumbered four to one. My slaves possess all my power and strength. I will end you, all of you."

"If that were true, demon," Dmitri said as he appeared in a shimmer of red light, "then you wouldn't be stalling right now." The other vampires, Carmen, Magnus, Adelai, and Donovan, appeared as well. Each of them took a defensive stance in front of the Millennials.

Dmitri rushed forward, to be shoulder-to-shoulder to Lucien. "Welcome to the twilight of the Ardent." His eyes were completely black, and his talons clicked in the quiet night. "You come at a good time, my lord. We were about to bring death to your old servants."

Lucien looked confused. "I didn't expect that you'd stand with us, vampire."

Dmitri smiled. "Even immortals can surprise you." He looked at Donovan. "Are you happy now?"

"Thrilled," Donovan said, his eyes already taking on a reddish glow. "The Ancient and I are totally square after this."

"No doubt," Dmitri said. He looked at the Morte-Veras. "So, *Sophia,* care to try your luck with all of us? Your odds aren't so good with those who you can't possess. Oh yes, how quickly they forget. Vampires are immune to possession."

The monster raised its arms to the sky. "Bear witness to my power."

"How about you bear witness to mine?" Dante said as he landed next to the creature. He wasted no time and grabbed her. "You're coming with me."

"I think not," Hope spat. She dislodged his hands with movement faster than the eye could track. She followed quickly with a sweeping grab of her own, her hands around Dante's neck. "Now you die, Truthsayer." She looked out to the group of amassed slaves. "Kill them. Let the ground be stained red with their heart's blood!"

Lucien launched forward. The column sealed, blocking Dante and Hope from Lucien and the others. The first line of knights let blue lightning fly from their gauntlets. Carmen and Adelai were hit, but shrugged off the impact.

"I think that was meant to hurt us, Carmen," Adelai said. Her eyes went crimson and her body twisted into a predatory animal's stance. She emerged with claws, fangs and a truly nasty disposition.

"What rank amateurs they are. I will show them how to bring pain," Carmen answered. She launched a bolt of fire at the first line. Instead of hitting the attackers, she aimed for the earth beneath them. The resulting explosion launched three knights into the air. They slammed back into another group of three, and soon all of them were in disarray. Carmen and Adelai shared a twisted chuckle and then moved back in.

Magnus stalked forward to engage. Four knights quickly surrounded him. They swung blades in an attempt to bring him down. The attacks weren't very successful, especially when Brett grabbed one off Magnus' back and flung him twenty feet away. Several powerful strikes from Magnus laid the rest of the four down. Before more knights could assault the huge vampire, the rest of the Millennials entered the fight.

Naomi stayed with Max. She sent bolts of fire down the line in an attempt to clear a path. "We have to get to Dante," she said. Max made a break for it, only to be brought down by several knights who remained in the way. "Damn it, Max!" Naomi spat.

Max socked a knight in the jaw. "It's no use, there's too many of them between us. He's on his own."

Cracks rang out as Hope squeezed Dante's neck. He gagged, life-giving breath fading fast in his lungs. "What is it, Empyrial? No witty line?"

"Actually," Dante answered as he grabbed Hope's neck in response. "Time to go home, bitch." Closing his eyes, he gripped *Ardent Vow*. Holding on tight, he commanded the Amphitheater to accept them, and it did not disappoint. The trees and cool night air of the park was gone, replaced with the darkened room and skylight of the Empyrial legacy. The creature let go of Dante immediately.

"No flesh, right?" Dante raised the *Ardent Vow*. "You can't use my girlfriend's body as a shield, now, shithead."

"You can't keep me here, Empyrial," Hope spat. She still looked like Sophia, but her shape was a little ghostly, and shifted into a shade-like monster. Her wings re-emerged and the creature roared at him. Hope drew a wicked blade from nowhere.

Pain cascaded in his head. "Uh oh, you just lied to me, so I guess things aren't so easy for you," he said jovially. "I'm so sorry, but you're stuck here until I say you can leave."

"I will end you."

"I heard that already. Let's try something new. How about you talk less and fight more?"

Hope launched herself at Dante. Her sword went low, attempting to cut him off at the knees. Seeing the attack coming, Dante flipped into a tucked position, landing on the other side of the swing. He spun around and swung *Ardent Vow* backhanded, aiming for Hope's head. The creature managed to get its sword up and deflect the strike. The blade scorched on contact with the Truthsayer's sword.

"Die," Hope roared. She lunged forward, blade first. Dante swung his sword in a half circle, knocking the enemy blade away towards the right. He pressed the advantage forward, striking with a quick thrust to the midsection. Hope rolled over the blade, twirling in the air and slashing Dante in the back. The blade was Ardent, and the strange burning sensation that went along with a wound from such a weapon, emerged immediately.

"Your Empyrial strength won't save you from my blade, Truthsayer."

"Yeah, yeah, you're all big and bad, aren't you?" Dante sidestepped forward and slashed straight down. Hope evaded the strike by inches. She swung across in response. The strike was horizontal to the ground. Dante leaned back out of the way, then spun around and struck Hope with a kick. The impact threw the creature back into a stone wall.

Hope pulled herself out of the impact site and ran back towards Dante. The monster slashed four times. Two of the four slashes hit Dante, one striking his thigh and the other his side. Blood dripped onto the floor. The burning pain rose in his blood. It became unbearable in seconds. Dante swung his blade wildly, forcing Hope back. He needed the time to recover.

Dante leaped up at the sky and began a flight towards the other end of the Amphitheater. Hope followed him up and tackled him in mid flight. The impact sent the both of them careening to the ground. They slammed into the fire cauldron at the bottom of the Amphitheater, stumbling around underneath the skylight which was streaming sun in.

"You can barely stand. You're all alone here. Perhaps once you are dead, I will possess your corpse. Even in death, the power of an Empyrial vessel would be very potent indeed. Would you like that?"

"You can go to hell. And you're wrong, by the way," Dante said as a trickle of blood lobbed out of his mouth. "I'm not alone. You forgot someone."

"And who might that be?" Hope said with a laugh. "Your entire people are dead, *Seraph*. What manner of help could you have *here*?"

"He has me," Sophia said, stepping into the sunlight. She swung her sword and slashed Hope in the chest. The creature roared in shock. "You forgot about real owner of that body you're walking around in. What, did Lucien never come out to kick your ass in here?" Sophia slashed her in the face. "How do you like that?"

The shock wearing off, Hope dashed forward and backhanded Sophia. The impact forced the other spirit down. "You defied me. That is not possible!"

Sophia rubbed her jaw. "What can I say? I'm a defiant person."

Hope stalked towards Sophia, its talons scratching against the sword it carried. "No longer will I compete for control of your body. Now you die."

"You first." A flash of gleaming metal struck the Morte-Veras through the chest plate. A sickening crack rang out in the Amphitheater. The blade crashed through to the other side, snapping and tearing as it reached the monster's spine. "August sends his regards." Dante pulled the blade out, and stepped back to Sophia's side.

"You think you've won, Truthsayer?" Hope spat.

"I'm more focusing on the fact that I think you lost."

"You don't know what is coming. You can't even begin to imagine the horrors that will face you."

"Well, I should be scared then," Dante replied.

Hope slumped over on the ground. A moment later, the shade dissolved into a fine mist which vanished immediately.

Sophia rushed over to Dante. She threw her arms around him.

"You did it." She kissed him deeply. It felt very real. She pressed into him, almost desperately.

Dante shrugged. "Was there ever any doubt?"

"Hate to break it to you, love, but you got seriously lucky," Sophia replied.

"I didn't have luck," Dante replied. "I have you."

"You reached me, didn't you?" Sophia said. "I was asleep one moment, then the next I saw that thing. My sword was right there, and voila!"

"I wasn't sure if it would've worked, but I took a chance. I'm so glad that's over," Dante replied. He kept her close, looking at the room of spirits within the Amphitheater. Dante waved his free arm and the scene of shades changed to the fight outside. The entire image was still frozen. "We need to get back."

"I wish we could stay here." Sophia threaded her fingers through his hair. "This is such bullshit." Her gaze went back out towards the center. The skylight streamed golden light into the room. The perimeter danced near Sophia. She stepped a little forward so that her head was coated in the sunlight.

"What do you mean?"

Sophia lowered her head. "It's par for the course, really. We get through this crap, and now things are going to hell."

"You *are* going to go back, right?" Dante asked.

Sophia nodded absently. "Yes, my body is waking up. I only have seconds left."

"Then we'll be together in a few seconds," Dante said with confusion in his voice. "What's the matter?"

"Dante, I don't know how to tell you this, but things are going to be a little different when I return."

"Yeah, you'll be free, and we'll be together," he said a little nervously. "Right?"

Sophia looked sad. "I wish it were that easy."

"You're not making sense, Sophia." Something was seriously wrong. "I'm getting a little freaked out here."

"You said you'd never give up on me," she stated quickly. Her spirit was starting to fade. "Did you mean it?"

"Wait, what?"

"Did you mean it?"

Dante closed his eyes a moment, then smiled. "With everything in me."

"You're going to have to prove it," she replied as she vanished. "I love you, my Seraph." Her words were carried only on the wind.

"I love you too," he replied to the empty Amphitheater.

Eighteen

Sophia nearly hit the ground before Dante could catch her. Her eyes were closed and her breathing was steady. For all intents and purposes, she looked like she was in a very deep sleep. Dante heard Lucien issue order for the knights to surrender, and witnessed them complying.

The cheers of victory around them should have roused her, but Sophia remained at peace.

"You did it, champ!" Max said. He rushed over to Dante. His clothes were ripped in places, and there was a nasty scratch going down his neck, but otherwise he had emerged unscathed.

"Hope's dead, I think," Dante replied. He knelt on the ground, still holding the unconscious Sophia. "I'll tell you about it later. Is she all right?"

"Let's check her out," Max answered. "Her vitals." He tapped a few keys on his armlet. "Scans say she's fine. Don't be such a worrier."

Naomi wandered over to Max. "Hey, big guy," she said without warning. He turned around just in time for her to press her lips to his. She pulled back quickly. "You weren't going to do it, so I did."

"Well, I'm very glad you have more guts than I," Max said. He took her hand, threading her fingers with his.

Dmitri walked over to Dante. The vampires were starting to leave. Carmen and Magnus already teleported away. "You honored our deal, Ancient. We will honor yours. Keep the Royals in line and there will be peace."

Lucien wandered over. "There will be no more war with the vampire in Louisville. The remaining Royals will now serve to protect the city from all threats to Ardent and mortal alike." The Royal Lord extended his hand to Dmitri. "Now, after so many years, I see the truth. Thank you for allowing us to win the day."

Surprising everyone, the vampire took Lucien's hand. "It was good to be in the light again." He turned to Dante. "Ancient, I leave you now. Donovan tells me you still owe him a rematch. If you choose to accept, or even if you just want to enjoy the music, we would be glad to see you at Bloodlines."

"I'll do that. Thank you Dmitri."

The vampire nodded and vanished. The Millennials were cheering and jumping up and down. Brett had been hurt, but Eve had quickly bandaged his wound, preventing any lasting damage.

"*Ardent Rising* kicks ass!" Brett yelled.

"You are such a moron," Eve replied as she tried to keep his wound from opening again.

Amanda and Jon embraced, screaming at the top of their lungs in triumph.

"They really did it," Dante said. He put a hand on Max's shoulder. "The Millennials really did it."

"You did it, champ, they just helped lead the way."

"We all did it, then," Dante replied. "Look, the knights are coming out of it." He pointed to Byron, who walked over towards Sophia's sleeping form. "Ah, Byron. Glad to see you made it through in one piece."

Byron spoke quickly. "Is she okay?" He looked a little embarrassed, but too proud to admit it.

Dante looked down. "I think so." As if on cue, Sophia's eyes began to flutter. The group that had amassed around her collectively breathed a sigh of relief. She was going to be all right.

"Wow, that was quite a concert," Sophia said. "Hold on. This isn't the Galleria." She looked around, confused. "Oh my God. Did I get drunk again?"

"Again?" Dante said. "Sophia, are you all right?"

She sat up slowly. "I think so. Oh man, what the hell happened? I feel like someone drove a pair of trains through my eye sockets."

"It's a long story," Dante answered. "Can you stand?"

"Yeah, yeah." She stood up. "Oh, hey, Byron. That was a seriously awesome concert. You should be proud that your stupid-ass friends were able to keep up with me."

"What are you talking about?" Byron said in confusion.

"The concert. You know, the concert you took me to last night? The concert where your band was opening for Sudden Evisceration?" Sophia looked at Dante. "Oh, hi. I don't know how I fell in your lap, but I'm Sophia. Who are you?"

Dante stood in shock. *"I'm sorry?"*

"I asked you who you are. Typically I get people's names before I let them sleep with me, or I sleep on them. Anyway, you get the idea. I must have been really drunk."

"I'm Dante," he answered. "You, you really don't remember me?"

"Why? Did we have a, um, tumble last night? I sure hope not because my boyfriend may have a problem with that. You'd defend my honor, wouldn't you, Byron?"

"Are you shitting me?" Naomi said. "What are you going on about?"

Max put his hand over Naomi's mouth. "Sorry, it's been a confusing night, and I think you've had a bump on the head. You should go to the doctor."

Sophia touched the back of her head. "I don't feel any bumps. You're drunk-pranking me, aren't you?"

"Sophia, let me get you to the hospital," Naomi said. "It's not far from here. I'll get you back in no time."

"Listen, shrimp, there's no way I'm going to go anywhere with any of you guys. I was taught very well that nasty things happen when you go off with people you have just met."

"Who are you calling *shrimp*?" Naomi said, heating up.

"You're not helping, love," Max said. He looked at the Truthsayer and pointed at Byron. "Dante, new plan."

"This isn't happening," Dante said under his breath. Max glared at him. Dante got the hint and looked at Byron. "Byron, it's probably a good idea for Sophia to get checked out. Would you mind taking her to the emergency room? We're not far from campus, getting your *car* won't be a big deal."

"Oh, yeah, that's cool. Come on, Sophia, let's get you checked out," Byron replied.

"I guess," she replied and followed Byron out of the clearing. "Nice meeting you, Dante!"

Dante nodded as the pair walked out of sight. He turned back around at Lucien, Naomi and Max. "She doesn't remember me," he said. "She doesn't remember *anything*. She told me that she broke up with Byron years ago. How could this have happened?"

"One of the possible side effects of possession is memory loss," Lucien stated. "It is why the Royal Lords do not use the power more often. Our servants could be harmed by the power coursing through them."

"Max, I thought your scans said she was fine."

"There's nothing physically wrong with her, as far as I can tell," Max said. "It must be in the old psyche."

"How serious is the memory loss?" Dante asked Lucien. "Do they recover?"

"Most of those injured in this manner never regain their lost memories. I am sorry."

"Without her memory, she's completely helpless. I need to get to the hospital," Dante stated. "I don't trust her with Byron. I didn't know what else to do. We didn't have a lot of choices."

"Indeed," Lucien answered.

Naomi, who had stepped back to talk to the Millennials, jogged back up to the group. "The others are heading back. With the problem contained, they're just going to take the night off. I said that was okay."

Max pointed at the former knights. "What about them?" They were all standing around, looking very confused.

"I will tend to them," Lucien said. "We will need to ascertain how far the Morte-Veras' possession extended. The ones who were my knights, well, as this body was the cause of their trouble, it is my responsibility to see them home, safely."

"What will you do now?" Dante wanted to know. Lucien hadn't seen the sun without Hope's influence in a thousand years. What is next for someone with a millennium of catching up to do?

"For now, I will serve the ones who served me," Lucien answered. "I will remain in the city, tending to the damage and repairing it. If you should need me, find me in your Empyrial Amphitheater."

"It sounds very strange to say this to you," Dante said, "but thanks for all your help."

"You freed me from a thousand years of living hell," Lucien said. "It was the least I could do." He nodded, and turned away towards the knights. "We'll meet again soon, Truthsayer."

"I'm going to go on ahead," Dante said to Max and Naomi. "You guys okay to follow in normal conveyance?"

"He means a car, Max," Naomi tousled Max's hair.

"I knew what he meant," Max answered. "Yes, we'll see you in a few."

"Go get her, Dante," Naomi said. "There's no telling what that creep Byron is going to do."

∴

"I'm sorry, sir, but you'll have to stay out here," the nurse said when Dante entered the ER. At his confused look, she continued, "Sophia's mother and boyfriend are in there with the doctor. There are only two people allowed in the ER at a time."

"Of course," Dante said. "Thank you." He walked over and sat down in one of the completely uncomfortable white plastic chairs. It was a surprisingly quiet night in the ER. Dante was the only person waiting. That, combined with his overwhelming emotion, tore at his core.

Thankfully, Dante didn't have to wait long for Max and Naomi to walk through the automatic double doors. Naomi, in her normal vibrant fashion, scanned the room and made a beeline for the seat next to Dante's. Max just walked up behind, never breaking stride.

"Did you guys teleport here?" Dante asked.

Naomi shrugged. "Nah, we teleported to the *car,* Max let me drive."

"Letting her drive, huh?" Dante smirked. "I thought you liked that car."

Max laughed. "Yeah, but I have a good insurance policy."

"Do you guys ever quit?"

"Not really," Dante answered. "At least we didn't bring up the cafeteria. Oops."

"Jerk," she said without malice. Naomi looked up towards the nurse's station. "Do we know anything yet?"

"She's being seen by the doctor right now," Dante replied.

Max took Naomi's hand. "She'll be okay, love. It'll only be a matter of time before she's back to her old loud mouthed self."

"I wonder if this is what she was like, you know," Naomi said, "before?"

"She seemed pretty carefree, doesn't she?" Dante replied. "Of course, she thought she was drunk."

"There's no way to know what's been affected. For all we know, this could be a complete aberration," Max stated. "It sucks, but only time will tell."

Dante caught sight of Byron walking out of the back. He was walking next to an older woman. Her stance, eyes and manner painted her as Sophia's mother. As Dante rose to his feet, she walked over to him aggressively.

"Are you Dante?" Sophia's mother asked. Her voice was adversarial and harsh.

"Yes, ma'am," Dante answered with a hint of confusion.

"I thought as much," she replied. Her eyes narrowed. "I have just one thing to say to you. Stay away from my daughter."

"I'm sorry?" Dante's face flashed open in shock.

"I said, stay away from my daughter. Do you understand me, boy?"

"Yeah, I get it," Dante said. He lowered his head slightly to avoid her gaze.

"Good," Sophia's mother stormed out of the hospital.

"Rough night, Ancient?" Byron wandered up to Dante with a smirk.

Dante's eyes flashed and he grabbed Byron's lapels. "What the hell did you tell her?"

"I told her that when she was with you, she got hurt. Isn't that what happened?" Byron made no attempt to resist Dante's strength. All things considered, that was probably best for everyone. "You may have won the battle, Truthsayer, but you lost the war."

"What are you saying?"

"Sophia and I were in love before Lucien entered the picture. It was something glorious," Byron said with hint of the wistful in his voice. "Then she got these powers and forgot the simple things in life. She stopped being herself, and had to transform into this crazy-ass Ardent warrior. You don't know her at all."

"That is bullshit," Dante snapped. "You don't know anything about me."

"I know that Sophia has no memory of the time she spent as an Ardent," Byron said. "She lost all her episodic memory for the last three years. She remembers her academics, her martial arts training, but she doesn't have a single experience after her freshman year. She has absolutely no memory of you at all. In essence, she's exactly what she would have been if Lucien hadn't taken her from me."

"You son of a bitch," Naomi spat. "She loves Dante. She nearly died for him!"

"That's my point," Byron said. "I'm done with this Ardent thing. I'm finishing up school and getting the hell out of this little town. You're the Seraph of *Ardent Rising*, or whatever your little club is called. Can you say the same?"

"It doesn't matter," Dante answered. "This isn't for me *or you* to decide. Sophia gets to make this call."

"And we're back to the part where she doesn't remember you." Byron patted Dante's arm. "Sorry, boy. You saved the day, but I get the girl."

"I'm going to roast you alive, you superfluous asshole," Naomi snapped. Max put his hand on her shoulder and pulled her back.

"Do we have a problem here?" The security guard said. He walked over to the gathering.

"Not at all, officer. We're just having a friendly chat. Isn't that right, Dante?" Byron said.

"We're leaving," Dante answered. He released Byron and made for the door.

Max shook his head. "Come on, Naomi. Let's get out of here."

"This is bullshit! It can't end like this." She shook her head.

"Things don't always work out, Naomi," Max replied. "Not like they're supposed to."

NINETEEN

THREE WEEKS LATER

"You have to tell her, Dante! She has to know the truth." Naomi said as she handed Dante his mortarboard. It was graduation day. The group was sitting in Dante's room as he got his robes on for the ceremony. "She's going to leave soon! You'll never get another shot!"

"We've been talking about this for three weeks, Naomi," Dante said as he fiddled with his tie. "There's nothing for me to do. I can't just go in there and declare my undying love. She doesn't know me. I'm a complete stranger to her. The last thing she needs is for me to scare her."

"But I thought you weren't going to give up on her," Naomi snapped. Her hands were fidgety, tapping on his closed computer keyboard and playing with stray locks of her hair. Max sat down on Dante's bed in easy reach of Naomi.

"Let me ask you something, Naomi," Dante said. His eyes turned to face her. She flinched slightly at the look he gave her. "Have you seen her recently?"

"Um, yeah?"

"Didn't she seem happy to you?"

"That isn't the point."

"It *is* the point, Naomi. I ask you, doesn't she seem happy to you?" Dante's voice was calm, but in full interrogation mode. This had to stop. She had to let it go, for all their sakes.

"Yes, she seems very happy."

"And you want me to dredge up all this stuff? Horror and death and destiny are things she doesn't have to worry about anymore. I'm supposed to do that just to try to win back her favor?" He gave himself a look in the mirror. "Byron is a completely opportunistic asshole, but he did have a point. He can escape from this. I can't. The Ardent are my people. With August gone, I'm the last Ancient alive. I can't forgo that responsibility. If I learned anything from Sophia, it was that the duty is more important than my feelings. I hate this, but I don't see that I have a choice."

"I didn't want to bring this up, champ," Max said, "but it may not be the end after all."

"What do you mean?"

"Sophia is still an active Ardent," Max replied. "I took the scans myself. She just forgot that she had the power. Someday she's going to remember, or she's going to figure it out again."

"If she does, then she'll get the help of the Seraph of *Ardent Rising*," Dante said, as his face made something nearly resembling a smile. "It's a great title, Naomi."

"It suits you. The Ardent Rebellion is dead, but *Ardent Rising* is alive and well. Many of the old knights have joined. I'm afraid to jinx it, but there's peace in the city."

"A peace that Louisville hasn't seen in decades," Max added.

"Exactly. Just like I helped Brett, Amanda and the others, I'll help Sophia when it's her time."

"You're really not going to go to her, are you?" Naomi asked.

"No, I'm not. I can't take away her happiness. I can feel her in the Amphitheater, and for the first time since I met her, she's truly happy. How could I say I love her if I'd take that away?"

"Do you really think she could be happy with Byron?"

"I wouldn't have thought so, but this Sophia isn't exactly the same as ours. She's a Sophia who never watched Rachel die, or had to kill someone in her service to Lucien. She never had to spy on her friends, or use a crowbar to disable a Royal knight. Sophia is a normal person, now, Naomi. An innocent."

"What if she breaks up with him?"

"If she does, then although a part of me would be tremendously happy, especially if she cracked his jaw again," Dante said, his eyes taking on a mock-sinister look, "I'm still the Seraph, and she's still not going to know me. That part doesn't change. Even if we could bridge the gap, it doesn't help that Byron got Sophia's mother to think I'm a demon straight out of hell. There really is no hope."

"This sucks," Naomi pouted. "This really, really sucks."

"Look, you guys have been great friends throughout everything this year. I couldn't have made it through any of it without you."

"Likewise, Dante," Max said. "I owe you a lot. We both do." Naomi nodded.

Dante smiled, shaking Max's hand. "This is something that I'm just going to have to live with. Sometimes, in life, there are no such things as happy endings."

Before Naomi could reply, there was a knock at the door. Dante looked confused for a moment and closed his eyes. "I'll take a look," Dante reached out to the Amphitheater.

"Who is it?" Naomi asked.

"Sophia. With Byron right behind," he sighed. Dante looked at his two friends. "This ought to be good. Would you mind giving us a minute?"

Max spoke up. "Sure, we'll just meet you after the ceremony. Remember, *Seraph,* there's the big hillside party tonight. You're not going to cheat us out of your company. You read me, champ?"

"Yeah, I read you," Dante smiled. "Thanks,"

Naomi threw her arms around him. "You're my hero, Dante, and more importantly, you were always *her* hero." The two of them stood up and walked to the door. Max opened the door and came face to face with his old friend.

"Um, hi. Is Dante around?" Sophia looked very different. She was robed in the graduation outfit, and she wore the same four-pointed hat that Dante did. The difference was her makeup. Gone was the preppy lip gloss and blush, and now she was pale, with blood red lipstick and heavy eyeliner.

"Sure, he's back there. We were just leaving." Max smiled and walked out into the hall. His hand was in Naomi's, giving Dante a little joy that at least *they* get to have a happy ending. Naomi glared at Byron, who smirked back at her.

Dante walked out to Sophia. "Hey," he said with a nervous chuckle.

"Hey, Dante, right?" Sophia said. Dante nodded. "You ready for the big day?"

"The big day?"

"Um, graduation, big boring speech, brave new world?"

"Oh, yeah, yeah, right, sure. I'm ready as I'll ever be, I suppose."

"I know what you mean. It's going to be hard to leave this place, especially considering how little I remember about it. Do you mind if we come in for a second?"

"Um, no, I guess not," Dante answered. He stepped back from the door and allowed the couple to enter.

"I see you started packing," Sophia said. "I did too, even though we can stick around in the dorms next week. I didn't want to leave it to the last minute."

"No, that makes a lot of sense."

"Sophia, darling," Byron said smoothly. "We don't have much time. The line-up for graduation starts in twenty minutes."

"Oh, right. Thanks, B. Would you give us a second? I'd like to talk to Dante for a moment."

"Okay," Byron said.

"In private, please?" Sophia stated.

"Um, sure. I'll be out in the hall." Byron smiled through gritted teeth at Dante, who smiled politely back to him. The door closed and Sophia breathed a sigh of relief.

"You did something to piss him off, I think," Sophia said. "He wouldn't tell me what, exactly, but he certainly has it in for you."

"Yeah, we don't really get along. We have some," Dante searched for a phrase, "differences of opinion on how to handle things."

"Sounds to me like there's a story there."

Dante smiled. "There certainly is, but I'd need far more than twenty minutes to tell it to you."

"It's too bad we're not together in the graduation line. We'd have something to talk about during the three hours of boredom that awaits us."

"It is too bad," Dante said. "I know just how much you *love* to sit still." He didn't mean to say it, especially like that.

"Dante, were we involved?" Sophia blurted out. "I know that sounds really out there, but I feel strange when I look at you, like we were really close and I knew you very well."

Dante wasn't going to lie, he wasn't even sure if he *could.* "Yes, we were involved."

"Oh, what happened?"

"Remember that story about Byron hating me?"

She nodded.

"This one makes the other story look infinitesimal."

"I really wish I could remember," she said, a little frustrated. "After graduation, do you think we could meet and talk? You know, just the two of us?"

"I'd like that, Sophia."

"Cool. Well, Byron's right, we do need to get going. Do you want to go with us?"

"I'll walk out with you," Dante said. "But I have a stop to make before I head to the graduation ceremony."

"Okay. So, meet you at the party tonight?"

"Sounds great," he replied.

"Cool. See you later, *Seraph,*" she said, before her forehead knitted together in confusion. "Seraph? I don't know where that came from."

"It's your nickname for me, Sophia," Dante said, his face breaking into a full-fledged smile. "We can talk about that tonight, too. Right before we walk into tomorrow, we'll talk about yesterday."

"Very poetic. It's like destiny, isn't it?"

"I hope it is."

The pair walked out into the hall. Byron possessively put his arm around Sophia's waist. Dante walked with them. His face took on a very sly smile. He reached into the Amphitheater one more time.

"Byron," Dante's mind called to his rival. "I know you can hear me, so listen up."

Byron stumbled and looked at Dante, who didn't even turn to face him as they walked towards the doorway.

"Sophia can't hear us right now. This is a little chat between you and me. As an Ancient, I am connected to *everything*, Byron. I see all. I can go into your teeny, tiny mind with as much effort as it takes me to flip a light switch. I will know everything that happens with Sophia. If I see that you hurt her, in even the most insignificant way, I will come back for you. You can't hide from me. No matter which corner of the world, no matter what rock you hide your sorry ass under, I will find you. You hurt her, and you'll see just how powerful the Truthsayer really is. I will torment you in ways that would make a vampire blush and make the most depraved Royal Lord look like a school child. Am I making myself clear?"

"Yes," Byron stammered out loud.

"Yes, what?" Sophia said in confusion.

"Yes, um, it's going to be a beautiful day," Byron said. "It will be a perfect day for stepping into a new life."

"It is. Don't you see, Dante? It's the end of an era," Sophia said. Her eyes looked a little sad at the statement.

"Maybe, but it's a beginning as well," he replied. "Maybe there's a place for a little of both."

"I hope so," Sophia said. "Well, this is our stop. I'll see you downstairs, after we've graduated, right?"

"Sure," Dante said. "I wouldn't miss it."

"See you around," Sophia said. Byron just nodded as the two walked away. The lines were starting to form down the long path in front of the ceremony room. Teachers, administrators and students all were chatting and trying to organize the procession into the place. Parents, siblings and old friends all pushed their way in and out.

"They can wait for a moment," Dante said to no one in particular. With so much focus on the graduation, he found himself alone on the hill in front of his dorm.

Dante leaped up into the air, soaring above the school thousands of feet. He brought his gaze to the sun, seeing the light cascade to the heavens above.

The world was very alive. Dante took a moment before returning. He landed behind one of the buildings on campus. Moving forward, out into the open, Dante took his place in the graduation line. As the group began the procession, He saw Sophia out of the corner of his eye. She smiled at him. It wasn't the beaming smile he remembered when she told him she loved him, nor was it the sly smile when they were shoulder-to-shoulder in battle. It was a sweet, genuine and happy smile. He returned that smile. She ducked her head a little shyly in response.

It was a good day, the first of many.

SNEAK PREVIEW

OF

ARDENT STAND

THE SEQUEL TO ARDENT RISING

COMING SOON

The place stank of decay, both through his nostrils and through his supernatural perceptions. The door itself was sturdy, the product of major reinforcement. This guy was a pro, or at least a well practiced amateur. Neither choice made Dante feel any better.

"Detective Rubicon," one of the officers called out to Dante as he examined the door. He was young, probably on his first rotation. He had that look of terror in his eyes. It was to his credit. A lot of the rooks who come out to a strike like this expect excitement, but what they get is a first-hand account how truly horrible people could become. The smart ones are scared *before* they go in.

The case had been very long and arduous, despite its start less than 36 hours ago. The abduction had been out in the open. The little girl, Sarah Richards, was plucked off the playground amidst several dozen other children, two security guards and a teacher.

Naturally, no one saw anything.

If Dante wasn't the Truthsayer and gifted with supernatural senses, they wouldn't have had a snowball's chance in hell of finding anything out. There wasn't even a stray fingerprint on the playground to go after. The mortal police were completely baffled. They had no concept of how such a thing could happen.

Dante knew it was a Portalis teleport, the kind that Royals use. Over the last few years, he'd had plenty of opportunity to examine the effect firsthand. At first Dante suspected that a Royal Lord might have been the culprit, but Lucien assured him that no Royal Lord had stepped into the city since the grand evacuation five years ago.

So it was perhaps a latent who had just 'popped'. Despite his inability to reach the Empyrial Amphitheater, the signature was easy to track with his senses. The harder part was to make sure that the police didn't suspect that he was using a supernatural ability to determine the abductor's location.

So, less than two days later, they were at the end of the line, standing outside the criminal's door, waiting to arrest him and save the kid.

"Backup will be here in ten, shall we secure the perimeter?" The rookie questioned, his eyes fearing the worst.

Dante nodded outwardly but cursed inwardly. Ten minutes was far too long. Sarah would already be dead by then. The clamoring moron from the news station sent far too much detail of their progress to the evening news. The serial killer was certainly tipped off. He had turned this place into a fortress. Normal methods weren't going to work here, and certainly not in ten minutes.

Time was running out. He had to act quickly. "Go," Dante replied. The officer left and Dante was once again alone in front of the door. He waited a few moments, making sure that the rookie would not be able to interfere.

Leaning back, Dante slammed a kick into the door. The metal creaked and moaned as the hinges blasted off. The entire door frame shattered. Dante moved through at inhuman speed, scanning the room for the abductor.

A gunshot fired to Dante's back left. His perceptions increased and time slowed, the bullet disturbing his shirt collar as it passed within inches of his body. The attack was good. If a child-abducting serial killer was shooting at Dante, he wasn't hurting the little girl.

If he were in tune with the Amphitheater, this would have been a piece of cake. Without that talent, Dante was forced to rely on his martial ones.

Dante swooped down and around, rolling behind a couch as bullets sprayed everywhere. They were close shots. The guy was pretty good with a pistol.

His view of the attacker blocked, Dante snaked his head around the corner of the couch. The monster turned and raised his gun back towards the kitchen, pointing it towards the sink. It had to be Sarah's hiding spot. Dante snapped up and dove in that direction.

The criminal's finger was on the trigger and his mind had already commanded the body to pull. Dante poured on the speed. He reached the wrist supporting the gun and flung it up as the pistol discharged. The bullet shattered the glass blocks over the sink. The sounds of sirens spilled into the room.

Dante grabbed the man and hurled him back out into the living room. The brute was strong, but not strong enough to stand against Empyrial power. Shielding the kitchen, he marched forward on the beast. "You are under arrest. You have the right to remain silent, Asshole." Dante said, walking forward as he pulled out his handcuffs.

The response was four heavy impacts to his chest.

Damn, the creep still had a gun. Dante walked over unfazed and snatched the gun out of the criminal's hands. "Anything you can say can and will be used against you in a court of law, prick."

The criminal opened a Portalis portal in the wall, and made a move towards it. Dante was too fast. A single grab to the crook's collar sent him flying back into the room. The portal closed on impact.

"I shot you," the brute stammered, "in the heart. You should be dead."

Dante bit back a curse. This was going to get complicated. Whatever, it would have to be up to someone else to figure it out. Dante was wearing a Kevlar vest (mostly for show, really.) Hopefully that would be plausible enough. He had long since stopped fearing small arms fire since his Ardent powers rendered him immune to them years ago. He was lucky that this idiot hadn't learned of Arcana bolts yet, as that would have been far harder to defend against.

He completed reading the abductor his Miranda rights and secured him, then walked back over into the kitchen. "Sarah?" He called under the sink. The emotions of the girl flashed into fright.

"Come here, Sarah. I'm going to take you home." She seemed to relax slightly, but was still terrified.

Dante grabbed the locked doors and snapped them like so much kindling. The little girl, barely six years old strained at the change in the light. Mindful of the shock, Dante waited with his arms outstretched. "It's okay."

The little girl anxiously crawled out and wrapped her little arms around Dante. He picked her up, cradling her, moving slowly. "Are you an angel?" she said, her eyes so innocent.

"Not exactly," he replied with a delicate smile. "My friends used to call me Seraph."

Sarah smiled. The police swarmed through the doorway, and ushered the light in.

Steve Marco lives in Louisville, Kentucky, with his family.